T0077887

PHENOMENAL

JEZREEL JONES

authorHOUSE®

AuthorHouse™
1663 Liberty Drive
Bloomington, IN 47403
www.authorhouse.com
Phone: 833-262-8899

Published by AuthorHouse 07/13/2021

ISBN: 978-1-6655-3132-0 (sc)
ISBN: 978-1-6655-3131-3 (e)

Print information available on the last page.

Any people depicted in stock imagery provided by Getty Images are models, and such images are being used for illustrative purposes only. Certain stock imagery © Getty Images.

This book is printed on acid-free paper.

For Olivia.
Thank you for always believing in me, and for pushing me to be the best I can be, even when I disappear into the worlds I've created. I love you endlessly.

JOCASTA

Waiting to go into the meeting, Jocasta couldn't help but tug at her jacket cuffs. This was HUGE. In the next hour, she could be working *with* the people she had studied her whole professional career. She was more nervous now than she had been over five years ago meeting Marcus Patton, the man behind the superhero persona "Protector", and who happens to be one of the wealthiest people alive. Now she was meeting with not only Marc, but four other enhanced individuals and two very important agents of W.E.I.R.D, the Worldwide Enhanced Individual's Reconciliation Department, which was a protective agency both focusing on keeping enhanced individuals safe in a biased society and on keeping everyone safe from outside threats like the aliens that invaded Earth when Jocasta was a child. That was really what started her journey to where she was today.

Jocasta Jones was the foremost doctor in her field. She was also the newest doctor, having received her degree barely a year ago. The problem was, there were only a handful of people in the world who got their doctorate in the study of enhanced individuals, so she felt like it wasn't *that* great of an achievement. She was a doctor of suprology, which to her was incredibly cool, but she knew that most people didn't think so. She thought it was so cool, in fact, that she got her masters at 22 and doctorate at the age of 24, while teaching. In her three years as a professor, she had come across enough skeptics than she'd like to think about. Even though enhanced individuals were on the news every other week, there were still students who thought that the powers of those people were elaborate hoaxes. How that could be possible still escaped her, but there were enough skeptics that someone had to be pretty convincing with their conspiracy theories. Of course, whenever she told these students about how she had met many of the individuals she taught about, they nearly always still argued with her, leaving her with a theory of her own. *Some people just choose ignorance over possibility.* Which is the nicest way to put how she feels about people who push her buttons. She had met and studied many people with less extreme powers, like being able to heat things up with their hands or being able to move small objects with telekinesis, but this meeting could open so many more doors for her studies. If this went well, she would be the in house suprologist for W.E.I.R.D. and she would be working with individuals with much greater powers. The power to harness the weather, super strength and flight capabilities that were much stronger than those she had met so far, currently inexplicable abilities that know no bounds (as far as she knew) would be at her fingertips to study and hopefully find out the reasons behind the differing strength in the powers of each person. She would have connections with the most incredible heroes in the world, some of whom were there when the attack happened that caused W.E.I.R.D to be established. It was becoming a little bit too real as she sat down in the chair outside of the boardroom where this life altering meeting would begin in minutes.

Trying to gain composure, she rubbed her temples and closed her eyes. *"Just breathe, idiot. You're going to do fine,"* She thought, and as she opened her eyes, the boardroom door opened. Out stepped the most incredible woman Jocasta had ever seen. She knew who she was from the news and from her studies, but Katerina Gradoff was a newer member of W.E.I.R.D, and her powers had not yet been extensively recorded, let alone studied. Jocasta was surprised she would be one of the members in the meeting, since she was so new. Based on watching the news stories, Jocasta had never seen power like hers from any enhanced individual ever before. Seeing her in person, the camera did not do her justice. She looked shorter on TV, but she was actually around four inches taller than Jocasta, and she was stunning. Long, wavy, auburn hair, skin so blemish free it could have been porcelain, and eyes that were as deep and mysterious as the ocean. Her suit was skintight, a black jumpsuit with red detailing and a halter top, and a long black leather jacket that reached her calves in the back. Her hair spilled over her shoulders and when she looked at Jocasta, long eyelashes rimming those intense eyes, she felt her stomach flip. Jocasta had never seen someone so captivating. She was so taken with her that she almost didn't hear Katerina say, "We are ready for you, Doctor." in an accent that made Jocasta afraid her knees wouldn't support her when she stood up. She managed to squeak out "Thank you, I'll be right in," before Katerina slipped back inside. *"Get it together, Jocasta,"* She scolded herself. She stood up and wiped her sweaty palms on her slacks before taking a breath and opening the door.

The room seemed like a pretty basic board room. There was a big table in the middle of the room with chairs surrounding it, and that was about it. The walls were a soft green, which was comforting. She knew green was the most comforting color scientifically because it reminded the mind of nature, but she was also just a fan of cool tones. The far end of the table was chock full of people she admired. There was Marc, Katerina, Arthur Johnson (Captain Honor), Carter Mills (The Crusher), The director of W.E.I.R.D Thomas Graham, and another Agent that Jocasta didn't know. Jocasta sat at the opposite end of the table, where there was a glass of water ready for her.

Director Graham spoke first, his English accent surprising Jocasta. She had never heard him speak, just seen his picture next to articles about W.E.I.R.D. He looked more severe in person. Dark hair, dark eyes, and the most neatly trimmed facial hair she had ever seen. "So, Dr. Jones, we are looking to add a position under the umbrella of W.E.I.R.D to start a study on our task force of enhanced individuals, the Phenoms."

"Essentially they want to figure out how we got our powers so that they can make more of us." Katerina interjected with a tone that suggested she was not keen on the idea. She wasn't looking at Jocasta, but at the Director.

"What Katerina means is that we are looking to find out if enhanced individuals are the next evolutionary step for humanity or if they are just incredible anomalies." Graham said with a hint of annoyance in his voice. There was a pause where Jocasta realized the Director was waiting for her initial thoughts. She cleared her throat before responding.

"Well, as far as we know, there is no consistent way that one would become enhanced. Some people are born with their powers, some are brought on by trauma, and some, like Marc's, are technically all science. What I mean by that is that Marc is exceptionally intelligent, but his powers come from his knowledge of science, they aren't biological. In fact, I don't know that Marc even counts as an Enhanced individual, since his abilities are not really his own, but his suits. Regardless, it would be incredibly challenging to see how someone would go about testing evolution in that way." Marc laughs, his pale blue eyes glistening.

"I told you she would see through that, Graham. He wants to see if we can reproduce our powers and if we would have to do that in the womb or if we can give an adult person enhanced ability."

"So, we are talking about studying which type of power would be easiest to reproduce and how to go about doing that," the Agent that Jocasta didn't know added. "My name is Rob Wright, by the way. Agent Wright." He reached across the table to shake her hand, "We all assumed you knew everyone else already." He leaned back into his chair, running a hand through his short blonde hair.

"I did." She settled back into her chair. "I know I'm a bit young, but I've been studying enhanced individuals for my entire career, and you couldn't ask someone more qualified to help you with this. I do have some questions, though."

"Shoot," said Carter, a smile on their face, "We have literally all day."

"What are the ramifications if we discover that the best way to create more enhanced individuals is to reproduce with enhanced individuals? Do we just tell everyone on Earth that if they aren't enhanced, they should mate with someone who is so we can evolve? That seems absurd. Also, how would we test that within this group?" This time it was Arthur who spoke up.

"I actually thought about that, and I think the best option is to have volunteers from outside W.E.I.R.D. Like a clinical trial for medicine, essentially. We wouldn't really be telling the public that they should try to evolve humanity, just seeing if that could eventually happen." The rest of the group made general agreement sounds and motions, except for Katerina who sat there with no expression, eyes glued to Jocasta.

"Okay, next, why would you want to create more enhanced individuals? I don't want to be a part of creating a privatized army or something." At that, Katerina's eyes lit up for a moment as she was studying her.

"We really just want to know if it is possible. If there is a way to prove that enhanced individuals are just like everyone else. We have been getting a lot of reports of groups who believe that enhanced individuals are not even human, and we feel that we can prove them wrong, we just need someone qualified to find that proof. It's a sentiment I know you wholeheartedly believe in." Marc was looking between her and Katerina as he spoke, as if assuring both of them that enhanced individuals would not be used as weapons. "We would again take volunteers if there's a way other than reproduction, but it wouldn't be going past proving that it can be done."

They spent another hour or so fleshing out what exactly it was that they wanted her to accomplish by taking on this position, and Jocasta felt herself becoming increasingly excited. Each time she felt herself looking toward Katerina though, she felt her stomach sink a bit. She was silent for the entire rest of the meeting, studying Jocasta with an intensity that was frankly intimidating. Once or twice, when Jocasta glanced toward her, she quickly looked to whoever was talking. It seemed that she was against the idea of bringing her on, but she also wasn't fighting anyone about it, so maybe that wasn't quite on the mark. Jocasta tried to ignore her unwavering gaze, hoping she wasn't reading her thoughts, but she was also having trouble not letting her own eyes linger as she passed over her when the others were speaking. Carter started going on a tangent about the way their hands might grow too big to study them in a small space like the labs here at the headquarters when Jocasta realized that they were clearly hiring her, and she wanted to seal the deal. She waited for Carter to finish voicing their concerns and assured them that it would all get figured out before she started studying them before addressing the whole group once more.

"Listen, this could change the future of humanity, and I am very much in, but under one condition." Jocasta leaned in toward the table for unnecessary dramatic effect. "I want to be set up in the Phenoms mansion. The more I can study their powers the better, regardless of whether or not they will be the ones whose powers I'm reproducing."

"When can you move in?" Marc asked, with a smile plastered on his face.

"The semester is over in a week, so I will let the university know I'm taking sabbatical after finals. I can be moved in by next Friday." Director Graham stood up.

"Welcome to W.E.I.R.D. Agent Wright will escort you back to the lobby, and we will be in touch." He shook her hand briefly and then left the room. As soon as he was out the door, Marc rounded the table and reached out to pat her on the back.

"I knew you would be on board. Between you and me, we didn't even call anyone else to invite them to the project." Agent Wright stepped toward the door to start leading her back out of the building, but Katerina stopped him.

"I'll walk her back, if you don't mind, Agent Wright." Katerina moved toward the door. Jocasta jumped; a bit startled that she had finally spoken up. But she decided that that was her cue, said goodbye to Marc, and followed Katerina out of the room. As they started walking, Jocasta couldn't help but notice just how young Katerina was, now that she wasn't staring intently at her. She wasn't sure, but she thought Katerina was around her age, which would make her the youngest Phenom on the team. The next youngest would have been Carter and Austin Greene, who were both twenty-nine. It had been a big deal when they became members at twenty-six, both joining when previous members were retiring. It was strange to her that a project like this would be in the hands of people who weren't even 30 yet. A good strange, but still. They were about 50 yards down the hall when Katerina stopped. "Doctor, why do you want to make more enhanced people?" Jocasta looked at her. Her eyes were genuinely curious, but Jocasta knew better.

"Haven't you already read my thoughts? You can do that, right?"

"I can, but I try not to invade the privacy of my colleagues. So, what is your answer?"

"I look at enhanced individuals and I see a minority group that is powerful enough to overthrow the entirety of society, but who don't. I see people who are judged because of that power and sometimes not even believed to exist, and I want to create a world where Enhancements are celebrated and normalized. If that means proving that everyone is the same by creating more enhanced individuals, so be it."

"You sound like an optimistic ally, but I'm honestly not sure that this study is a great way to change the minds of the public. What will people think if powers can just be given to someone willy nilly, or if we say we should be creating more enhanced people? I'm worried that we will just become bigger targets for the general public, who might think that we are seeing ourselves as a 'master race' of sorts."

"I think that it is going to take a lot of study to even get to the point of reproducing enhancement if it is possible, and that study can teach me endless things that can help with that bit." Jocasta looked into those infinity pool eyes. "I just sincerely hope that trauma is not the most effective way to gain Enhancement. Because I know that some people would monopolize on that, and I do not want to cause even an ounce of pain." She knew that Carter had gotten their powers after going through a horrific car accident, and the thought of having to put someone through physical or mental trauma made her sick.

"I am glad to hear that. Now, let's get you out of this maze of a building." Katerina smiled, and the whole hallway got 50 times brighter as relief filled her eyes.

"I really hope she did not look at my thoughts just now. That was cheesy as shit." Jocasta watched Katerina as she thought that, but Katerina just turned and began to lead the way again. Jocasta noticed the gentle sway of her hips as she walked. Katerina had left her jacket in the boardroom, and Jocasta was having trouble keeping her eyes off of Katerina's frame. Her suit really was skintight, and Jocasta was admiring how muscular her legs were as she turned a corner and they arrived in the building's lobby. "This is where you came in, yes?" Katerina turned, and Jocasta tried to hide her ogling.

"Uh, yes. Yep. I can get to my car from here. Thank you." She reached out to shake Katerina's hand.

"Of course, Doctor. I will be glad to see more of you soon." Her hand grasped Jocasta's firmly, her skin soft and warm against Jocasta's clammy hand.

"You can call me Jocasta, you know. I mean, I like Doctor, it's still really cool for me to hear that title, actually, but we are probably going to be working pretty closely, and I don't want you to think you *have* to call me that." She smiled again, and Jocasta felt heat rising in her cheeks.

"Okay, Jocasta. I would also prefer it if you called me Katerina." Her accent was incredible, and Jocasta tried to say her name as correctly as possible, but she was pretty sure it sounded as American as ever coming out of her mouth.

"Well, see you soon, Katerina." Jocasta turned to go, silently cursing the week of grading she still had ahead of her. *"Why couldn't I just quit before finals?"* She thought as her hand touched the door.

"Oh Doc-Jocasta!" Katerina grabbed her arm to stop her from walking

7

away. "I wanted to give you my contact information in case you would like to touch base or if you have questions before you move in."

"Thank you, but I have Marc's phone number, you don't have to-"

"Nonsense, you'll need my number soon enough." She held out her hand, and Jocasta handed Katerina her phone. As she typed in the numbers, Jocasta watched her fingers. They were delicate, swiftly tapping the screen. Katerina's hands were as elegant as the rest of her. She handed the phone back. "Okay, you can go now." She turned around and walked back into the hallway they had just left, her auburn waves bouncing as she went.

KATERINA

Katerina had never once felt the attraction she felt toward the Doctor. *Jocasta*. She would never have offered to walk a stranger back to the lobby, that was unnecessary time where someone could try to talk to her. But the Doctor hadn't. She just followed Katerina's lead and walked in the quiet of the hallways. It was Katerina who felt the need to break the silence, and for what? To ask a question that barely made sense and to get an answer she didn't need to hear out loud. She could have just read the Doctor's thoughts. They weren't friends or anything, but when she looked at her, the idea to take a peek seemed... *dirty* for some reason. She was so small, it was hard to believe that she could really do the things they talked about in the meeting, and she had such an innocence and optimism in her eyes that Katerina felt if she had looked into her mind, she would have been tarnishing something pure.

Doctor Jones was a bit of a mystery to Katerina. She was small and sweet upon a first glance, but when they were talking about her research possibilities within W.E.I.R.D., she had a real power behind her words, strength and intellect beyond her years that she didn't show on the surface. It had made her suspicious in the meeting. Katerina felt that many people had underestimated the woman she just left at the door, and she did not want to be one of them. In fact, she wasn't sure if what she was attracted to was entirely professional curiosity, especially after their conversation in the hallway. Jocasta's eyes were mysterious as they were gorgeous. A caramel brown that made Katerina feel warm inside, like stepping into the sun after a long winter. Her slight build only accentuated how lean she was, small but strong. Katerina had never seen someone who made brown hair and eyes look like the most rare and beautiful thing on Earth, but the Doctor did. Katerina was a little bit worried about working with her now that she knew just how distractingly beautiful she was. She had been so distracted in the meeting that she almost didn't hear anything her fellow Phenoms had said. Just Jocasta's responses. Watching the Doctor as she got increasingly excited for the opportunities this position would give her was mesmerizing. It was definitely safe to say that Katerina had a bit of a crush. Now just to try and ignore that so that she could remain professional. She was already the youngest person ever on the team at 24, and there was no need to embarrass herself with a schoolgirl crush on their newest addition. The teasing she would have to endure from Viktoria would be unbearable. She would have to just get over it, and fast.

As she pushed open the doors to the boardroom, she overheard Agent Wright laughing, "That doctor is quite a looker, I wonder how she feels about workplace relationships, because I could see a fight breaking out over someone that pretty with all this testosterone everywhere."

"Oh please, she's only 25, Wright, half of us are old enough to be her father." Marc scoffed. "You included."

"I am not! I'm 38! That's only 13," He paused and chuckled, "Yeah, too much for me."

"I have a feeling it won't matter anyway, boys." Katerina said. "According to my research, she is a lesbian."

"How come I don't know that, and I have known her for years?" Marc seemed genuinely surprised. "Maybe our relationship is more professional than I realized."

"I'm sure she just never felt the need to say anything. Or she assumed you knew already. I mean, I only know because it is in her author's description in her book." Katerina realized it might have been a bit too much preparation to read all four hundred pages of Dr. Jones's book before the meeting, because everyone looked at her like she had done something strange.

"Were we supposed to familiarize ourselves with the Doctor's work before this meeting? Because I *definitely* did not." Carter sighed, "I did google her, but I didn't read her book. Was I supposed to?" They looked at Marc, genuine concern in their eyes, "I assumed the meeting was a formality, since you already knew her."

Marc patted Carter on the shoulder. "No, you didn't have to do that at all, Katerina is just overly prepared to meet new people. She doesn't want any surprises, good or bad." Carter's shoulders relaxed, and they looked at Katerina.

"It's true," she shrugged, glad that Marc understood her apprehension at bringing outsiders into their group. It had taken her long enough to let herself become as close as she was to the current team members. "The Phenoms are my family, I'm always worried to bring in a new person."

"Okay," Carter drew out the word. "Well, I am hungry, and it seems like a good time to get home and eat! Everybody on the same page?" They looked around; excitement written all over their face. For someone who was older than Katerina, their energy was so much younger and lighter than hers was. She envied them of their optimism and seemingly eternal joy. Especially after all they had been through. As they all said their goodbyes to Agent Wright, Arthur pulled Katerina away for a moment.

"Are you okay, kid? You seem a bit off." He looked at her sincerely, worry starting to crinkle his eyes.

"Yeah, Art. I'm fine. Just nervous to have someone studying us *and* living with us."

"Marc has every confidence that this will be a great thing for the team, and I actually agree with him for once. You can relax! We will all be there with you and for you."

"Thank you, Art. Let's get home." She didn't want to tell Arthur that she was more concerned because she felt like melting in a puddle when the Doctor's eyes met hers than she was because she would be studying their powers. That she was more nervous that the whole team would see her melting and would tease her relentlessly. The science didn't worry her, Doctor Jones was a great doctor. Her book was well written, and she backed herself up with incredible amounts of research. Katerina thought that with as young as she was, Jocasta probably never slept, with the amount of work she had already accomplished. Anyway, it was the chemistry she was worried about. Or lack thereof, which she wasn't sure would be better.

She followed her friends to the private jet they had taken to get to the W.E.I.R.D. headquarters and took a seat next to Carter. They gave her a quizzical look, probably wondering what Arthur had wanted to talk about. She shook her head, and they didn't press. This was the kind of thing that made her feel so comfortable with the group of people she called her family. Nobody pressed her or made her feel like an outsider if she didn't want to talk, and if she did want to talk, they would listen and not judge her. Not that she ever really talked to anyone other than Viktoria or Art about anything really deep.

Viktoria was the only other woman in the main group of active duty Phenoms. Well, the only one that stuck around most of the time anyway. There was Heather, who controlled the weather, funnily enough, but she was usually off base, working with meteorologists and natural disaster efforts to help with predictions and damage control. Katerina admired her and the work she did, but they weren't really that close. Usually, it was just her, Vik, Carter, Austin, Marc, and Arthur who stayed and worked at the mansion. There were plenty of trainees and kids who learned how to hone their powers, not to mention medical and research staff that worked there every day, but most of them only stayed during their training. Many of the enhanced individuals that trained at the mansion worked abroad or as special agents with non-enhanced agents of W.E.I.R.D. They were all technically Phenoms, but they were almost never called in to assist with the missions the six of them went on, except for Heather, who worked with them semi-regularly. And the kids that learned how to control their powers only came on the weekends, supervised by either one of the main six Phenoms or a group of trainees if they were on a mission. Katerina let out a small sigh of relief when she saw the mansion out the window of the jet, glad to be home.

As they landed, she couldn't help but look at her phone, wondering if Jocasta had sent her a text. There was one message from an unknown number, telling her that it was Jocasta, in case she needed to reach out to her instead of the other way around. She grinned and saved her number as a contact. As she typed her name, Katerina couldn't help but smile at how beautiful it was. *Jocasta*. It rang a bell for some reason. She kept pondering her name as the guys got some lunch made, and she ate quickly, excusing herself to her room as soon as she was finished. She quickly looked it up, and immediately found why it was so familiar. Jocasta was a Greek name, specifically the name of Oedipus's mother-and wife in the famous story. Katerina wondered if that was ever an issue in Jocasta's life. And then wondered why her parents would ever choose that name, not just because of the unfortunate connection to an incestuous mother, but because according to her author's notes, Jocasta grew up in the Midwest to a couple of 'all American parents' in her words. Maybe they just thought it was pretty, or maybe it had another meaning.

She dug a little deeper and found that Jocasta's name meant 'shining moon'. She thought that it might be odd to mention it to her, but that made it seem much more fitting. She kept thinking about it. Jocasta, shining moon, beauty, mystery, strength. The moon controlled the tides, but Jocasta was controlling Katerina's thoughts, and that was going to be a challenge.

What was it about this woman that made her think like this? She had had romantic relationships before, but no one had ever captivated her from the moment she met them before. Just sitting outside the boardroom, Jocasta had been mesmerizing in her suit. She had an undercut, and the top had been pulled back into a tiny bun, very neatly, like she wanted every strand to be perfect. Her hands had been sweaty when she shook Katerina's, and she thought it was very attractive that she had been so nervous and eager for an interview that she could have crushed in her sleep. She decided to go downstairs and train to try and get her mind off of Jocasta, but she had a feeling she would be glued to her phone waiting for a text message for the next week.

JOCASTA

The week had passed excruciatingly slowly for Jocasta. Grading finals felt like torture when she knew the possibilities awaiting her at the week's end. Not to mention that this semester's batch of students seemed to have taken her class as an easy credit. None of them had shown the interest in her teaching that she was hoping for. She knew her field was small, but this semester had her afraid that suprology would become extinct before it had even gotten fully established. A colleague of hers had been asked to take over her classes in the fall, as the University had not been too happy about her leaving, and he seemed up to the task, so she could only hope that he could get some shining new faces into the field. Clinging to the hope that her W.E.I.R.D. research would change that situation for the better was what got her through the dismal papers.

Now, she was incredibly excited, so much so that she was almost not nervous when she pulled up to the mansion that would be her new home for the foreseeable future. She had never seen a place so gorgeous. Not necessarily the architecture, it was just a big, modern, window-filled building. It was the knowledge that her whole life was going to change in that building that made it so beautiful.

The drive up here was peaceful, and the excitement had really started to get to Jocasta. This really would be the beginning of a whole new chapter for her and for suprology itself. Not to mention, she would be seeing Katerina again. She had been occupying the corners of Jocasta's mind since the meeting. She kept seeing those deep blue eyes whenever she closed her own. There hadn't been any time to reach out since the meeting, between the dismal grading and panic packing. Plus, she couldn't figure out what to say, anyway. And apparently, neither could Katerina, as she hadn't texted Jocasta either. She was incredibly interested in learning more

14

about Katerina, though, and it wasn't just because her powers had yet to be studied intensely. She felt drawn to Katerina, both because of her mysterious powers and because she was being featured in Jocasta's daydreams more and more as the week went on. Jocasta couldn't stop thinking about her, and even now she was starting to let her mind drift to what it might be like living in the same building as someone that stunningly gorgeous. *"Don't start again. You just met her, you hopeless romantic."*

She parked in front of what looked to be the main entrance of the mansion and looked around. Was someone coming to greet her? They couldn't possibly think she would just let herself into their home. She had received a key in advance, but she was still an outsider, it would be very strange if they wanted her to enter unannounced. Before she could finish pondering whether or not to get out of her car, Katerina stepped out of the door, and Jocasta tried not to let her jaw drop at how beautiful she was. Even her imagination couldn't compare to her in real life. She was followed by Viktoria Antonov, another member of the Phenoms, and an incredible inspiration for Jocasta. Behind them, Marc and Arthur waited by the doors for her to start gathering her things. She opened her car door and stood up just in time for Katerina to reach out her hand to shake. "Hello again, Docto- Jocasta." She caught herself before Jocasta could remind her to use her first name. "I would like you to meet Viktoria Antonov, who I'm sure you know as 'Noxia'." Jocasta reached out to shake Viktoria's hand.

"You are an inspiration, Miss Antonov. I actually wrote my thesis paper for my doctorate about you. It's an honor."

"Likewise, Doctor." Viktoria's grip was even stronger than her Russian accent. "And please, call me Vik."

Jocasta was awestruck for a moment, this woman who had saved the world countless times had just said it was an honor to meet her. She even told her to call her by a nickname! This was better than a dream. "Please, call me Jocasta."

"Alright Ladies, now that we're all introduced, can we please get all of this luggage?" Art called, heading their direction.

"We didn't want to overwhelm you with the whole rest of the team, right when you showed up, so I asked if everyone would wait a bit to meet you. Arthur is anxious to make the introductions." Katerina chuckled.

"Do you think you two can handle the bags? I want to show her her living space." She called to Marc and Arthur, who were waiting by the trunk.

"Obviously, what else would I be using my enhanced musculature for?" Arthur laughed.

"Just pop the trunk before you go, would you Jocasta? I don't think you want Artie over here to 'accidentally' break your car." Marc was smiling ear to ear as she reached down to hit the button. "We should be getting you a better car though; this is going to look dismal in the garage here."

"Hey! I like my car! I've had it since I was 16!" She laughed as the women began to lead her away.

"And it was already old nine years ago!" Marc shouted after them. Viktoria opened the door and ushered the other two into the building.

"Let's hurry before those two really get started with the jokes. They both think they are the most hilarious man alive. It's ridiculous." She smiled, and Jocasta giggled.

"I think it's sweet that they act like that. It makes you guys really feel like a family. My parents were always like that, having contests to see who could make me laugh harder, or who could make pancakes better... It's nice."

"Well, it is also a bit annoying sometimes. Especially when we are in the middle of a mission, and they do it while we are actively participating in a fight. But here I guess it is kind of cute." Katerina looked at her as they walked down a hallway. "My parents were also silly, but never competitive like those two."

"Maybe it's an American thing." Viktoria stopped at a closed door on the right side of the hallway. "This is your room. Every room has its own attached bathroom, too, so do not worry about having to share with all of us."

"I'm right across the hall, and Vik is down that way," Katerina said, pointing further down the hallway. "We can wait here if you want to get acquainted with the space."

"Thank you, but I actually want to check out my workspace before I get settled, if that's okay with you guys." She paused for a second, "Unless I'm supposed to meet everyone else first. I almost forgot!" Katerina and Viktoria exchanged a glance, and Katerina turned to Jocasta.

"We actually were going to have everyone meet you in the new lab, and then Marc has a cocktail party planned. Don't tell him we told you, it is supposed to be a surprise." She smiled that intoxicating smile. "I can stay with you in your room for a bit if you want. The boys should be bringing your things in a few moments."

"I'm going to wrangle the rest of the team. Marc put me in charge of setting up. See you this evening, Jocasta." Viktoria disappeared back down the hall the way they had come, leaving Jocasta alone with Katerina. She had a sneaking suspicion that Katerina might have planned this. Or was that just because she had been daydreaming about being alone with Katerina since the moment they met?

"Uh, sure. I'll probably need some help unboxing some things if you wouldn't mind." She looked at Katerina, trying to get a read on whether she was right about her suspicions. There was a glint in her eyes that made Jocasta nervous. *"Are you reading my mind? No? I would probably feel something if you were doing that...right?"* She realized she had been staring at her new colleague. Great. *"Can I get even more awkward?"* "Um, I should probably open the door." She muttered, reaching for the handle.

"Were you just trying to see if I was reading your mind?"

"What!?" Jocasta feigned, "I mean, no! Not at all. Nope."

"I'm used to it, really. I can actually tell when someone is doing it without reading them at this point. It has become obvious." Katerina giggled. "Sometimes, men will do it so hard that I'll pretend I am reading them, and they always apologize for whatever sexual thing they were thinking about. Women are a little harder to read."

"What about nonbinary folx?"

"It depends. For example, Carter is incredibly easy to read, Austin, not so much. Oh, you'll meet Austin later." She followed Jocasta into the room. "They're super sweet."

Jocasta looked around the room. It was huge, clean, and modern. The furniture was sleek and gorgeous, black dresser and bed frame, black nightstand. The walls were a robin's egg blue, that made Katerina's eyes pop just a little more when she entered. Well three of them were. The far wall was entirely window, and the view was immaculate. Beautiful trees as far as she could see, and a good view of the training grounds as well. She looked to her left and saw a door that must lead to the bathroom, as well as a very cute reading nook and gorgeous white chair. She took a seat, admiring the luxurious fabric. "This is incredible. My whole apartment is the size of this room. Wait. Did you mean Austin Greene? Like the fastest enhanced individual ever recorded? Snap Speed?"

"They are a Phenom, and they live here...so obviously you would be meeting them. Would you like a list, or?" Katerina smiled again, and Jocasta felt like the Earth was moving.

"Knock Knock, luggage is here!" Marc walked in with about a fourth of Jocasta's things from the trunk, sweating profusely. He was followed by Arthur, who held everything else, and was not even breaking a sweat. This was going to be the most incredible job ever. They sat her things in the corner of the room next to her now favorite chair and left to go "prepare the others to meet her" which Katerina promptly explained to her that was code for helping Vik decorate her new lab for the big reveal. She had explained to the men that she would stay with Jocasta to keep her company while she unpacked, but she was also giving her a bit of a rundown of the mansion and the grounds. They had been talking for quite some time now, and Katerina had even asked her about the origins of her name without making fun of the fact that Oedipus's mom shared her name, which was refreshing.

Jocasta looked at Katerina, who was explaining that the tennis court literally opened into a pool, as if any of the Phenoms had relaxation time enough to develop a tennis *or* swimming habit. She looked so much more at ease here in the mansion than she had at the W.E.I.R.D. headquarters. Her cascading auburn locks shone in the natural light of the window, and Jocasta could actually see a few scattered freckles on Katerina's cheeks and nose. She was wearing jeans, a t-shirt, and a cardigan, which was much different from her super suit, which is really all Jocasta had seen any of the Phenoms in, save for Marc, who was always swarmed with press and wearing the best suits. Today, everyone had been in casual clothes, and Jocasta felt like she was in a slightly skewed version of reality, where she was actually friends with these incredible people, which of course, was probably going to be the case very soon. Katerina looked up and tilted her head to the side. "I'm sorry. Am I overwhelming you?"

"Oh! No, you aren't. I just, um. This is an incredible opportunity and I really do not want to blow it." Jocasta met her eyes and for a second, she almost felt a spark. Of what, she wasn't sure. Attraction was obvious, but was this professional excitement, or something more? She desperately wanted it to be the latter, but that would probably be something that would lead to the aforementioned 'blowing it' so maybe she didn't want that. The more time she was spending with Katerina, the more confused she was becoming. "You seem different though. You were much quieter last week. And much more serious." She lifted her eyebrow. "Is this the real you, or are you as nervous about this endeavor as I am?"

"I, as you may have noticed, have tasked myself with making you feel at home. I am probably more nervous than you are, and that is definitely why I'm so, uh, talkative." She deflated a little bit. "Seriousness comes with the job."

"I'm sorry, I'm not trying to push your buttons or anything, I'm just curious about you." She realized what she said, and she felt her heart jump into her throat. "I mean, professionally. Um, there are some theories that powers are connected to emotions and personality, and um yeah." She dropped off, silently praying to whatever god was listening that Katerina was honest before about not listening in on her thoughts. She had a feeling she would be praying that a lot more often. Katerina finished the box of shirts she had been unpacking and opened another box of Jocasta's things. Jocasta watched as her cheeks flushed and her eyes widened.

"Um, I think this was a private box." She swiftly closed the lid. "I'll just put this somewhere else for now." Jocasta looked up as Katerina stood to move the box and recognized the label. [Literally a Box of Socks] It was meant to be a joke for herself later because it was actually a box of her... intimate things.

"I didn't want my landlord to show up and go through my things while I'm gone. He is quite nosy." She blushed. "I am so sorry I didn't hide that before we started."

"It's okay. You might want to keep it somewhere pretty safe, some of the trainees tend to be the snooping type...I'd hate for someone to think you were getting freaky with one of us." She winked. "What else do you want to unpack?"

"How about we just take a break? I bet they'll be wanting to escort me into the lab soon, and I am pretty exhausted." Jocasta got up and sat at the foot of the bed, gesturing for Katerina to join her.

"Sure you don't mean embarrassed? Don't be, really. I have no business judging your private life, and I never would, even if I had the business." Katerina smiled and sat on the bed next to her. "But, now I know a secret about you, so I guess you owe me for not immediately telling everyone that you own handcuffs for," she cleared her throat, "fun." She smirked. "I'm surprised though, you seem more vanilla than that box suggested."

"I am going to pretend you didn't say any of that and stay embarrassed." Jocasta laughed. "And for the record, how would anyone be 'getting freaky' in this mansion of windows?" She gestured at her expansive window of a wall.

"Like this, obviously." Katerina leaned over her, and Jocasta could feel her heartbeat start going double time. Katerina reached past her and grabbed a remote on her bedside table, and she tried to calm her heartbeat. Jocasta heard a beep and the whir of automatic privacy drapes covering the window wall as Katerina moved back to where she had been sitting. The smell of her shampoo lingered in Jocasta's nose, and she had to take a steadying breath before responding.

"That's cool! Does the remote control anything else?" She reached behind her where Katerina had left the remote. It was small and had about a million buttons. *"That's not confusing at all."* "Um, that is a lot of buttons."

"Yes, it controls many things in the room. I can have Marc explain it to you, he is a *lot* better at explaining technology things than I am."

"Oh okay." Jocasta sighed. "This is all a bit strange. I mean, this mansion is huge, and I'm not used to that. Space, that is. And how many people live here? The team has at least 6 people regularly seen on missions, but do you *all* live here? And does anyone else live here? Security? Intelligence? I am beginning to realize that some of you must have families. What is that like? Oh my GOD. Does anyone have kids? Are there CHILDREN who live here?" Jocasta realized how many questions she had just thrown out and blushed. "Sorry. I'm just getting nervous and excited again."

"It's okay, honestly. This place is really odd when you first arrive. Many Phenoms are not part of the 'main group' and live off site or abroad, working in different capacities with W.E.I.R.D., and I'm honestly not sure how many people live here full time, other than the 6 of us. Heather is here every so often, but she doesn't stay full time. There are definitely no children here though. Unless you count the teenage enhanced individuals who come here on weekends to train and practice their powers in a safe space. Two or three of them spend the night on those weekends though." Katerina put her hand on Jocasta's. "We are all very excited to have you here. Me especially. You don't have to worry." Jocasta looked into her eyes and felt it again. The spark of something inexplicable.

"Um Katerina? I'm sorry I didn't reach out this week. I was so busy finishing the semester and packing. I also didn't really know what to say."

"What do you mean? We've been talking for hours, and you knew what to say the whole time. I had trouble too, but I regret it. You're very easy to talk to, Jocasta." It was the first time she had said her name without almost saying 'Doctor' first, and it literally took the wind out of Jocasta to hear it on her lips. It was almost like hearing her own name for the first time. She felt the heat rise in her cheeks.

"Hey! You didn't say Doctor first! Does that mean we're friends now?"

"I-I guess I just had to get used to it. I would like to be friends if you would." Katerina pulled her hand away and looked at her watch. "It is about time to head down to your lab; I'll leave you to change if you want."

"Oh no, I don't need to change, we can head down." *"What I mean is don't leave."* She thought. This whole 'friends' idea was going to be a challenge, especially since Katerina just kept getting more beautiful with every interaction. They stood up and Jocasta followed Katerina's lead down two floors and to her new lab. It was absolutely incredible. Everyone was wonderfully kind and welcomed her with open arms. She got to know some of the techs and doctors that she would be working with, or rather, overseeing, and they all seemed great. She couldn't believe how lucky she was.

<hr />

KATERINA

Jocasta was probably the most entrancing person Katerina had ever seen. She couldn't stop thinking about how soft her hand was when she had comforted her earlier, and now, watching her talk to Austin at the party, all she could think was that if her hands were that soft, how soft would her lips be? Not that she would be finding out, like ever. They were friends now. Friends. That would be fine. She could handle friends. But *friends* could lead to late nights, and drinks, and hugging, which. She stopped herself. *"Do not even let yourself think that you imbecile."* She knew that was a dangerous train of thought to follow. They were coworkers and friends. That's all. Plus, Jocasta would be studying her, and wouldn't a romantic relationship cause a conflict of interest? And, who knew if she was even single? There were enough *things* in that box she had opened to suggest a full sex life. She tried to hide the thrill she got when she thought about what she would like to do with some of those things and tuned back into whatever it was that Vik was saying to her.

"And anyway, that's when we all decided to get the hell out of there, you know?" Vik was saying. She looked at Katerina. "You weren't listening, were you?"

"Sorry, I'm a bit distracted tonight."

"Clearly. What on Earth has she done to you?"

"What? Who? Jocasta? Nothing. Why do you ask?" Katerina could feel herself beginning to blush. Viktoria was better at reading people than anyone else, and she had been caught daydreaming.

"You're staring at her like she just ran over your puppy. Are you sure?"

"Yes. I am fine, Vik. She's actually wonderful." She was definitely blushing now. "I just um, I'm worried about what the testing is going to consist of."

"Okay, well I'm sure the doctor is still working that out herself, and I doubt it will be too invasive. She seems," Vik paused for a moment, "like she really respects privacy." At that, Katerina choked back a laugh, thinking of the privacy she had invaded earlier.

"Yes, she really does. I'm going to head up to bed, it's getting pretty late." As she started walking toward the door, Jocasta ran up to her.

"Hey! Where do you think you're going? We were just going to start a dance!" Jocasta reached for her hand. "You've got to dance with me." Katerina felt a tingle run up her arm at the sensation of Jocasta's fingers wrapping around her hand. She pulled her to the center of the room, where Austin and Carter were waiting. As soon as she was about to ask what song they were dancing to, the Cupid Shuffle started playing and Katerina laughed.

"Dating ourselves with this one, huh? Not something newer?" Katerina nudged Jocasta with her elbow.

"We're still the youngest people here, Katerina. Enjoy it while it lasts!" The four of them giggled and danced until the song ended, and then Marc's voice came over the speakers.

"We have received some new intel on the terrorist cell we've been tracking in Germany. Everyone let's get to bed, I will be calling on a few of you in the morning for a new mission. Welcome home, Doctor Jones, and goodnight, everybody." He was standing in the corner of the room, and when he locked eyes with Katerina, she didn't need to read his mind to know she was going to be in Germany tomorrow. This group was small and didn't have a name that had been found yet, but they always used the same weapons and left a spray-painted symbol. They had set off quite a few bombs internationally, all government buildings that housed offices of people who were advocating for clean energy.

"Come on, I'll walk you back to your room, Jocasta." She grabbed her hand and headed toward the doors. Everyone else was already leaving the room, and she wanted to tell her that under no circumstances should she request to come on the mission to study them. She could begin with whoever was not on the mission.

"Actually, I need to speak with Marc before I go up." Katerina felt Jocasta's hand leave her grip and turned. "Don't worry, not about you." Jocasta laughed.

"Well, I can wait." Katerina offered, hoping she would still be able to ask her to stay behind for a while.

"Okay, it'll just be a minute. I definitely couldn't find my way back without you, this place is even bigger than I realized." Jocasta smiled and made her way over to Marc. Katerina realized she was directly in the way of the people who hadn't left yet, and she slipped out the door to wait for Jocasta. This group was incredibly dangerous, and if the intel they received was what they had been hoping for, the team would be heading directly into their base of operations. They kept moving it every few months, and this was the quickest they had found the new base, so they were confident they would still be operating out of this location. *"I should have just read Marc, then I wouldn't be so anxious."* But that was a violation of her own personal rule not to spy on her friends and coworkers' thoughts.

As soon as she could control it, she made sure not to violate anyone's trust. That didn't mean that she *never* read her friends, though. Sometimes someone would fixate on a thought so much that it would just pop into her head when she looked at them. She would never tell anyone though. Of course, she might have to tell Jocasta with her research. That could prove to be interesting. She could only imagine Jocasta focusing intently on the phrase "Can you hear me?", her nose all scrunched up. It was a very cute image if she was being honest. She kind of hoped it *would* happen now that she was picturing it. She felt a flutter in her stomach at the thought of seeing Jocasta's face when she would respond *"Yes, I can hear you, Jocasta."*

She waited for another few minutes, trying not to let her mind wander too far, or fixate on the smooth lines of Jocasta's jaw, or the way her body moved when they danced together. She needed to focus on the upcoming mission, and that was becoming increasingly difficult waiting for Jocasta to finish talking with Marc. What could she be talking about? She hoped it wasn't the mission tomorrow. Jocasta was not ready to accompany them on a mission so soon. Katerina hoped she would never have to accompany them on a mission. People always thought 'mind control' seemed cool, but her powers were much uglier in practice. She didn't want Jocasta to see it in real action and change her mind about being friends. More than one person had done it before, and she was already nervous to be friends with this woman who was becoming increasingly, well, distracting. Just as she was thinking she might have to knock and see if Jocasta still wanted her to wait, the door opened. Jocasta stepped out, a grin on her face, and closed the door behind her. *"Marc must be staying to plan the mission."* She worried about him sometimes, he seemed to never rest. "Are you ready to get to bed?" Katerina grinned at Jocasta, "It'll be a big day for the whole mansion tomorrow."

"I honestly don't know how I'm going to sleep. Marc just told me that I get to accompany you all tomorrow." When she smiled, Katerina felt her throat close up a little bit. "Virtually, of course. I'm not trained to be in the field, obviously."

Katerina let her throat muscles relax before she responded. "That's great! I doubt I'll get much sleep either. I'm still a bit jittery before a big mission."

"Maybe it's not the best idea, but seeing as how we both won't be sleeping very well, do you want to study up on the terrorist group with me? I don't know much about it, and I was hoping to get at least generally up to speed, so that I can focus on studying the way everyone's powers work in the field, instead of on the actual mission. If I don't learn about them, I'll be distracted with questions about the mission rather than focusing on my work." She laughed. "Sometimes I wish I wasn't so curious." Jocasta reached up and pushed back her hair, which had fallen into her face. Katerina felt that flutter again.

"Um, sure. We can use the screens in my room if you'd like. It's a little less daunting than our command room." She started walking toward their rooms. "I'd probably also change into something more comfortable, in case we actually end up getting tired."

"Fat chance," Jocasta giggled. "But I do really want to get into some sweatpants."

They walked quickly, and they were in front of their doors in no time. "Just knock when you're done changing." Katerina said as she popped into her room. What on Earth was she thinking? She really was jittery before a mission, but there was no reason to do anything other than try to sleep right now. Except for that she wanted to spend more time with Jocasta before she started to get busy with her work. And when Jocasta was excited, she looked so cute, Katerina wanted to pick her up and hold her in her arms for the rest of forever. So, it seemed getting over this crush was going to be a lot more troublesome than she was prepared for.

She changed into a comfortable pair of sweats and a tank top and began getting the screens on her wall set up. The privacy drapes were much more than just drapes. As she tapped the buttons on her remote, multiple different screens came to life on the drapes, displaying as much information on the terrorist cell as she could fit onto the wall. When she had the information she wanted to display all ready, she heard a soft knock at the door. She stopped herself from calling "It's open!" and walked to the door so that she could sneak a peek at Jocasta.

She didn't want her to notice if she accidentally stared too long when she came in. She looked out the peephole to see Jocasta standing there in an oversized henley style shirt and what looked like fuzzy pajama pants. She had a notebook hugged to her chest, and a pair of wire framed glasses sitting delicately on the bridge of her nose. She reached up as if to knock again, and Katerina realized she had been staring a bit too long, and she opened the door before Jocasta's hand could hit the wood.

When the door swung open, Jocasta's eyes grew wide. "Is that what the privacy drapes do? I thought all those buttons were for like hidden screens on the wall, but that is a whole other level. Also, sorry, hi, hope you don't mind that I went straight for pajamas instead of sweats." She gestured at her pants, which were definitely fuzzy, and pink. She looked up at Katerina, and her glasses slid down her nose a little bit, making Katerina smile.

"I don't mind. Come on in." Katerina opened the door wider to allow her to pass. "Are those glasses for reading, or for blue light? They're very cute." Katerina tried to hide her blushing.

"Oh! They're actually for both. My good 'ole work glasses. I get migraines without them at this point. Do you wanna try them on? They were only like $15, which is pretty good for blue lights." She reached up to take off the glasses, "I'm sorry, I'm rambling a little bit, aren't I? I think I might still be a little jazzed from the party."

"No, you are absolutely fine. I'd like to try them on." She took the glasses from Jocasta's hand and when their fingers brushed, Katerina felt that tingle up her arm again. She put the glasses on, and looked up to see Jocasta blushing, eyes wide. "How do they look?"

"Um, they're, ah, really cute!" Jocasta cleared her throat. "Uh, do you want to get started? I brought my notebook, but I think maybe it would be easier to just send me a file of highlights while we're doing this." She tugged at the ends of her shirt sleeves and bounced on the balls of her feet, and Katerina had to look down at her own feet to escape the urge to scoop her up and kiss her.

"Okay, but I have to make sure that W.E.I.R.D. gave you clearance to access this information, it is pretty confidential." She paused before realizing she had made a mistake. "I probably should have done that before pulling it all up, shit." Katerina went to grab her remote and turn off the blinds so that she wouldn't get in trouble in case Jocasta wasn't allowed to know about the classified intel splayed across the wall.

"Marc said I have the same clearance as any of the team would. Except for him and Arthur, obviously. They have a bit higher clearance than everyone else." Jocasta reached into a pocket on her fuzzy hip and pulled out a W.E.I.R.D. identification badge. She started rambling again. "This says clearance level D. Is that high enough? Did you just break a rule? I am so sorry, Kat-"

"Yes, D is high enough, Jocasta, calm down." Katerina cut her off, noticing that 'Kat' sounded much more appealing coming from Jocasta's lips than when anyone else had tried to call her that. "Let me just turn the screens back on, and we can start."

At that, Jocasta sat down on the end of Katerina's bed and breathed a sigh of relief. Katerina had a flash image of Jocasta, tangled up in the sheets she was sitting on top of, and had to turn away from her, afraid she would see the deep red that her cheeks had just turned. *"Stop thinking that way, god."* "Hey, Jocasta, I have a small table if you do want to write anything down, it's over by the chair." She said, hoping Jocasta would sit somewhere less, she flushed, distracting.

"Oh cool, thanks." Jocasta stood back up and walked over to the chair and table and hit her palm to her forehead. "I'm sorry, I shouldn't have just sat down on your bed without asking, that's shitty of me. A bed is an intimate piece of furniture. I should have thought about it."

"Jocasta, it's fine, really, I just thought you would want something to write on." Katerina bluffed. "Plus, that's my spot."

"It is a very comfortable place to sit." Jocasta teased, then paused, her face falling slightly. "Sorry, that was probably inappropriate."

"We all have the same beds, so, not really. Now, if we didn't all live in

the same house and have identical furniture here, I would agree with you."
Katerina smiled. "But I would have allowed it from you, anyway." She felt
her skin go cold and clammy at the realization that she said that out loud.
"Uh, you know, because you're new here and all. Probably a bit nervous."
She hoped she hadn't embarrassed herself too much.

"Katerina?" Jocasta sounded like she was smiling, and Katerina looked
up to see those caramel eyes earnestly trying to meet her own. "I um, well,
it might be crazy, but I feel connected to you. Like, I don't know, like
we've only known each other for literal hours, but I can tell you that you're
going to be really important to me." Jocasta looked down at her hands.
"Sorry if that was whack. You can just send me the info and I'll study it by
myself." She stood up and started to leave, but Katerina felt herself reach
for Jocasta's hand.

"Would you stop apologizing immediately for things that you do not
have to apologize for? So, you are nervous at a new job, and you are not
afraid to say what you think or feel. That does not make you *whack* or make
me want you to leave. I like you. You seem fun to work with and you seem
like a good friend. I do not usually like making friends or really even *want*
new friends, but I want you. As a friend. So, please, let's just get to work
and prepare you for the mission tomorrow." Katerina had never spoken like
that in her life. Why was she so determined to be close to Jocasta? Jocasta
had said it right, they had known each other for literal *hours* and Katerina
was making speeches about how great Jocasta was? It was absurd, to say
the least. It honestly felt like she was in someone else's body. She did like
Jocasta, and she was probably going to be a good friend, but what was
making her act the way she was acting? Surely not the tingling sensation
Jocasta's touch gave her, or the way her stomach felt like it was flying out of
her body when Jocasta's eyes met hers, or that thought earlier about sheets,
and now her mind was drifting again. "*Ugh I'm insufferable*," she thought.
"*I'm acting like another person because I want her to be sexually attracted to
me, and I am not even trying to stop myself. I'm a mess. Katerina Gradoff is
not a mess. I need to get it the fuck together, or I have to stop being around
her. It has literally been one day.*" She grabbed the remote and selected the
'overview' file on the screens. "Ready?" She asked through tight lips.

"Yes. And thank you. For that, uh, pep talk? I needed it." Jocasta gave her a smile so sincere, her internal 'pep talk' to herself melted away from her thoughts, replaced again by thoughts of tingles and butterflies and rivers of caramel. She was going to need a cold shower before the mission if she was going to be able to focus at all.

~~~~~~

JOCASTA

Jocasta was pumped, to say the least. Marc got her set up with a communicator and a screen so she could see everything from his perspective in his suit of armor. She would be able to hear everything they said to each other, and see the mission firsthand, but she was set to mute so that she wouldn't distract anyone. Which, after embarrassing herself repeatedly in Katerina's room last night, was probably a great idea. She did not want to say something stupid again, especially when it might get someone killed. Although Katerina had said her nervousness and over talking was not something she should apologize for, she was a bit colder to Jocasta when they were studying up, and Jocasta couldn't help but wonder if she had already messed up her friendship with Katerina before it had even really begun. Not that she *wanted* it to just be a friendship, but that was neither here nor there.

The team was about to enter the facility and capture the leader of the terrorist cell. Marcus turned his head, and Jocasta saw Katerina, eyes shining with power, taking over the guard at the door they were about to enter. She used her powers to make him open the door with his fingerprint, then Marc knocked him unconscious. As she was controlling the guard, Jocasta couldn't help but think that she wouldn't mind Katerina taking her over like that and blushed even though no one was in the room with her. They entered the facility and just as Katerina was about to engage another terrorist, Jocasta heard a loud crash and a bang. As Marc turned toward the noise, the screen went dead, and her sound turned off. Marc had said if anything started to get a little bit dicey, she would be cut off, but now that it was happening, she felt a chill run down her spine. They were supposed to be entering the facility stealthily until they reached the center, where the leader was, but that sound had been anything but stealthy.

She waited for another hour, nerves running her raw, thinking about what could have happened to the team, and decided she probably would not be patched back in. She went up to her room and sat on her bed. Maybe if she tried out the remote some, it would ease her mind. She played around with the buttons and eventually figured out how to get her streaming set up on the screens. She didn't feel like watching anything though; she was still on edge. She got the drapes to retreat back into the ceiling and pulled her chair over to the window. A few of the Phenoms stayed behind, and Austin and Carter were out on the training grounds. It looked like they were playing some sort of "keep the balloon off the ground" type of game, but they were using their powers to do it. She looked further out and tried to find some way to calm her nerves in the trees. The forest was expansive, and so bright and green in the late spring that she did feel a bit of comfort in its beauty. Also probably in the color green, which hadn't been her favorite color, but had recently been so comforting, she might just change that. She tried to hold onto the little bit of calm she got from the trees, and unpacked a bit more of her things before she went back down to her set up of the mission, just to check if Marc had patched her back in.

She walked in to see that the screens were now showing the inside of the Phenom's jet, and that the team seemed to be debriefing. She watched for a moment to make sure all four of the people who left that morning were still there, and then she turned off the screens. They would be back soon, and she could ask Katerina what she missed. She knew that after watching as much as she did, she would rather not watch a mission from the sidelines again. Maybe if she had some field training, she would like to *go* on one, but until then, she would be studying everyone right here in her lab. Or maybe outside. There was not a ton of space in here for powers like super speed. There were a lot of breakable things too. Maybe she should go on the training grounds to study. That would definitely work better than her lab, but it was also outside, so it was subject to weather. Maybe she should ask if they did training anywhere inside the mansion.

As she continued to plan where and how she should really begin her studies, she got into a head space she hadn't been in since her first study in college. She felt an excitement for her project and her theories that made her remember why she went through all of that school in the first place. It was these moments when she didn't mind the mountain of student debt she had to pay off, if it meant this was her job. As she was working, Katerina entered the room, but she didn't see her until she was right next to her. "Oh! Hi! You're back! What happened? I got cut off, and I waited for a while, but then I didn't get patched back in, so I just thought I would wait until you got back. Sorry, it's probably overwhelming for me to bombard you with questions right after that, isn't it? My bad."

"It is okay, Jocasta." Katerina's accent melted Jocasta to the bones. "Everything went according to plan; you were accidentally cut off. Marc is not used to having a camera wired into his head gear." Katerina rested her hand next to the keyboard Jocasta was currently typing on, and Jocasta felt a tingle of excitement at her being so close with those powerful hands.

"Oh, that's good. I was worried when it cut out, and I had to go distract myself."

"What were you worried about? It is our job to do that sort of mission, we train for it, and we are very well prepared, you don't need to worry." Katerina leaned against Jocasta's desk, and her hip grazed Jocasta's arm in the process, making her feel the heat rise in her cheeks just a little bit.

"Well, I saw you and then I heard a crashing sound, and then everything cut out. I was worried you got blindsided or something!" Jocasta smiled. "I guess you think I'm pretty silly, worrying about that sort of thing as a civilian, when like you said, you are well prepared and trained, but it is not something I've ever seen before." Katerina looked down, either sad or embarrassed, Jocasta wasn't sure.

"You saw me use my powers?" She said softly, sounding a bit worried herself.

"Yea, of course I did, and it was amazing! The way you took control of that guard and used him to get into the building stealthily, it was so cool to watch. Your powers are so much more than I thought they were, I mean I knew you had telekinesis abilities, and you can read minds, but to essentially control someone even just a little bit? I mean, you are one in a million, you're just amazing." Jocasta felt her blush fully reach across her face as she was talking, but Katerina had gotten a bit of a shadow over her own face.

"It is not all that amazing. It is actually very dangerous. Most people think my powers are evil." Katerina looked like she was going to walk away, so Jocasta grabbed her hand.

32

"Your powers are beautiful, Katerina." She paused, weighing whether or not she should say the next thing. She must have decided that she should just say what she thought, because before she knew it the words were out of her mouth. "*You* are beautiful. All of you. And that means your powers are beautiful, too." She felt her whole body get hot and she knew her blush had deepened enough that her face was probably bright red. Katerina looked like she had just slapped her. Just completely shocked. They were both silent for a few moments, until Jocasta dropped her hand and said "Honestly, I am looking forward to figuring out your powers the most. I have a sneaking suspicion you are even more powerful than you think you are."

"Thank you, Jocasta. That means more than you can possibly know." Katerina managed, her eyes shining. "You are a good person, and I am very glad you're here." She smiled, and Jocasta felt a pang. She had just called Katerina *beautiful,* albeit accidentally and while rambling, and she responded with 'you're a good person'? She couldn't help but feel a little bit disappointed that Katerina hadn't returned the compliment. Maybe she just really wanted Katerina to think she was beautiful, but still. She *was* glad Katerina thought she was a good person and that she was glad for her being here, but it was not quite the response she longed for.

If she was honest, the response she *really* wanted was a very long, romantic kiss, but that would probably never happen at this point. She was going to start her research tomorrow, and they had already established their relationship as friends. There was not going to be an opportunity to try to date *anyone* in the near future, let alone her coworker/subject. Plus, she probably shouldn't try anything romantic with someone she was studying in the first place, that probably broke some sort of unspoken rule, even if most of suprology was uncharted waters. Best not to complicate anything.

"Jocasta? Have you eaten yet?" Marc popped his head into the lab. "Oh, hey Katerina, there you are. Do either of you want to come up to the kitchen? I think Austin made something. They're a pretty good cook."

"Uh, I think we're good." Katerina replied, and Jocasta gave her a side eye. "I wanted to take Jocasta to the cafe in town, if you don't need me." Jocasta smiled. Maybe Katerina was thinking the same things she was. Or maybe she wasn't even gay, and Jocasta was just an idiot. She hadn't even thought to ask, she just daydreamed and felt butterflies and never once focused on the harsh reality that Katerina might not even feel the tension she did. Maybe Jocasta was just losing her mind.

"Oh sure, go ahead! See you two later." Marc disappeared around the door frame, and Katerina grabbed Jocasta's hand, pulling her from her chair.

"Come on then! I really want you to try their grilled cheese sandwich. I know, you Americans think it's a basic sandwich, but I have never had one so good." Katerina paused and looked at Jocasta. "Were you finished? I'm sorry, I didn't think to ask."

"Oh yea, sure, I'm done. Um, hey Katerina? I wanted to ask you something, but I also hate asking people this because they always think I'm being creepy or hitting on them, but um are you, maybe, perchance, someone who dates women?" Jocasta's blood froze in her veins, hoping she hadn't ruined her new friendship. She honestly kind of hoped she was straight, because then she could stop torturing herself with what if scenarios. Katerina blushed though, and then she gave Jocasta a little wink that made her knees feel like Jell-O.

"Exclusively. The team doesn't know though, I never felt the need to tell them. So, it's a good thing you asked me and not anyone else, because then you wouldn't have the look on your face that you have now." Jocasta felt herself panic.

"What? What look?" Her legs were mere seconds from either collapsing or sprinting away, and she felt sweat on the back of her neck. Why did Katerina do these things to her?

"You just look relieved that there's another lesbian here, and also terrified because you thought I was going to be offended." Katerina laughed. "It's a cute combination of emotions." *Cute.* She called Jocasta *cute.* That had to mean something. She was a strong empowered woman; she wouldn't call another woman cute condescendingly. Maybe Jocasta shouldn't have asked. Now she was going to triple analyze everything Katerina said to her. Jocasta brushed her hair back and sighed.

"Well, let's get to this grilled cheese. That's a comfort food for me, so it better live up to your talk. That *was* pretty high praise for a grilled cheese, you know." Jocasta hoped Katerina couldn't hear the straining in her voice, trying not to sound as conflicted as she was feeling.

"I know, I know, but it is truly amazing." Katerina giggled. "I'll show you to the garage, I don't think anyone has shown you where it is yet, have they?"

"Uh, nope. And honestly if they had, I wouldn't remember, this place is huge. I barely remember how to get here from my room and vice versa. Thank you, by the way, for making sure I feel welcome. It means a lot that you would do that for me, especially since we just met, essentially."

"It was not long ago that I was the new girl. I wanted you to feel like you had someone to talk to, because I know how much I appreciated that with Arthur and Vik." Katerina smiled at her. "I wanted you to have a friend from the start."

"That's so sweet of you, really. I just want you to know how much I appreciate it. It's been a crazy two days, but I am excited to really get started in the morning."

"Oh, who are you starting with?" Katerina turned down a hallway. "I was kind of hoping it could be me, just because I kind of want it to be over with." She hesitated for a split second before adding "Because I'm nervous, not because of anything to do with you. You're great."

"Thanks, Katerina, but I was going to start with some more surface level powers, like strength or speed. Yours is much more in depth of a study, and I wanted to get through the others first." Jocasta unconsciously mimicked Katerina's hesitation. "Not because I'm nervous. Because my method makes more sense that way." Jocasta giggled. "I'm glad you want to do the study though. You were so quiet in the meeting that I thought you would be against it."

"I was just, uhm distracted." Katerina stumbled through the sentence, and Jocasta thought that was odd, since she had been staring right at her the whole time. They went through a door and entered the world's biggest garage. There were so many cars to choose from, all brand new and all pristine. All that is, except for her own car, which looked like a literal bucket of bolts lined up next to the other cars. "Do you want to take your car?" Katerina laughed. "It looks a bit out of place in here."

"Sure, as long as you tell me how to get there." Jocasta jumped into her driver's seat, the worn leather sagging comfortably under her weight. She found her keys already in the ignition and she started the car as Katerina settled into the passenger seat.

"I hope you're a good driver." Katerina smiled. "I wouldn't want anything to happen to your *gorgeous* car."

"Oh, come on, it's a perfectly fine car." Jocasta laughed. "Why does everyone hate my car?" She pulled out of the garage and headed down the long path to the main drive.

"I don't hate it; I just think you could use an upgrade. It is very old." Katerina laughed. "You don't even have an aux cord, let alone Bluetooth." Katerina went to rest her hand on the center console, but Jocasta's arm was sitting there already, so Jocasta felt Katerina's fingers just brush her forearm before she moved her hand to her lap. "Oops, sorry." Katerina blushed, the pink in her cheeks making Jocasta smile.

"It's cool." Jocasta rolled down her window, which was not automatic, as Katerina gasped. "What?" Jocasta asked, jerking her hand back to the wheel in preparation for whatever she was about to hit.

"You have MANUAL windows? Jocasta, *please* get a new car!" Katerina laughed harder than Jocasta had heard her laugh before. Her laugh was like an extension of her voice, bubbling out of her chest and bouncing in the air. It was incredibly contagious, and Jocasta found herself laughing along.

"You know, I know you're right, but I just can't get rid of this car. I'm too sentimental, you know?" Jocasta was a little bit embarrassed to admit it, but she had been through so much in this car, she felt like it was a part of her. She was so sentimental sometimes it was a little bit upsetting to her.

"I think it is nice to have things that mean something to you. I know how it feels to have a thing that you really care about that other people make fun of. I won't make any jokes about it anymore." Katerina looked sad, but sincere. It made Jocasta want to ask her what had made her feel the way she felt about her car, but it seemed like it might be deeper than her situation. She let a beat pass before reaching into her center console for a folder of CDs. "Got any tune preference?" she giggled, handing the folder to Katerina. "I have just about everything." Katerina thumbed through her prized collection, occasionally making a face or a small sound, sometimes even saying 'Ooh!' or 'Ugh!'. Jocasta wondered which albums she was reacting to, but she kept her eyes on the road. She felt more content driving with Katerina than she had felt in a long time. There was an ease in her body that she missed. Tension began to melt away the longer she was with Katerina, and her chest felt less tight.

Katerina really had made her feel at home already, and it was only day two. Katerina directed her into the closest town and to a small cafe, where Jocasta had to park on the street. She received more teasing from Katerina as she admitted that she couldn't really parallel park, and had to watch, embarrassed, as Katerina parked for her. Katerina climbed out of the car and joined her on the sidewalk, holding her keys out to her. "Will you be able to get out? Or will I have to do that for you as well?" Katerina was teasing still, but more gently this time. Jocasta had a feeling she would have driven the whole way home if she asked.

"No, I can get out myself, thank you." Jocasta playfully snatched her keys back from Katerina. "This grilled cheese better not disappoint if I had to go through all of this incessant teasing to get it."

"Oh, it will be worth it." Katerina laughed and opened the door for her.

"Hey there, Miss Katie-rina!" The person behind the counter called, and Jocasta noticed Katerina stiffen slightly. "I see you've brought a friend with you today! That's new!" The person turned to Jocasta, "Do you want a grilled cheese too? It comes with a soda and a cup of tomato soup!" Katerina closed her eyes for a moment, and Jocasta just nodded at the person, whose name tag she now saw read 'Katie'. "I'll have those right out to you, take a seat anywhere!" The cafe was empty, just her and Katerina, so they sat in a spot by the window. The Formica tables and tiny space made her think of a cafe like this that she went to as a kid, and she started to feel a bit more comfortable as she pulled her chair closer to the table.

"So," Jocasta cleared her throat. "'Katie-rina', huh?"

"I do not even want to explain." Katerina ran a hand down her face and rolled her eyes. "I think it goes without saying that I hate it."

"Oh, most definitely."

"But they are a small business, and I like the food. I was just hoping it would be one of the two people other than Katie that would be working." Katerina lowered her voice. "She tends to be a bit, well, much."

"I can see that." Jocasta giggled. "I think she likes you."

"I know she likes me; she has asked me out to dinner four separate times," Katerina whispered, glancing toward the kitchen.

"Well, why haven't you gone out with her?"

"She is very much not my type." Katerina looked at Jocasta, the look in her eyes making her gulp. Katie was just about the exact opposite of

Jocasta, tall, long blonde hair, seemingly confident. She couldn't help but wonder if Katerina's look was pointed for that reason.

"Oh, I see, so you want me to chase her off for you?" Jocasta was joking, trying to hide how glad that comment made her, but she would definitely chase this girl off for Katerina.

"That was not my original intention, but now that you mention it, it could be kind of fun." Katerina grinned. Jocasta felt herself becoming emboldened by her.

"In that case, put your hands on top of the table." Katerina gave her a questioning look but did it. Jocasta felt her heart speed up as she grabbed both of her hands, rubbing circles with her thumbs across Katerina's skin. She glanced over toward where Katie had been. "Is she cooking, or is there someone else back there?"

"Usually, she is watching me from the kitchen." Katerina glanced as well.

"Ew. Okay, well if she comes out here and I don't see her first, squeeze my hand, and I am going to giggle like you are the funniest person around."

"Jocasta, this isn't a romantic comedy."

"The movies are a reflection of real life, Katerina!"

"Okay," she sounded skeptical. "Well, she is probably coming out soon, she'll want to get your soda choice."

"Right, because she has yours memorized." Jocasta joked, but Katerina's face told her that it was true. "In the meantime, do you want to talk about the mission?"

"It was pretty straight forward, got in, got out, left the arresting to the German authorities." Katerina seemed bored by the thought of talking about her work.

"Well, um, did anything exciting happen?"

"Vik used her powers to make about 45 men unconscious at once, which was a bit of a record, but it was because so many people were in the same room."

"I mean, that's cool."

"Yes, I was proud of her." Katerina looked down, and Jocasta wondered if she was still embarrassed about her own powers.

"Hey, I meant what I said before. I think your powers are amazing."

"You say that, but you've never had them used on you."

"I still don't think I would mind at all." Jocasta thought, but what she said was "I guess not, but don't think that everyone should be scared of your powers, that's a mindset I would expect from those people that judge you. Don't do it to yourself."

"Thank you," Katerina looked back up to her, "Also, your thoughts were quite loud just now." She smirked, and Jocasta burst out laughing in embarrassment. The timing could not have been more perfect, as Katie sauntered up to them as Jocasta was letting go of Katerina's hand to wipe a tear. She took Jocasta's drink order and then glanced at Katerina before focusing back on Jocasta.

"So, how long have you two known each other?" She turned to Katerina again, "You've been coming in for such a long time and you've never brought anyone else in." There was sugar dripping from her voice, but ice in her eyes.

"We met at work," Jocasta answered, "How long ago do you think that was, hon?" She smiled wide at Katerina, who blushed deeply.

"Oh uh, you know, I am not sure, it feels like we've known each other forever." Katerina's eyes were pleading for her to save her from this nightmare.

"Yeah, it does." Jocasta sighed, "She finally got to drag me out of the office to take me to her favorite local restaurant. Katerina tells me you guys are the best."

"Oh, well, thank you." Katie looked at Katerina.

"Of course." Katerina looked at Jocasta before adding, "What kind of girlfriend would I be if I didn't get her to try the best grilled cheese on Earth?" As soon as she said 'girlfriend', Jocasta's stomach flipped, and her hands went clammy in Katerina's grasp. She looked down, away from Katerina, and hoped that Katie just thought she was blushing, which she was, but she didn't want Katerina to see just how much. She glanced up to see Katie grimace before turning back toward the kitchen. When she was gone, Jocasta looked back at Katerina.

"Do you think it worked?" She whispered, still struggling to meet her gaze.

"Well maybe. At least she might lay off the flirting for a little while."

Katerina pulled her hands away. "Maybe we shouldn't have done that. It feels a bit mean."

"I mean, sometimes people can't take a hint, and if she made you uncomfortable, I say it's worth it." Jocasta played with a napkin to avoid looking at her, trying to regain her composure.

"It seems like I made you uncomfortable." Katerina almost mumbled it, and Jocasta snapped her head up to meet her eyes, forcing her awkwardness down.

"No, not uncomfortable, just, um, well, you're very good looking and you called me your girlfriend and it made me flustered for a second."

"I got flustered saying it, so I think we are even." Katerina smiled, and just like that, Jocasta felt at ease again. They chatted a bit about Jocasta's plans for her study so far before Katie brought them their soup and sandwiches, and Jocasta was very much not disappointed.

"Okay, you were right, this is the most perfect grilled cheese I have ever had in my life." Jocasta told her between bites. "The soup is amazing, too."

"Everyone thinks I am wrong; you'll have to tell them they can't judge until they try it." Katerina smiled at her around her own sandwich.

"Oh, I will."

When they had arrived back at the mansion, Jocasta did just that, telling anyone they came across that they had to try the grilled cheese Katerina was so obsessed with, and after she had told the fifth person, while they were sitting in the common area, Katerina nudged her with her elbow.

"You can stop now."

"Oh, but only if you agree to hang out with me again tomorrow." Jocasta was surprised by herself. She would never usually be so pushy or forward with a new friend. She tried not to think it was because she wanted to be much more than friends with Katerina. Before she could say anything else, Katerina reached over and touched her elbow.

"I could do that."

"Really?"

"Yes, just don't start spiraling into a ramble again, okay? It seemed like that was about to happen." Katerina pulled her hand back and sunk into the couch. "You're fun to spend time with."

"Well, I hope so, you've been with me for most of the time I've been here so far, I'd hate for you to have been bored." Jocasta felt herself getting a little bit nervous again, her eyes scanning the couch instead of looking at Katerina, who moved her hand to Jocasta's.

"I mean it, I wasn't teasing you." Katerina whispered, and Jocasta nodded, pulling her hand back. They talked for a while longer, and then both made their ways to their rooms. When Jocasta said goodnight to Katerina, she felt a bit of a pang, not wanting to be away from her. She shook her head and went into her room, trying to get her thoughts trained on work.

KATERINA

Katerina was exhausted. Training this week had been extra tough since she was trying to push herself for Jocasta's sake. It had been three weeks since Jocasta had moved in, and just about everyone had already been through her rigorous testing. Heather had even come up for a few days to be tested. Katerina's was to begin tomorrow, and she was trying to keep her powers nice and ramped up so that Jocasta could see her at full capacity. Since the mission on Jocasta's second day here, they hadn't had a whole lot to do. A few emergency responses, so it was mostly assisting local first responders with extracting victims of large crashes or fires, and she was only needed if someone was pinned by rubble or a car or something like that, so she had been pretty bored these past few weeks.

What made her boredom even deeper was that she hadn't really had a chance to spend much more time with Jocasta, since she had been so busy with her work. Save from a few instances of her getting lost and needing Katerina to come find her, Jocasta really hadn't been around during the day. She did live right across the hall, but it seemed like Jocasta may have slept in her lab more than a few nights, which was honestly very attractive in Katerina's opinion. To be so passionate about her work that she literally forgot to go to bed was something to be admired. Just thinking about Jocasta falling asleep while waiting on a result to come through a machine-made Katerina smile bigger than she had since they went to get dinner three weeks ago.

They had eaten together four times over the past three weeks, but they hadn't really gotten to talk too much, as they were always rushing off to do something else, or the rest of the team had been there. A few times during these meals though, Katerina had noticed Jocasta leaving her hands somewhere in between them, or moving just a bit closer to her, and gotten a little bit tingly. She had hoped it was an attempt to touch her 'accidentally', and more than once she had brushed her arm or bumped her, softly apologizing to Jocasta. Every time they touched, she felt shocks traveling from the spot their skin met. The morning would bring her some nerves with the testing, but it would also bring her a lot of excitement because she would finally be spending actual time with Jocasta again.

She stared out the hallway windows, not really looking *at* anything, just taking comfort in the monotony of the forest view. It was probably ten minutes before someone came up behind her, pulling her out of her trance. She turned to see Jocasta, head in a folder, her work glasses sliding precariously to the very end of her nose. She was walking a bit fast for someone who wasn't looking where they were going, and Katerina couldn't resist the urge to startle her. She used her powers to turn a page in Jocasta's folder, making the scientist jump, and that caused her glasses to fall. Before they could hit the ground and possibly shatter, Katerina caught them with her telekinesis and brought them to her own hand. "You looked to be lost in your own world, and I couldn't resist startling you, I'm sorry." She laughed, watching Jocasta's hand leave her chest where she had been clutching the folder.

"You got me good, that's for sure. I probably shouldn't be walking around like that anyway; I *have* gotten lost in this mansion. More than once." Jocasta met Katerina's eyes, and Katerina felt her insides twist. Those swirls of caramel made her melt every single time. It was kind of embarrassing, she thought, as a grown adult. That was something teenagers in books talked about, but here she was, mid-twenties, feeling it. She knew Arthur would laugh at her for even thinking that, but she couldn't help it. Being even a little bit emotionally vulnerable seemed silly and childish to her as someone who literally threw themself into danger for a living. She should be a rock, not a butterfly-stomached idiot. "You ready to get to work with me tomorrow, Katerina? I was actually doing some reading for prep."

"Yes, I am very excited. I've been making sure to train harder this week just for you." Katerina felt her cheeks getting warm and handed Jocasta her glasses. "So that you get the best results, obviously."

"I'm also glad to see you more. I feel like I haven't really seen you for a while." Jocasta's cheeks were matching Katerina's, which made Katerina feel simultaneously like she was flying and like she might throw up. "Speaking of what are you doing this evening?"

"Oh, nothing. Probably just going to bed early, why? Did you want to get started tonight?" Katerina felt her whole body get tingly at the idea of spending the evening with Jocasta, even if it was just for work.

"Actually, a new movie just came out, and I was hoping you would want to watch it with me...I am not good at scary movies alone, but it looks *so* good." Jocasta smiled, and Katerina couldn't say no, even though she hated scary movies. The characters always did the *stupidest* things, it was just annoying. But Jocasta was so entrancing, with her gorgeous eyes pleading her to say yes behind those adorable rose gold frames.

"Sure, that sounds fun." Katerina wasn't lying, the time with Jocasta did sound fun, even if the movie didn't. "I should probably clean up first though, I'm still in my training gear." She fought the urge to invite Jocasta into her shower, which was very strong, standing so close to her for the first time in weeks. She smelled like fresh linens and a rich, warm perfume. Katerina realized that Jocasta could probably smell her as well, so she stepped back. Training was not something that made one smell good, and she didn't want Jocasta to think she smelled bad.

"Absolutely! I'll just get everything set up and you can come on over to my room when you're ready." Jocasta smiled with all of her face, lighting up the corridor, and they started walking toward their rooms. The quiet as they walked felt comfortable, and neither of them spoke until they got to their doors. Jocasta turned toward her, her eyes glowing with anticipation. "I'll see you soon!" She smiled and wiggled her fingers "Prepare to get scared!"

"I don't think that will be happening, but I will prepare to be amused at your fear."

Katerina wiggled her fingers back and went into her room. After showering, she threw on some comfortable joggers and a tank top, sprayed a little perfume on, and padded across the hall.

She reached up to knock, more nervous than she was expecting to be. She was conflicted, wanting to spend time with Jocasta both because she thought it would be nice to have her as a friend, and because she wanted more. She felt it might be smarter not to do this. It was becoming clear to Katerina that the time apart had only strengthened the attraction she felt for Jocasta.

She stood there, with her hand frozen in the air, trying not to overthink things. After all, they would be beginning their work together tomorrow, and Jocasta seemed to genuinely appreciate her as a friend. She didn't need to worry. Her hand finally found the surface of the door, and Jocasta immediately swung the door open. She was wearing a tank top as well, although hers had thinner straps than Katerina's did, and she had on a pair of shorts that seemed like they might give her a heart attack when Jocasta eventually turned around. Her glasses were gone, leaving no barrier between Katerina's eyes and those sweet pools of caramel. "Hey! I made a blanket nest on the floor for us! This is gonna be so fun! Oh, I should have gotten some popcorn."

"We can go downstairs and make some if you want," Katerina offered, "I know we have microwaveable popcorn, but we also have a kettle that we can pop our own on the stove with, if you like that better." She hoped Jocasta would take her up on the offer, because then she might be able to get over the feeling she was getting seeing her in those shorts before they started watching the film.

"Oh my god, home-made popcorn? I haven't had that in, probably, 15 years! My dad used to make it a lot." Jocasta's joy dimmed a little bit before she added, "Before he passed."

"Oh, I'm so sorry, Jocasta. We don't have to if it's too emotional. I am fine with-"

"It sounds great!" Jocasta cut her off. "Sorry to bring down the mood. He passed when I was 10, so it's really okay, it's not fresh or anything." Jocasta's smile was so genuine that Katerina knew she was being honest. They started walking to the kitchen, and Katerina felt like she should say something, as she did just kind of open a wound by accident.

"Do you mind if I ask?" Katerina wanted to know everything about her, even the devastating parts. "It's absolutely okay to say no."

"Oh, it's okay, he and my mom were in a car accident. She survived, but she ended up being diagnosed with cancer, and she passed when I was a freshman in college. The memory of the accident really haunted her, but she was really strong for me. We leaned on each other a lot when I was a teenager. We were really close." Jocasta didn't seem sad, just a little bit far away when she talked about her parents. She looked wistful, her eyes thoughtful and her expression sincere as they made their way around a corner and into the kitchen.

"So, are you an only child then?" Katerina was hoping she had *some* family, because she knew what it was to have no one.

"Yeah. It was just me and my parents, so now it's just me. Both of their parents died before I was born, and they were both only children, so." Jocasta shrugged, like she hadn't given much thought to being without a family. "I kind of like being on my own. I don't have anyone to worry about disappointing, so I can really just do whatever I want, there's nobody to answer to. That's why I can really just jump into my work and not worry about my family missing me or anyone being mad if I miss a holiday. My parents are always with me, and that's all I need."

"That is a beautiful way to look at it. I know a lot of people would be angry about being alone like that. Angry at the universe, god, whatever. You are a very strong woman, Jocasta." Katerina found herself admiring Jocasta more and more with every interaction. She truly was a wonderful woman.

"Oh, I went through the angry phase. Twice. I was an awful tween, and then an awful young adult. It took a lot of therapy both times to get where I am now." Jocasta's honesty was beautiful to Katerina. She didn't hide her thoughts, she just said what she felt. It made Katerina want to do the same, just for her. She wanted Jocasta to know her in a way nobody else did. She wanted to tell Jocasta secrets and confide in her in a way she had never wanted to with anyone else ever before.

"I was angry at first too, when I became alone." The words were out of her mouth before she could think to stop herself. "My family abandoned me when I started to show my powers. I was eight years old, and I stayed angry until I was twenty. I just wanted my family to know how lonely they made me feel, I wanted *everyone* to feel what I felt. I was in a very dark place when I realized how toxic that ideology was. I'll spare you the details, but just know, what you told me the day we met, about making the world more accepting? It really struck me. I am very glad to participate in your work." She felt like someone had punched her in the stomach. She had never opened up like that to anyone. Let alone someone she had only known for a short while.

"Oh, Katerina, I had no idea. That's honestly the worst thing I can imagine. I'm so sorry. It's unacceptable, truly." Jocasta reached out to touch her, to comfort her, it seemed, but Katerina felt an overwhelming urge, and she just let herself follow it. Next thing she knew, her hands were on either side of Jocasta's face, and she was kissing her. She felt Jocasta stiffen, and then melt into her embrace, returning the kiss with a fierce passion. Jocasta's hands circled around her waist, and Katerina felt goosebumps raise from her touch. Her hands slid up into Jocasta's hair, the right hand circling to the back of her head, the softness of her undercut luxurious and smooth, while her left hand tangled in the hair that fell from the top of her head over to the side, fingers curling into the gorgeous locks. Jocasta slid her hands up Katerina's back, making her shiver as one hand gripped the hair at the base of her neck.

Katerina deepened the kiss, tasting the sweetness of Jocasta's lips, pushing them both into the kitchen island, and causing Jocasta to gasp. Their lips met again, and Katerina felt like time had stopped moving. Nothing mattered except Jocasta, and Katerina kissed her with everything she had. As she poured herself into the kiss, she felt herself lifting off the floor, and wrapped one arm around Jocasta's waist, holding her firmly to her own body, allowing her power to lift them both into the air. Jocasta pulled away from the kiss and giggled "We're flying, Kat-" Katerina cut her off with another kiss and lowered them to the ground. Jocasta nipped her bottom lip and Katerina smiled. She leaned her forehead to Jocasta's, taking in the moment.

"I'm sorry," she breathed "Sometimes it just happens with a surge of emotion. It hasn't happened in a long time."

"No, don't be sorry, that was," Jocasta paused, shyly meeting Katerina's eyes, "um, it was incredible, Katerina." She tilted her head up to kiss Katerina again, softly. "Incredible."

"So," Katerina straightened up, away from the kiss. "Did you still want that popcorn?" As she was finishing the question, Viktoria came around a corner, and she jumped away from Jocasta. "Oh, hey Vik. What are you up to?" She hoped her lips weren't as swollen as they felt, *and* that her voice wasn't as shaky as she thought it sounded.

"I was about to make a protein shake, but what's this I hear about popcorn?" Vik's voice didn't contain any trace of suspicion or teasing, so it seemed she hadn't caught them. Katerina almost wanted to read her thoughts, just to be sure, but she didn't break her rule. Jocasta gave her a quick glance before responding to Vik.

"Oh, we were going to make fresh popcorn and go watch a movie in my room. Did you want to join?" The invitation caught Katerina off guard, but she didn't say anything. If Jocasta wanted to invite someone else, by all means, it was her room and her movie. Katerina would have a tough time being close to Jocasta on that 'blanket nest' with someone else in the room, but that was probably smart, considering the fact that just the presence of Vik had made Katerina realize just how stupid she had been. Maybe that was why Jocasta had invited Vik, she realized it as well, and she thought it would be safer for them to have a chaperone. Just as Katerina had decided she wanted Vik to accept the offer, Viktoria shook her head.

"No, that's okay, I might snag some popcorn, but I'm heading to bed early tonight. Katerina had me working hard in training today, I'm surprised she's willing to stay up." Katerina felt her face begin to flush as Vik winked at her. "Have fun though, you two." Vik reached into a cabinet for the blender and began making her shake. That wink made Katerina think that Vik had *definitely* seen or heard something. She made a mental note to ask her later. Maybe it was just Vik being her normal, suggestive self, but it seemed too on the nose. She wasn't the type to tell anyone what she saw if she *had* seen anything though, so Katerina was good to just wait it out. She walked over to a different cabinet and grabbed the popcorn kernels and the popcorn maker. They were in the same cabinet because as Marc had told her "When will they ever be used separately?" Never mind that one thing was a food item and the other was a cooking tool, which in her mind should always be in a separate cabinet. She set the items on the island and reached back in for the butter sauce, just as Vik hit the start button on the blender, startling Katerina, and causing her to bump her head on the cabinet. She grunted softly and pulled back out of the cabinet, straightening up and rubbing the back of her head. The idea of Vik eavesdropping, however unintentionally, had apparently put her more on edge than she thought it had. Katerina turned to see Jocasta looking at her with an expression that Katerina could only describe as dreamy, and she couldn't help but smile. If Vik *hadn't* overheard or seen, she definitely would have questions about the way Jocasta was staring at her. *That* was one hundred percent something Vik noticed, as Katerina saw her observing the two of them.

At this point, Katerina was just glad it wasn't Arthur who had interrupted their moment. He would have been unbearably awkward. As Katerina started to get the kettle ready, she felt Jocasta's fingers lightly graze her arm, and she felt electric shocks spread from each finger. "Can I help you with that?" Jocasta asked, and reached for the handle of the kettle. "I feel awkward just watching." Katerina handed it to her and let her take over making the popcorn.

She tried not to watch too closely, as Viktoria was quietly finishing up with her shake, but it was difficult not to look at how gorgeous Jocasta was. Her hands moved delicately, and she jumped when the kernels started to pop, making Katerina smile larger than she meant to. Jocasta's hair was tousled a bit from their kiss. It was bouncing gently as she moved, and she kept trying to tuck it behind her ear even though it was slightly too short to stay tucked. She chewed on her tongue as she worked, which Katerina thought was absolutely adorable, and she could feel her cheeks reddening the longer she watched.

Katerina turned to talk to Viktoria, hoping she hadn't seen her blushing, only to see Vik scrutinizing her. '*What is going on here?*' Vik mouthed at her, slyly gesturing between her and Jocasta, so that Jocasta wouldn't see. Although Jocasta was so focused on her task, Katerina doubted she would have noticed anyway. She looked at Jocasta for a second before mouthing back that she didn't know. Vik shrugged and mimed texting at her, washed out her cup, and then left, leaving her alone with Jocasta again. She felt the air immediately crackle with tension as Vik got far enough not to be able to hear them anymore, and Katerina chanced a look at Jocasta, who was pouring the now finished popcorn into a bowl. She seemed overly focused, like maybe she was trying not to look at her, so Katerina walked over to the refrigerator and started looking for something to drink. There weren't any fun options, really. Basic cola, juices, and water was generally all they had on hand in the fridge. She was about to ask Jocasta if she wanted a soda when she heard a sniffle.

She peeked around the fridge to see Jocasta softly crying, holding the empty kettle. Katerina grabbed a couple of drinks and shut the fridge before heading toward Jocasta on the other side of the island. She reached out to cover Jocasta's hand with her own and put the kettle away, and Jocasta let her, still quietly sniffling. "Thanks, sometimes it just hits me. I didn't think it would since I already said something." Jocasta sniffed and wiped a tear from her eye. "I'll be good in a sec, let's head on up."

Katerina looked at her, and her tension melted away. "Is a soda okay?" she asked, holding one toward Jocasta. Jocasta picked up the bowl of popcorn and took the soda from Katerina, a smile plastered on her face.

"Absolutely! Let's get this party started!" Jocasta started back toward their rooms, and her gait was so bouncy and light, it was hard to believe Katerina had just seen her crying. She sped up so that they were walking side by side, and she bumped into Jocasta playfully. "Hey! Don't make me drop this popcorn I so painstakingly labored over!" Jocasta laughed, throwing her head back a little bit, and making Katerina's heart skip a beat. Jocasta was truly gorgeous.

"Uh, I was there, and it took *maybe* ten minutes, Jocasta." Katerina teased, and they walked the rest of the way to Jocasta's room in a contented quiet. When they got there, Katerina reached out and opened the door, since Jocasta's hands were pretty full, and she couldn't resist saying "Milady," as Jocasta squeezed through the door, which earned her an adorable giggle, complete with a tiny snort.

"Thank you, Katerina." Jocasta smiled and set the popcorn down on the floor in the center of what she had called a 'blanket nest' and gestured for Katerina to sit down. There was a wall made of pillows against Jocasta's bed, where they could lean against her bedframe and look at her screens to watch the film, and there were probably 10 blankets arranged for them to sit on or cover up with. The whole setup was very cozy, and now that they had kissed, Katerina realized that it was also a pretty romantic scene.

As she sat down, Jocasta got the screen turned back on, as it had returned to a blank screensaver mode while they were gone. The film was set to play in the middle of the screen, and Jocasta had somehow set it up to have twinkling lights displayed around it. Katerina realized that Jocasta really had spent time making her room nice just to watch a movie with her, and it made her heart flutter a bit, knowing that she thought enough about her to want to do that. That wasn't something anybody had done for Katerina in a long time. She settled into her spot, and Jocasta pressed play on the movie, doing the same.

They spent the first twenty minutes just eating popcorn, occasionally drinking their sodas, and trying to pay attention to the movie, but every time that their hands touched in the popcorn bowl, Katerina felt an electric bolt go up her arm, and it was becoming increasingly difficult to pay attention to the film and not think about the way Jocasta's hair felt between her fingers, or the way that her lips felt on hers. She reached back into the popcorn bowl, hoping to find Jocasta's hand again, and felt that the bowl was actually empty, so she moved it to the side of their blankets, leaving nothing but space between them. After a few more minutes, Jocasta paused the movie and turned toward Katerina. "So, um, I can't focus on this at all." She blushed, and Katerina felt butterflies in her stomach.

"Oh?" Katerina was too excited and nervous to say anything else. All she wanted was for Jocasta to close the space between them. It was only a few inches, and Katerina was itching to do it herself.

"I really want to kiss you again," Katerina felt her heart rate skyrocket, and then at the next word, the same heart dropped to her stomach. "But I just think that maybe we shouldn't?" Jocasta said it like a question, and when Katerina didn't respond, she continued. "I mean, I'm supposed to study you, and we work together, and I mean, there are no rules against it here, but I think that maybe if someone found out, my study's findings would be questioned or maybe thrown out, and I don't know if it is a good idea at least until we're done with my work, but then, will that be next week, or next year? So, then maybe we should just say 'fuck it.' you know?" Jocasta looked genuinely conflicted, and her eyes said she was expecting an opinion from Katerina.

"I understand where you're coming from. Although, I have been thinking about it a bit, and I don't see how exactly involving yourself with me would change anything about your study. Maybe I don't understand the science behind it, but how would your feelings change anything about it?" Katerina hoped that there was some sort of recording device or fact checking system with Jocasta's study that would allow her to refute anyone if they tried to say that she was doing anything wrong. It seemed like it would just be data, and why would Jocasta's feelings have any effect on data? Katerina saw Jocasta's gears turning, probably going over her process to see if her integrity would be compromised. She watched as Jocasta bit into her tongue, which now seemed like it might be a little habit when she was concentrating.

"I do record everything and keep everything on the cloud, with backups, so I would be able to prove that I hadn't done anything sketchy, just in case." Jocasta finally said, a smile creeping across her face. "I literally even record myself typing in data just because the field is so small and I want people to see that I do real science, and it isn't just a show. I want people to know that suprology is real, so I record excessively. The lab has cameras everywhere. No one could successfully accuse me of falsifying data with that much proof!" Jocasta had leaned closer to Katerina as she got excited, and now the space between them was so small, Katerina could have easily kissed her.

"That is the best thing I have heard in a long time." Katerina looked at Jocasta's lips, now centimeters from her own, and leaned in.

JOCASTA

Jocasta woke up three minutes before her alarm went off. 4:57 am, and she was as giddy as can be. Katerina had left a couple of hours after they had paused the movie, and Jocasta couldn't wait to start their work today. They had spent those few hours finishing the movie in between breaks to kiss and cuddle, but they hadn't done anything else. Jocasta had felt it was too soon to escalate anything right now, and Katerina hadn't tried to escalate it.

She walked toward her bathroom, preparing to hop in the shower before heading down to the kitchen for breakfast, but a piece of paper slid under her bedroom door, catching her eye. She picked it up and saw that it was a note from Katerina, telling her to meet her for breakfast in 30 minutes on the roof. Now even more excited for the day, Jocasta got ready as fast as she could and started to head toward the roof. That was one place she definitely knew how to get to. There was a garden on the roof that Jocasta had found to be a great place for reading, and she went up there a few times a week to decompress. After the third time, she didn't get lost anymore.

When she got up to the rooftop, Katerina wasn't there yet, so she just went over to her usual spot. There were rows and rows of flowers and herbs, leading toward a greenhouse, where her bench sat, between the far wall of the greenhouse and the railing of the roof. There were vines that were a bit unkempt there, as it was the most out of sight area of the roof, but Jocasta liked it that way. The way the vines felt more wild over here made her feel safe and secluded, away from the world. That was why it was the perfect place to decompress with a good book. She stayed in her spot for a few minutes, looking at the stars that were beginning to fade, as the sunrise would be starting soon, and soaking in the peace of the early morning.

Just when she was about to go see if Katerina was up there yet, she poked her head around the corner of the green house. "I see you've found the best spot on the entire grounds." She smiled and pulled a breakfast sandwich from behind her back and handed it to Jocasta. It was a biscuit with eggs and cheese inside, and it was still warm. Jocasta took a bite, savoring the warmth in the cool of dawn.

"That is a good sandwich." Jocasta smiled and patted the seat of the bench for Katerina to join her. When she did, Jocasta leaned her head on Katerina's shoulder. "Did you make it?" She asked, hoping the answer was yes and that she could get many more of these in the future.

"I did." Katerina smiled and let her cheek rest on Jocasta's head. "This is my favorite thing to do here, watch the sunrise. This bench is in the perfect spot for it." Katerina rested her hand on Jocasta's thigh, sending shockwaves through Jocasta's body. Katerina was able to excite her with one touch in a way that she hadn't experienced in quite some time.

"I love this bench," Jocasta said quietly, thinking that loud noise would ruin the serenity of the moment. "By the way, where is your breakfast? Please do not tell me you made me food and didn't make any for yourself."

"I ate it while I was cooking yours, Jocasta." Katerina smiled, and Jocasta could feel her face muscles move as they rested on the crown of her head. This was already the best morning she had had in a long time. The sky was starting to bleed color as the sun began its rise, and Jocasta finished her breakfast. "So, what is the plan for today?" Katerina asked her, and Jocasta's heart felt like it was growing. Her job was so important to her that when anyone asked her about it, it made her happy. In this moment with Katerina, she was overjoyed.

It had not been common for Jocasta to meet a woman she was interested in who cared much about the day to day of her job, and although Katerina might be interested because she was involved, at least she was asking. Something as small as that was a big deal for Jocasta, and she couldn't suppress a gleeful giggle as she detailed her plans for the day. Katerina nodded and listened, even when Jocasta started rambling on a tangent about the specifics of a test and the ramifications that the data she would be collecting would have on her initial findings. She told Katerina that she was excited to see the differences between a more physical power and her powers, because she had only worked with people who had light telekinesis powers, and nobody she had worked with could read minds, much less control people the way she had seen Katerina do in that mission weeks ago.

"I don't like to call it 'controlling' someone," Katerina interjected, and it was the first thing she had said for a few minutes. "I think it is more of a suggestion. A very strong suggestion, of course, but 'control' has such a negative connotation, and I do not like to think of myself that way. I don't want others to feel that way about me." Katerina was someone who had a sincerity about her that made Jocasta wonder if she chose this terminology because people tend to see a more serious personality like Katerina's and assume negative things already, without a phrase like 'mind control' being attached, and she immediately felt bad for describing her powers that way.

"Oh my god, I'm so sorry, I'll make sure to put a note in my records to change my terminology." Jocasta knew that positivity was so important in representation, so she wanted to make sure that anyone who wanted to say enhanced people were inherently bad would not use their own terminology against them. It happened too often with marginalized groups, and she couldn't be part of the problem within her research. This was the sort of thing she was adamant that suprology was the best at, and she felt honored to be able to make real change in her field.

As she was telling Katerina a bit about how she is adamant that she work with as many enhanced individuals to keep terminology updated and as positively connotated as possible, she saw Katerina start to smile. "I'm rambling, aren't I?" Jocasta blushed.

"You are, but it is very cute." Katerina chuckled and kissed Jocasta on the nose. Katerina's face turned a bit more serious as she pulled away, "I do have a serious question about work."

"Anything!" Jocasta was becoming increasingly excited to get down to the lab, even if this was the most perfect morning she could have imagined.

"Would you mind if we just remained one hundred percent professional in the lab and around others? Not that I want to hide anything, but it is very new, and I've never really let anyone here know about my more intimate relationships before." Katerina gestured between them, "Whatever this is, and I don't want the rest of the team to start asking questions that we don't even know the answer to." She looked a little bit nervous, and it made Jocasta feel a little softness in her chest.

"Of course! I say let them find out naturally, if we want to make this," she copied Katerina's gesture "a *thing*. If someone asks, then we don't lie, but I don't see the need to tell anyone just because, ya know?" Jocasta watched Katerina's nervousness melt away as she was agreeing with her. "If you want to have a discussion about what we both want from this at some point, obviously I am down, but for now, we need to get going to the lab!"

The next few days felt like they went by in a flash, but they say time flies when you're having fun, and everything about Jocasta's work was fun to her. She was buzzing with anticipation for the results of some of their tests they had finished today, but nothing would be conclusive until the morning, and they decided it would be a good idea to go ahead and be done for the day, rather than run any more tests. Katerina had gone up to the training room on the main floor to train in hand-to-hand combat with Vik again, so Jocasta was editing her notes from their tests to make sure they were legible. Sometimes she would type so fast that she would have a full paragraph with no punctuation, or she had been using her stylus to write and her computer misinterpreted her handwriting. As she typed, Arthur popped his head in and knocked on her door frame. "Everything going well?" He asked, entering the room, and finding a seat at a table a few feet from Jocasta's desk. Jocasta smiled, thinking *"You have no idea how well."* She stopped typing and looked up.

"Yes, it is! I am having the best time with my research; I actually only have to finish up with Katerina and then I'll be done with the first round of testing!" She gave Arthur a big smile. He had been asking her about her work since her first day of testing, but she thought it might be because he was curious about his own results, which she would not be sharing until the first round was complete. He had been the first Phenom to participate.

"So, I get to learn more about myself soon then?" He sounded excited, albeit a little nervous. Jocasta liked Arthur a lot. He definitely cared what she thought of him and respected her research enough to be worried that his results could somehow be bad. She had told him that at this point, no information could be bad news, as they weren't really sure what they were looking for. The only thing she knew at this point was that she needed to talk to the team about making her a permanent fixture. No research of this extent had ever been done before, and she was now sure it would be years of research instead of the few months they had been hoping for.

"I'm hoping the results of the testing can lead to *me* learning something soon!" She laughed. "This is a whole new world of science, Arthur, it might not be anything definitive for a long time."

"Well, I know you can do it! I think Marc is going to want to keep you forever, we all really like having you here." Arthur leaned back in his seat, content to just keep Jocasta company, as he had done a few times while she was editing notes like this. "Fixing your notes again?" He nodded at her desktop.

"You know it! I hope Marc can get W.E.I.R.D. to keep me forever, I can only imagine what we would be able to learn. Plus, I love this mansion." She winked at him "And all of you goof balls." Arthur laughed, and Jocasta joined him. Arthur had such a contagious joy, which was rare for someone who had experienced as much trauma as he did. He was almost 70, but his enhancements kept him in incredible shape, so he never retired from being a fighter, and Jocasta knew he had seen some horrible things when he was a soldier, let alone as a Phenom.

She was hoping her research with him could help to extend the human lifespan eventually, because not only was he in ridiculously good shape, but he definitely looked like he was in his 30s, and she suspected it was because he aged slower than an average human. No one had really looked into it, so it was something she had put on her list of things to do. She actually had a specific doctor under her that she had assigned to the task, but Arthur didn't need to know that until they had confirmed it. No need to worry him, he did enough worrying already.

He may have looked young, but he knew his age, and he really felt like a dad to the team sometimes. Both him and Marc, even though Marc was in his mid-40s. They really ran the team together, no matter how much Arthur downplayed his role. Marc paid for a lot of the team's extra things that W.E.I.R.D. didn't cover, and worked closer to the organization, but he saw Arthur as an equal, and it was clear to everyone.

"I'll let you get back to work, Jocasta. I can bring you down some food in a little bit though if you want. I know you spend a long time down here and forget to eat." He waited for her to decline, like she always did, and he left. This time she really *was* almost done, and she and Katerina were going to order a pizza and go sit on the roof again. They hadn't had time for more than a stolen kiss here and there between work and training sessions, and she had been anticipating this date since Katerina had suggested it on the way down to the lab this morning.

Katerina had told her that there was another spot in the garden that was a little less private, but her favorite place for watching the sunset. Jocasta had finished up her notes and was double checking her drives when Katerina came into the lab. "Are you off the clock yet?" She asked, excitement in her voice. "I did already order the pizza, so I really hope it is not another late night for you. Sunset is in," she checked her watch, "forty-five minutes." She looked up expectantly at Jocasta.

"I am off the clock," Jocasta paused, closing out of her work, "now. Do you mind if I go change, maybe take a shower before we head up?" She grabbed her water bottle and edged around her desk, walking between the rows of lab equipment before reaching Katerina at the door. "You look incredible, by the way. How do you look like that after fighting with Viktoria? I would look like a hot mess."

"*You* would be dead." Katerina laughed. "I took a shower already. It did not take very long for her to beat me. Twice."

"Well, she has years of training and experience, so. I'm sure you did well." They walked toward the end of the hallway, where the stairs and the elevator were.

"Actually, I do tend to beat her fairly often, I was just distracted today." Katerina grinned slyly at her. Jocasta had made a habit of not using the elevator, but thought maybe they should today, since Katerina had just been training. She knew it would have been exhausting, as Vik had been training in combat since she was a kid. She told Jocasta it was because always knew she wanted to be a hero one day, which gave Jocasta an image of a tiny Vik, punching a punching bag with a sheet tied around her shoulders like a cape. It was sweet, she thought, but sometimes she wondered how true it was. As they approached the elevator, Katerina veered toward the stairs, and Jocasta followed. "Not too tired for the stairs I see."

"You always take the stairs, so I just assumed." Katerina replied, surprising Jocasta. Katerina knew she took the stairs every day? Who noticed stuff like that unless they were always with someone? She thought it was so cute, like a high schooler knowing their crush's class schedule.

"Have you been spying on me?" Jocasta joked, nudging Katerina's shoulder with her own as they began their ascent. Katerina's cheeks reddened, but she giggled.

"I'll have you know that I am just very observant, as I have been trained to be, for my job." Katerina nudged her back.

"Are you sure you don't just have a crush on me?" Jocasta's giggle became a real laugh, and Katerina joined her. Katerina's laugh was so bouncy and sweet, rising up and making Jocasta melt. Katerina's smile took up her whole face when she laughed, and it was becoming Jocasta's favorite way to see her smile. When they got to the ground level, Katerina decided to go ahead and wait there for the pizza. They would be meeting on the roof when Jocasta finished with her shower. She moved as quickly as she could, borderline running up the stairs and down the hall to her room. She sped through the shower and was trying to decide what to wear when she got a text from Katerina.

Pizza in hand, heading up to the roof now! :)

They had been texting a lot since she moved in, but since the kiss, they had been texting like their phones were attached to their hands. Jocasta typed out a quick response, threw on a fluffy sweater and joggers, slid into a pair of slippers, and headed out of her room. As she was coming out of the doorframe, she almost ran right into Vik, who must have been heading to her own room. "Oh, Vik! I'm sorry!"

"Where are you off to in such a hurry?" Vik looked her up and down, and Jocasta felt like she was being scrutinized, but not in a bad way. "You're awfully comfortably dressed, so I doubt you're going out."

"Oh, um, yea, I'm just going up to the roof, Katerina and I ordered pizza." Jocasta waved her hand like it wasn't a big deal, but just saying Katerina's name out loud had made her stomach give a little flutter. Plus, the way Vik had just looked at her, she felt like she could tell Jocasta was downplaying her excitement. Viktoria's eyes lingered for another moment, as if she was vaguely suspicious of Jocasta, and making her feel exposed.

"Well, have fun. The roof has some particularly," she paused, seemingly finding the right word, "pretty spots." Vik winked and headed down the hallway, leaving Jocasta wondering if maybe Katerina had said something. When they had kissed in the kitchen, Vik hadn't seemed to notice anything. At least, Jocasta didn't think she had. She had been a little distracted by her own emotions both about Katerina and her dad, which had been incredibly embarrassing. Katerina was so kind and gentle about it though. Jocasta was just glad that Katerina knew it wasn't about her kissing Jocasta. That had been absolutely amazing, no complaints from her. Just thinking about it now, Katerina's arm slipping around her and holding her in the air as her powers lifted them, Jocasta was starting to get hot. She hurried up the rest of the stairs and opened the door to the roof. There was Katerina, pizza in one hand, two empty wine glasses in the other, a small smile turning the corners of her mouth.

"Hey, are you ready?" Katerina asked her, motioning with her whole body the direction they would be walking. Her hips swiveled toward the opposite side of the roof from where they had been that perfect morning a few days ago, and she raised her eyebrows.

"Absolutely," Jocasta smiled. "I'm starving." They headed through some rows of flowers and over to where there were a few small trees growing to find a bench with an archway overtop of it. There were vines growing on the wooden arch, and a few small flowers poked through the greenery. Plants were not her forte, so she had no idea what anything over here was, but it was gorgeous. She saw that Katerina had laid out a picnic blanket by the bench, which faced the west edge of the roof, and there was a bottle of wine in an ice bucket, with a candle lit next to it. "Katerina…" Jocasta trailed off. This was so beautiful and romantic. Jocasta had not been on a date as well thought out as this in such a long time, and for Katerina to have taken the time to set this up for them, she felt that it meant she must really like her.

"There is water in the bucket too, if you don't want the wine. I wasn't sure if you would want to have any, since we have more work in the morning. "Katerina set the pizza down next to the bucket and candle and sat herself down across from where Jocasta was standing. When Jocasta didn't sit down as well, Katerina looked up at her. "Is it too much?"

"No, of course not, it's perfect, Katerina." Jocasta sat down and reached for one of the glasses that Katerina was still holding. "I'm just surprised at *how* perfect. When did you have time to set this up?"

"In between training with Vik and coming to get you. It didn't take that long, Jocasta, it is just a blanket and some wine." Katerina said it like it was nothing to pick a gorgeous spot and set up for a date like this.

"Well, it is just too romantic to act like it's no big deal, so thank you."

Jocasta leaned over and kissed Katerina's cheek. "I appreciate it." At that, Katerina opened the pizza box, and they dove right in. They ate quietly for a while, just enjoying each other's company. When the sun was just about to sink below the skyline, Katerina turned to Jocasta.

"You are absolutely incredible, Jocasta." The compliment surprised her, and Jocasta almost choked on the wine she had been sipping.

"Wha-" she started, but Katerina was quick to continue.

"When you work, your passion for the job is contagious, and you have this intense beauty that takes me by surprise. You're breathtaking, honestly. And you're so smart, it's like watching a human computer when you're working on a problem. You can almost see all of the calculations and processes going through your mind as fast as lightning." She paused for a split second before adding "*Without* looking in your mind." She smiled the way she did when she was laughing, and Jocasta just wanted to kiss her. Katerina's smile was so brilliant and wide, it made Jocasta feel like she was the luckiest person on Earth because she was smiling at her. Her face lit up, and Jocasta could only think about how much she wanted to be the reason she smiled like that forever. With Katerina looking at her, with her impossibly blue eyes, she wanted to leap across the blanket and tangle herself into her. As the light of the candle hit Katerina's irises, Jocasta realized that they were changing color a little bit, turning almost green. as if having blue eyes wasn't hot enough, she had the audacity to have eyes that shifted between blue and green. Before she could stop herself, Jocasta blurted out what she was thinking.

"You're fucking joking." and then, "I mean, thank you. Sorry, it's just - I was listening. I just noticed your eyes change color." She blushed and gave Katerina a small smile. "And they're the most beautiful eyes I have literally ever had the pleasure of seeing. Sorry, I ruined the moment, didn't I?"

"Absolutely not." Katerina reached out and brushed Jocasta's hair out of her face, resting her hand on her cheek. And just as the sun sank below the horizon, Katerina kissed her. This time, the kiss was softer, less urgent. Katerina kissed her with a sweet sincerity, and Jocasta melted into her. When she pulled away, their little corner of the roof was lit up with fairy lights, and Jocasta giggled.

"There is no way *this* didn't take long to set up, Kat-" Katerina cut her off with another kiss, and then laughed.

"I'm sure that it took forever, but I can't take credit. The lights have been up here for a long time. I think Marc had them set up for some date with Lauren, and they never got taken down."

"How *is* Lauren? I haven't seen her around at all." Lauren was Marc's longtime partner. "Don't tell me she finally left him. I don't know how long she'll wait for him to propose."

"Longer than any of us can imagine, I suppose. I think she's been out of the country with work." Katerina laughed and leaned back on her hands. "So, tell me, are we ever going to talk about ourselves, or are we just going to spend all of our dates kissing and laughing." She smirked, and Jocasta copied her stance.

"Well, I don't see anything wrong with kissing and laughing." Jocasta winked, and smiled slyly. "But I guess that I could tell you a little more about myself. It's not like we text all day or something. Let's see, you know I don't have family, you know what I do for work. What else is there? Oh, I like to play board games, watch movies, read, and listen to music."

"Oh, come on, there's more to you than that. We mostly text jokes and flirt with each other. I want to know more! Where did you grow up?" Katerina sat back up off her hands and grabbed her wine glass, her fingers delicately caressing the stem. She finished off the glass and poured herself another while Jocasta answered.

"I grew up in Ohio. I know, gross. Small town, most people never left. I'm just glad I did my undergrad in New York and never looked back. I love the East Coast."

"Oh, I knew you grew up in the Midwest, but isn't Ohio supposed to be the epitome of boring or something? It's always the generic state in movies and such."

"Yes, and now you know why I said 'gross'. Nothing that special about Ohio." Jocasta chuckled and poured her own fresh glass of wine. "Tell me about your hometown."

"There is not much to tell. Borovia is a small country. Not very much to look at, and not very much to do even in the capitol. Not to mention that I was in an orphanage for most of my childhood, and they didn't do a whole lot of outings. I came to America because I knew people like me were not quite outcasted like they were in Borovia, and I found W.E.I.R.D. They put me in contact with Marc and Arthur, and the rest is history."

"Were you here for a while before you became a Phenom?" Jocasta may have joked about it, but she did want to know everything about Katerina, and to tell her everything about herself, as well.

"I moved in when I was 20, and they trained me until I was ready. I joined the team 2 years later, but I wasn't on any public missions until I turned 24. W.E.I.R.D. was concerned about how the public would react to my specific skill set."

"Well, fuck that! Your powers are *incredible*." She leaned in closer to Katerina, surprising herself a bit. She didn't feel tipsy or anything, but maybe the wine was affecting Jocasta a little more than she realized. She hadn't drunk much recently, and what percentage was this bottle? She hadn't checked.

"Thank you, Jocasta, but not everyone thinks that." Katerina put her hand on the blanket next to Jocasta's and linked their pinkies. Jocasta looked at their hands and blurted out.

"You want to know a secret?" When Katerina nodded, she continued. "When you use your powers, the way your hands move is really sexy." She felt her face turn bright red as Katerina laughed hysterically. When she had caught her breath enough, she replied.

"My hands. Are sexy?" She breathed in between laughs, and Jocasta nodded at her and giggled.

"It's also sexy when you tilt your head when you look into someone's mind. It isn't every time, but it looks like whatever you saw was intriguing in some way. I like it."

"Good to know." Katerina smiled that smile again, and this time Jocasta couldn't help herself. She put her hands on both sides of Katerina's face and kissed her, hard and hungry, and Katerina returned the kiss with the same intensity. The bucket and candle were in the way, or Jocasta would have escalated the situation. Instead, she pulled away and rested her forehead on Katerina's.

"Wanna go downstairs?" The question was out of her mouth before she realized that she had just asked Katerina if she wanted to have sex on their first actual date. She squeezed her eyes shut. "Shit. Sorry, I didn't mean to ask, I mean, first date and all. Not that I don't want to, but. Um, I'm gonna stop talking."

"That would be helpful," Katerina said softly. "I can't do this when you're talking." And suddenly, Katerina had moved the bucket and the candle, and she was kissing Jocasta. Her hands found Jocasta's waist and wrapped around her, pulling her close. Jocasta smiled into the kiss and pulled Katerina so that she was essentially on top of her on the picnic blanket. Katerina giggled "J-" she started, but Jocasta didn't let her finish whatever she was going to say to her, reaching up and kissing her again, trying to show Katerina how much she wanted her. Katerina pulled back again. "Jocasta. I want to go downstairs." Her eyes glistened with desire, and all Jocasta could do was nod. Katerina pushed up off of her and grabbed the bucket and their glasses while Jocasta grabbed the pizza box and blanket before blowing out the candle and picking it up as well. They went to the door of the roof and Katerina stopped short. "VIKTORIA?" she shouted, scaring the crap out of Jocasta, and making her jump. Before she could ask Katerina what the hell that was about, she heard Vik behind them.

"Well, you didn't text me, and this one was acting real skittish, so I thought I would come ask you what was up, but I did not expect to see what I just saw." She looked genuinely shocked, but then so was Jocasta.

"So, you hid in the bushes? Vik, what the fuck?" Katerina sounded more betrayed than angry, but both were applicable to describe the look on her face. Jocasta could feel the warmth leaving her cheeks, and realized she really hadn't been buzzed at all, just intoxicated by Katerina.

"What was I supposed to do? You two have been hanging out, clearly texting constantly, and both of you have been sneaking around this past week. I thought maybe you were planning a surprise party for Arthur's birthday, not making out on the roof under the stars. I didn't even know you were gay, Katerina."

"Why would it matter?" Katerina sounded defensive.

"It doesn't, obviously, I'm a lesbian. I just mean it never crossed my mind that I would be crashing a date is all." Vik ran her hand through her hair, and Jocasta tried not to dwell on the fact that her professional idol had just come out to them. "Look, I won't say anything, you know that, Katerina."

"And?" Katerina's eyebrows rose.

"And I'm sorry I hid, but in my defense, I didn't want to ruin the mood. I would have talked to you privately in the morning." Vik looked to Jocasta "I hope you can still enjoy the rest of the evening. Here, I can take your picnic things to the kitchen if you want. To make up for it." Vik reached for the blanket and pizza box, and Jocasta looked to Katerina before letting her take them. Vik hesitated to take the glasses and the wine, but Katerina offered them. The bottle was close to empty anyway.

"You can finish the wine. We will talk more tomorrow, okay?" Katerina seemed to have forgiven the intrusion, and Viktoria relaxed her shoulders as she went through the door and presumably headed to the kitchen. Jocasta was still so surprised by the whole interaction that she didn't say anything for a minute. When Katerina opened the door to go inside, Jocasta followed.

"So, mood ruined then?" She asked quietly just in case anyone else was heading up to the roof and could hear her.

"No, I don't think it is." Katerina grinned and grabbed her empty hand. "In fact, I'll race you, whoever gets there first is whose room we go to."

"Oh, you're on." Jocasta returned the grin, and they both broke into a run. Jocasta had never descended a flight of stairs that fast, and her grip tightened on the candle. She did not want to have to stop to clean up broken porcelain. They were neck and neck at the bottom of the stairs, but Jocasta was not an athlete, and she sorely regretted entering a race with a Phenom as Katerina zoomed ahead easily and beat her by a mile. Katerina stood there waiting as Jocasta reached their rooms, breathing heavily. "So, as you can see, I can't resist a competition, even if I am sorely outmatched."

"Noted." Katerina smirked as she took her candle from Jocasta. "Shall we?" She tilted her head to indicate her door and reached over to open it for Jocasta. They went inside, and Jocasta lingered by the door while Katerina put her candle on a side table. "Nervous?" Katerina walked back toward Jocasta and placed her hands on Jocasta's hips. "You can come sit down if you want." She gently tugged on Jocasta's hips, pulling her further into the room.

"I'm not nervous." Jocasta giggled. "I mean, I'm not *overly* nervous. Just the normal amount. It's just that this is your space, and I don't want to be rude."

"Oh, is that it?" Katerina laughed. "I guess I'll have to make you feel at home in here then." She winked and kissed Jocasta softly, first on the lips, then moving to her cheek, and then her jaw before Jocasta interrupted her.

"Um Katerina? Who do you share walls with?"

"Nobody on one side, and Carter on the other, why?" Katerina stopped kissing her and relaxed her grip on Jocasta's hips.

"Just because, you know, sounds." Jocasta blushed bright red.

"Don't worry, Carter's got soundproof walls that work both ways. They have a habit of accidentally waking everyone up when they have a bad dream. They may or may not have crushed a couple of beds and side tables in their sleep." Katerina slipped her hands around to the small of Jocasta's back and pulled her closer. "Pretty lucky for us, huh?" She bit her bottom lip, and Jocasta felt her heart rate tick up.

"Incredibly lucky." Jocasta kissed Katerina and wrapped her arms around her neck. "It's almost like you planned that or something, asking me to race you."

"Maybe, maybe not. I'll never tell." Katerina giggled and spun Jocasta around, giving her butterflies. "Now let me kiss you for more than two seconds." Jocasta giggled and obliged. Katerina's kisses were soft but sure, trailing a path from her mouth to her jaw and down to her neck, making Jocasta gasp as Katerina led her toward her bed. Katerina's hands traveled up and down Jocasta's back, her fingers flirting with the hem of her sweater. Jocasta let Katerina guide her to the edge of her bed before letting Katerina pull it off.

She watched Katerina's eyes as she took in the sight of a shirtless Jocasta. She had worn a lacy black bra that she kept for special occasions when she needed to feel confident, and she could see that it was doing the trick as Katerina's eyes lingered on her chest before she pulled Jocasta back in for a kiss. Jocasta grabbed the hem of Katerina's shirt and tugged her closer, breaking the kiss to say, "My turn." before pulling Katerina's shirt over her head. Jocasta sucked in a breath at the sight of Katerina in a blood red bra, her skin gorgeous and perfectly smooth.

Katerina's training really paid off, she looked like a bikini model or something, just all muscle and perfect skin. And her breasts. All Jocasta wanted to do was kiss every inch of her. To taste perfection. "You're perfect, Kat-" she began, but Katerina was kissing her again, and before she knew it, Katerina had lowered her onto the bed. Katerina pulled away for a second and looked at Jocasta's body, making Jocasta feel exposed in the best way. She was about to reach for Katerina's neck to pull her back down into another kiss when Katerina sat up, straddling Jocasta.

"I like when you call me that." Katerina smiled down at Jocasta and ran a finger down her body from in between her breasts, past her navel and stopping at the hem of her pants, keeping her eyes locked on Jocasta's.

"Call you what?" Jocasta asked, smirking a little bit. "I always call you Katerina." She was teasing her, and Katerina knew it.

"Not when I cut you off." Katerina hooked her finger into Jocasta's waist band but didn't pull on it. Instead, she leaned back down, pinning her arm between them, and got close enough to kiss her again. "Let me show you. Say my name." Jocasta felt the heat in her body spread as she smiled and bit her lip.

"Kat-" and just like all the other times she had done it, Katerina kissed her, preventing her from finishing her name. This time though, she didn't stay locked onto her lips. Instead, she moved to kiss Jocasta's neck, just underneath her jaw, making Jocasta let out a soft groan. When Katerina heard it, her other fingers joined her pointer finger in Jocasta's waistband and she tugged on her joggers, making her waistband snap back against her skin. Jocasta grinned, bucking her hips toward Katerina as she sat back up. "Are you gonna take those off for me, Kat?" Calling her that on purpose sent a thrill through Jocasta.

"Patience, Jocasta." Katerina chided as she maneuvered backward on the bed so that she could lean back down and kiss Jocasta's chest. She trailed kisses down to that damn waistband and back up, her fingers flirting with the lace of Jocasta's bra. Jocasta ran her fingers through Katerina's auburn locks, delighting in the silky softness of her hair. She tried to be patient, but Katerina was proving to be quite good at teasing her, so she locked her fingers into her hair and pulled her up to kiss her lips again. Kat obliged, but too quickly she pulled away again. "Not your strongest virtue, is it?"

"Patience?" Jocasta giggled. "You do know how much you're teasing me, right?" She raised her eyebrow at Katerina and pushed herself up to try to kiss her again.

"Ah, ah." Katerina tutted and put her finger to Jocasta's lips, guiding her back down to lay on the pillows. "Don't make me have to tie you down." Jocasta felt her heart skip a few beats. She held her hands together and lifted them to Katerina.

"Please, do." Jocasta bit her lip and gave Katerina the biggest puppy dog eyes she could muster. Katerina just chuckled and went back to kissing Jocasta's chest. She let her tongue flirt with the edges of Jocasta's bra, making her squirm with anticipation. She pressed a palm to Jocasta's stomach and looked up at her, her eyes piercing into Jocasta's soul.

"I knew you were a bottom." She smiled and reached under Jocasta's back, unhooking her bra. She lifted an eyebrow as if to ask, "May I?" and Jocasta nodded as fast as she could. Katerina pulled her bra off with ease and looked at Jocasta a moment before taking her own bra off and kissing Jocasta again, this time with a passion that made Jocasta lose her breath as Katerina opened her mouth and traced Jocasta's tongue with her own. Katerina's hands slid up her body and landed on her breasts, cupping them. She continued kissing her as she caressed her chest, rubbing her thumb over Jocasta's nipples, making them perk up. Katerina smiled into Jocasta's mouth and moved her mouth to her jaw, licking the edge of her jaw and up to her earlobe. She whispered into Jocasta's ear "I think you're a little bit *too* clothed, don't you?"

"Yes." Jocasta breathed and grabbed Katerina's wrists, pushing her hands toward Jocasta's hips. She was grinding her hips into Katerina's, begging her to pull her pants off. Katerina wrapped her fingers into her waistband at her hips and Jocasta gasped as Katerina tugged them over her hips and down to her knees. Katerina scooted down and ran her hands over Jocasta's thighs, squeezing them before she pulled her pants all the way off. Jocasta's boxers were the same color as her bra, and they were currently soaked as Katerina lifted her left leg to rest on her shoulder and began placing kisses along her lower leg, slowly moving up. When she got to Jocasta's mid-thigh, she could feel her heartbeat between her legs. Katerina nipped her skin softly and suddenly she was all the way back down to Jocasta's ankles, kissing her right leg now.

As much as Jocasta liked symmetry, she was becoming unbearably wet waiting for Katerina to touch her where she wanted. She started to pull her leg away from Katerina and take off her boxers herself, but Katerina swatted Jocasta's hands with one hand and tightened her grip on Jocasta's leg with the other. Jocasta met Katerina's eyes and stuck out her bottom lip in a big pout. "Please, Kat." Instead of responding, Katerina used the hand she had swatted Jocasta with to grind her palm into her center, rubbing her clit through her boxers. Jocasta let out a moan that surprised even herself, and she couldn't help but hope that no one was walking down the hall. Apparently satisfied, Katerina pulled her hand back and continued kissing Jocasta's leg. When she got to mid-thigh again, she bit into Jocasta's leg, much harder than she had bit the left leg, making her gasp with pain as well as pleasure.

"That's for not letting me finish." Katerina smiled, stood up off the bed, and pulled her own pants off, shimmying them off her hips and absolutely spellbinding Jocasta. Her panties were a match for her bra as well, and Jocasta had never been more attracted to the color red. Upon seeing the way Jocasta was looking at her she grinned. "It's only fair." Then her hands were on Jocasta's hips, pulling her closer to Katerina. "Are you sure?" she asked, hooking one finger into the already lowered waistband of Jocasta's boxers.

"Are you fucking kidding me? Of course." Jocasta answered in almost a yell, scared that if she didn't say it fast enough that Katerina would decide that she was the one that was unsure.

"I don't know if you want it enough." Katerina laughed and threw her head back, her hair cascading down her back and making Jocasta's stomach flip.

"Pleeease, Kat?" Jocasta whined, hoping she didn't sound as needy as she felt, practically begging Katerina to fuck her. But it seemed that Katerina had wanted her to beg, because she smiled that big smile and tugged, pulling Jocasta's underwear off faster than she had thought possible. She lay there, letting Katerina look at her for a second, before sitting up and grabbing her arm, pulling her to lay on top of Jocasta. She wrapped her arms around Katerina's neck and kissed her hard. She unwrapped her arms and started to touch Katerina, cupping her perfect breasts, and moving down to tug on Katerina's waistband, before slipping her hand around and squeezing as much of Katerina's ass as she could fit into her hands. Katerina awarded her a soft grunt before pushing herself off of Jocasta and trailing her tongue from Jocasta's neck all the way down to just above her clit, a sly smile playing at the corners of her mouth. She stopped before Jocasta could feel her mouth on her center and put her tongue back in her mouth.

"Beg for it, Jocasta." Katerina whispered, locking eyes with Jocasta.

"PLEASE, KAT." Jocasta was definitely yelling this time, and she didn't care if there was anyone close enough to the door to hear. Katerina grinned.

"Good girl." She licked her lips and bent forward again, finally giving Jocasta what she wanted. She gasped as Katerina's tongue swiped at her clit and then lapped at her slit, sucking her juices from her labia, and making Jocasta shiver. Katerina's tongue entered her, and she could feel her muscles squeezing around it as she pulled it back out and licked back up to her clit. She gently sucked as she let two fingers enter Jocasta, pressing her g-spot. It didn't take long for Jocasta to reach climax, practically screaming as her muscles tightened around Katerina's fingers.

"Oh my god, Kat!" She held Katerina's head to her center as the aftershocks began to subside. When she felt like she was done shaking, she pulled Katerina's hair toward her face and Katerina pushed herself up to kiss her. Jocasta could taste herself on her lips and she felt herself shiver again. Katerina pulled back and stared at Jocasta as she licked her fingers clean. She leaned down and gave Jocasta another kiss.

"Good?" She smiled at Jocasta.

"Incredible, Katerina." Jocasta felt her head sink into Katerina's pillows, and she couldn't believe how tired she suddenly was. She hadn't had an orgasm that good in quite some time.

"Well, I think I tired you out, so I'm going to go get ready for bed." Katerina began to get up.

"No! I'll be good in," Jocasta yawned "in just a second." Katerina just laughed at her and walked into her bathroom. Jocasta heard her turn on the faucet and presumed she would be brushing her teeth. She was determined to make Katerina feel just as good as she did right now, so she forced herself out of bed to follow her into the bathroom. "Please, Katerina, it's your turn!" she whined as she walked in. Katerina was leaning over the sink, splashing water onto her face. Jocasta reached out and held her hips, pulling her into herself. "I want you to feel this good." She leaned over and kissed Katerina's back. "I promise I'm not too tired."

"You really want to?" Katerina giggled and turned around, slipping her arms around Jocasta's waist.

"Yes, Kat. I *really* want to make you cum like that. Right now." Jocasta kissed her, opening her mouth, and tracing the opening of Katerina's lips with her tongue. She hadn't brushed her teeth after all, because she still tasted of Jocasta. "Please?"

"Okay, okay. Can I dry off my face though?" Katerina laughed, and Jocasta realized that she had been washing her face, and there was still a little bit of her face wash clinging to her eyebrows. She handed Katerina the towel that was sitting on her counter and nodded. As soon as she put the towel back down, Jocasta grabbed her wrist and dragged her back to bed.

They spent the next several hours taking turns making each other scream, each climax they caused giving them the energy to go another round, until Jocasta finally felt like she couldn't stand any more. "I owe you one more!" she giggled as Katerina got back up out of bed, the early morning sun beginning to stream through the bottom of her blinds.

"Jocasta. You can barely move." Katerina smiled and leaned down toward Jocasta. "I think I got enough pleasure from the way you screamed my name that last time." She winked and Jocasta shivered.

"I should probably get to my room and get showered anyway; we have to be ready for work soon." She started to get up herself, but Katerina was right, she was wiped out. "Or not. Your bed is so comfy." She pulled the covers up to her chin and smiled at Katerina. "Maybe I can tell my team that we need to take a day off today. You know, for morale, or something."

"Yeah, right. Jocasta Jones, taking a day off. They wouldn't buy it. Work isn't work for you." Katerina laughed and pulled the covers back down. She slipped her arms under Jocasta and carried her to the bathroom. "Let's take a shower together, and then maybe you'll be ready to work."

"If work doesn't involve me getting to see you naked, I don't want to do it." Jocasta giggled and rested her head on Katerina's shoulder. "I'll probably never want to do anything else again." she laughed.

"I was that good, huh?" Katerina laughed and set Jocasta on her feet. She got the water running in the shower and grabbed them two towels while Jocasta leaned on the door frame, watching her.

"I don't see how you could improve." Jocasta pushed herself off the door frame. "Honestly, the best sex I have ever had, hands down." She felt herself blush, waiting for Katerina to respond, hoping she felt the same way. She turned to her, and Jocasta felt herself tense up, waiting to hear the worst.

"Good to know. You're not so bad yourself, Jo-" Now it was her turn to cut off Katerina with a kiss. It was a softer kiss, but it still made Jocasta's stomach feel like it was floating when Katerina reciprocated her pressure.

"Are you sure we have to go to work?" She asked, surprising herself yet again.

"Who are you?" Katerina laughed and stepped into the shower. "Get in here already."

Later that day, Jocasta was thinking about how hungry she was while they were doing the last few tests they needed. She had burned off enough calories last night that her breakfast and lunch were just not cutting it. That thought made her blush a little as her mind drifted to thinking about Katerina, how she smelled, how her eyes flashed when Jocasta called her 'Kat', the way her voice dropped when she was telling her what to do, the flush in her cheeks when she came up for air…

"Earth to Doctor Jones!" Her favorite tech, Gary, was trying to ask her if they needed to run any more tests. She glanced at Katerina to see if she might have overheard her thoughts before responding.

"Sorry, Gary, my mind got away from me. Yes, just one more, then we will be compiling all the results from round one tomorrow." She handed him her clipboard that detailed how to record the data for the last test and felt eyes on her. She glanced up to see Katerina blushing. So, she *had* been fixated on those thoughts enough for Katerina to overhear. "*Sorry.*" she thought hard, and Katerina smiled. Then, "*No need to be.*" She heard Katerina's voice in her head. "Gary, hold on, I need to speak to Ms. Gradoff first." She called to Gary, who was getting the equipment ready to track Katerina's vitals. He nodded and set his things down on a table. "Excuse us," she said as she ushered Katerina into the hall. "Um, how come I didn't know you could do that?"

"What do you mean? Talk to you through thoughts?"

"Yes, Katerina, that is kind of a big deal! No other telepath has ever been recorded to be able to do that."

"I mean, they haven't been recorded as being able to suggest people either, it's just part of that I think."

"So, in doing what you just did, was that like what you do to bad guys?" At that, Katerina laughed. "What?"

"Bad guys. You sounded like a little kid." Katerina laughed again, so Jocasta glared at her. *"Oh, yes, I'm so scared of the woman I absolutely dominated in bed last night."* Jocasta heard in her head and blushed. "No, this is just an easy way to connect to someone. It is easier to do when I know the person, but suggestion is much harsher, so I don't do it to people unless I need to.

"Okay, well if it is different than when we recorded the suggestion, I need you to do that when we do this last test." Jocasta blushed again when she heard *"Yes, Ma'am."* They turned to go back into the lab, and Gary jumped when the door opened. "Everything okay, Gary?"

"Absolutely, Doc! Are we ready now?"

"Yes Gary. Just so you know, for this last test, you may hear Ms. Gradoff's voice in your head. It won't hurt, I just need her to do it on record."

"Are you sure?" He seemed more nervous than she had expected him to.

"Yes, Gary, she just did it to me, and it was fine."

"Um, Jo- Doctor? I can always just do it to you again, I don't know Gary as well as I do you, it would be easier." Katerina interjected. *"Look how nervous he is, Jocasta."*

"That's fine, but don't distract me from my notes, Ms. Gradoff." *"I mean it, Kat."* She thought, and Katerina smirked, clearly hearing her. Gary hooked up the equipment and Katerina started moving the designated objects, talking to Jocasta in her mind.

"Tell me what you're writing about, Jocasta. I love it when you talk about your work."

"The point is for you to project thoughts into my head, not the other way around."

"Aw, but where's the fun in that? You look so cute with that notebook."

"It's a tablet. And you're distracting me." Katerina tilted her head a little bit, and without filtering her thoughts Katerina heard *"There's that sexy head tilt. Shit. Sorry. You weren't supposed to hear that."*

Katerina laughed out loud, and Gary looked up from his computer. "What's so funny? Oh, are you guys talking now?"

"Yes, she is being more distracting than I would like." Jocasta smiled.

"Would your conversation explain an uptick in her heart rate? About 2 seconds before she laughed?" Jocasta felt the color start to drain from her face as she tried to think of an explanation.

"It might have, Gary. The doctor is quite the charmer." Katerina laughed. "I'm kidding. It was probably just because she was misspelling things in her notes. It was amusing."

"Wait, you're able to read my mind while also talking to me internally?"

"Yes."

"Incredible." Jocasta scribbled more in her notes. "Also intimidating. I'd better watch my thoughts from now on."

"You couldn't be thinking anything worse than what I did to you last night," Katerina laughed again.

"Your heart rate spiked again, Ms. Gradoff." Gary informed them, and this time Jocasta laughed.

"She's just teasing me about my notes, Gary. I'm going to assume it's normal conversation habits." Jocasta waved him off and he left the computer for a minute, instead watching Katerina as she moved more objects. She lifted a table and chairs, keeping them in their proper places, then moving the chairs in and out, as if people were getting up from the table. *"I am never going to get tired of watching that."*

"Good, because you are very sexy when you take notes on me."

"Oh, should I start taking notes during sex?" Jocasta's cheeks were turning red, having this conversation in front of her employee.

"I don't see how you can take notes with your hands tied to the bedposts." Katerina tilted her head, pretending to focus on lifting place settings up to the table.

"Ms. Gradoff!" Jocasta exclaimed without thinking. She cleared her throat. "Um, I think that is good enough. Gary, let's start cleaning up for the day, shall we?"

"Uh, yeah, sure, Doc." Gary began getting the equipment unhooked from Katerina while she set everything back down.

"Did I get you flustered, Doctor?" Katerina laughed in her head.

"I cannot believe you." Jocasta tried to get her notes finished up so that she could start editing them when Gary was finished. The rest of the techs were further back in the lab, running the samples and calculating data from earlier in the day. When Gary was finished with his computer, he looked up at Jocasta.

"Hey, doc? Should I go tell everyone we are good to go for the day?"

"Yes, Gary, please do. I'll just be here for a bit-"

"Editing your notes?" Gary laughed. "I'll see you tomorrow." And with that, Jocasta was left virtually alone with Katerina.

"I like getting you all hot and bothered in front of your employees. I should do that more often."

"I should have you banned from my lab." Jocasta was mostly joking. "That was over the line, Katerina." She spoke softly, so that nobody leaving the lab would hear.

"And your sex comment wasn't?" Katerina hissed. "It's not like I said anything out loud, Jocasta."

"Gary probably doesn't believe that your heart rate spiked because you saw some misspelled words, Kat. He's a smart guy." Jocasta felt herself getting angry. *"Look, my point is, we have only been on one date. One absolutely out of this world, perfect date, but still. Only one. It is a bit soon to be flirting with me at work, even if it is just in our heads."* Then aloud, "I have to edit my notes, Ms. Gradoff, I'm sure I will see you later."

"I'm going to pretend you didn't just blame me, when you were flirting just as much as I was, Doctor *Jones."* Katerina's thoughts were harsh, but her words weren't. "Yes, later." Katerina walked out of the lab.

"Kat, I'm just trying to stay professional, come on."

"Should have thought of that before you had sex with your coworker, Jocasta."

"That's not fair. You're the one who said we should keep it professional."

"I'm sorry, you're out of range from this person's mind. Please leave a message." Katerina sounded like a voice mail machine. She had clearly changed her mind since last night, but Jocasta hadn't.

"Hey, I'll be done in like 30 minutes, please let me come talk to you." Jocasta waited for a response, knowing that she wouldn't really be out of range unless she was about a hundred miles away. She thought as hard as she could *"Please, Kat."* After another minute, she heard Katerina say that it was fine if she wanted to meet in her room, and Jocasta spent the next 30 minutes rushing through her notes, editing as fast as she could. When she was finishing up, Arthur popped his head in.

"Hey there, kid. How's the study going?" He asked, coming into the room, and heading for his usual chair.

"Great, Arthur, It's just that I have somewhere I need to be, so I'm heading out."

"Oh, I just wanted to check in with you, go on ahead."

"Thanks, I'll see you tomorrow?"

"I'll bring you dinner then! You can't say no this time!" Arthur beamed.

"Yes, absolutely, I'll see you then." Jocasta practically ran out the door and up the stairs to her room. She threw on some deodorant and changed her shirt before walking across the hall and knocking on Katerina's door. When she answered, Jocasta darted in and waited for Katerina to shut the door behind her. "I'm sorry, you just surprised me, and I was definitely flustered, but we *have* only been on the one date, so I'm not entirely wrong to think it's a bit inappropriate, am I?"

"I think you're right, but you also were flirting with me, Jocasta.

"I know, I got carried away and then I was embarrassed, and I blamed you. I'm sorry." She paused, *"You were getting me a bit too horny for the workplace."* She thought; and then *"Oh fuck, are you listening in?"*

"You just went pale. Did you think something embarrassing?"

"Maybe, but you're not listening?"

"No, should I start telling you when I pop in?"

"Yes, but *have* you popped in before today?"

"Maybe once or twice to see if you were thinking about me at all."

"Katerina! That's a huge invasion of privacy!"

"I'm kidding. I only heard your thoughts if they were extra loud, like they were today. Mostly it was if you were thinking about a specific bit of your notes or something."

"I really *do* have to start controlling my thoughts more." Jocasta sighed. "Are we good, then?"

"Oh, I'd say we're more than good, Jocasta. We'll just have to both be a little more careful." Katerina's voice dipped a little bit as she wrapped her arms around Jocasta's waist. "I think I'd like to cash in on that debt you owe me."

"Is that so? It's pretty soon, don't you think? Don't you want to bank some interest first?" Katerina shook her head. Jocasta giggled and kissed her, guiding her to the bed.

⌐⌐⌐

KATERINA

Katerina woke up with a sense of optimism that she was still not used to. She had been seeing Jocasta for a few months now, and she was hoping that tonight she would be making their relationship 'official'. She had booked a reservation at the best restaurant she could find within a reasonable distance, and she had even gotten a hotel room nearby, so that they wouldn't have to come back to the compound after dinner. Viktoria had offered to cover for them if anyone asked where they were, or if Marc called a meeting and they took a while to get back.

Nobody but Vik had caught on to the fact that they were seeing each other, and Katerina thought it would be nice to spend the night somewhere other than her room for once. They hadn't really spent the night anywhere else, not even Jocasta's room, since she didn't have the luxury of soundproof walls. She rolled over to see that Jocasta hadn't come to her room last night and felt a pang of disappointment. She had been working late in the lab, and probably didn't want to wake Katerina, but recently, any time she woke up to an empty bed, she felt a bit disappointed. She got up and got dressed, slipping on the most comfortable jeans she owned and a faded old t-shirt she hadn't worn in a while. She was about to pad across the hall to see if Jocasta even made it out of the lab when her phone buzzed. It was a text from Marc.

New intel about an Anti-Government terrorist group.
Meeting in 5.

She pocketed her phone and threw on some shoes. She apparently would not be checking in on Jocasta this morning. She could only hope they wouldn't be leaving right away, as she headed down to the meeting. When she walked into the board room, she overheard Arthur asking what "Anti-Government" was supposed to mean.

"Is that Anti- the US government, or Government in general?" It was Marc that answered him.

"It's anti all government. These people believe humans should govern themselves, individually. They are currently US based, but their manifesto they've published online says their mission is to 'liberate the world'." Marc put air quotes around the last bit.

"I love the smell of extremists in the morning," Katerina said, walking in and finding a seat. "Does it look like a big mission?"

"Not yet, but I am going to bet that we will all be needed soon." Marc leaned against the wall and crossed his arms, "This group seems to be gaining traction fast. It seems like it's mostly teenagers and younger adults, and everything is online, so they can really get tons of followers very quickly." Marc sighed, rubbing a hand down his face. "But I'll save the rest for the team as a whole."

"Whenever they all show up," Arthur joked, nudging Katerina with his elbow.

"They still have a few minutes, Art, I just happened to see the text when I was already about to leave my room."

"Early bird gets the worm, huh?" Art smiled, and Katerina felt her cheeks warm at the reason she was really up.

"Something like that." She didn't say anything else as they waited for the others to arrive. When everyone was there and settled into their seats, Marc started briefing everyone on this group, who called themselves The Freedom Brigade. She tried to pay as much attention as she could, but her thoughts kept drifting to her date that would definitely not be happening now. Maybe Jocasta would want to go spend the night off base by herself. Katerina hated to waste the reservation. Or maybe the restaurant and the hotel would let her change her reservations to a different date. Not that she would know when that would be. She needed to focus on this meeting, then she could worry about the other stuff. Jocasta would understand, it had happened before, a mission would come up, and they would have to change their plans. Although, they never had plans that were this concrete. Katerina forced herself to tune back into Marc.

"So, we will be sending in some agents to try and get intel. Fortunately, we have some young folx around now that would be able to infiltrate this group easier than some of us old timers. Katerina, we were hoping you would go, and Carter, you'll be on the older end, but it should be alright. I have also been speaking with Doctor Jones, who feels that with her training with Viktoria that she is ready to study some field work, so she will also be joining you two. I need you to be extra vigilant for her sake and try to make sure that she never has to use that training."

"Of course," Katerina said, and Carter just nodded.

"Good, she has already been briefed, so I expect the three of you to be ready by tonight. We will be using whatever you can gather to plan our next move, so good luck. You are all dismissed." Katerina debated staying and asking Marc to detail the plan one more time, since she had been distracted, but decided she would just ask Jocasta, since she apparently already knew about it. She headed up to Jocasta's room and knocked on the door.

"Hey Jocasta, you up?" she called, and didn't receive an answer. Katerina used her powers to scan for someone in her vicinity, careful not to linger on anyone too long so that she wouldn't hear specific thoughts. She found Jocasta in her lab and headed down there. When she got to the door, she heard a soft snore coming from inside the lab. She quietly edged into the room, and walked up behind Jocasta, who was laying on her desk, head resting on her arms, a pen clutched in her hand. She reached her arms around either side of her, and gently plucked the pen from her hand, setting it on the desk. Then she checked to make sure they were alone before brushing the back of her neck with a soft kiss. "Wake up, sleepy head," she whispered, and Jocasta snapped her head up, almost smacking Katerina's head. Katerina backed up to give Jocasta some room as she spun around, eyes wild.

"You scared the shit out of me! God, Katerina, you can't wake someone up like a normal person?" Jocasta was flustered, her face red from laying on her arms for who knows how long. Katerina had to suppress a smile. She was too cute.

"You're not just *someone*, Jo," she teased, knowing Jocasta wouldn't be too keen on someone overhearing the nickname she had started using. It did the trick though because Jocasta looked around frantically as soon as she heard it.

"Katerina, please don't give me a heart attack so early in the morning."

Jocasta sighed. "I'll be dead before I'm thirty." Katerina reached a hand out to Jocasta and lifted a brow.

"You'd better not be, I like having you around. Let's go get you some breakfast before you start working again." She gestured at Jocasta's desk. "You know I had to take a pen out of your hand before I woke you up?" Katerina smirked as the red in Jocasta's cheeks deepened with her embarrassment. Jocasta's voice came hushed.

"I'm sorry I didn't come to bed last night, I got carried away."

"With the new mission?" Katerina gave her a knowing look as they began their walk upstairs to the kitchen. "When did you tell Marc you were ready for that, by the way?"

"About a week ago." Jocasta looked down, then back up at her, a little bit of fear in her eyes. "Do you not think I'm ready?"

"No, if you think you're ready, by all means, I was just a little bit surprised to hear about it in the meeting this morning." She didn't want Jocasta to think she was upset about her not knowing, because she really wasn't, but she realized as the words came out that it sounded exactly like that. "I'm not upset about not knowing, Jocasta, I know that might have sounded like I was." Katerina had learned that Jocasta couldn't help herself from over analyzing everything she said and had adopted a habit of making sure Jocasta knew exactly what she meant.

"Thank you." Jocasta almost whispered it, acknowledging Katerina's effort. "So, are you ready to go on a mission with me? I bet I'll surprise you in action!" Jocasta jumped a little bit while she was walking and held her hands like she was going to chop a wood plank. "I think I'm getting pretty good."

"Your endurance has definitely improved, that's for sure," Katerina laughed. When she saw Jocasta's eyes widened at her comment she spoke in her head, *"Nobody can overhear us, Jo. The closest person is over 100 ft away."*

Then she heard Jocasta retort *"Vik could. She has enhanced senses, Kat."* Which made Katerina laugh again. They had been practicing, and Jocasta was really good at projecting her thoughts to Katerina so that they could talk like this without Katerina actually entering her head. It felt strange and special at the same time.

"Vik has known we're seeing each other the entire time. Plus, Vik has the ability to knockout rooms of people with noxious gasses too, but I don't see

you worried about that." She looked at Jocasta to see that she was smiling now. Her smile had a way of making Katerina's stomach do a little jump that made her both excited about the idea of furthering their relationship and terrified that her feelings would begin to compromise her work. She had been trained not to let anything come before a mission, but Jocasta was making her want to step away from that ideology in a way that was thrilling. Not everyone she worked with was as staunchly dedicated to the mission as she had been and Viktoria was, and for the first time, she could see herself being one of the team members with a life outside of W.E.I.R.D.

"Jocasta? I think you need to take today off from the lab." Katerina realized that they didn't have much time to prepare for the mission, and she also still needed to talk to Jo about the date they were supposed to have been going on that evening.

"I- um," Jocasta tilted her head quizzically, "You know what? You're right," she smiled wide. "I think maybe we should do a little extra training session so you can see what you'll be working with." An image of Jocasta trying to spar with her flashed across Katerina's mind, making her grin.

I can't imagine someone as submissive as you being able to put up much of a fight." she thought to Jocasta, and seeing her cheeks turn red she laughed "I'd love to see how much you've learned."

"I am a sponge for information, you know."

"Yes, but how much does that translate into your *actual* fighting? I've never seen you do anything athletic." Katerina teased her, and Jocasta decided to respond in thought.

"*I'm pretty sure you have seen me do some acrobatics, Katerina.*" Jocasta smirked before out loud saying "I will have you know I took karate classes in the second grade. It did not last very long, but I did it."

"Karate Kid lover?" Katerina giggled.

"Maybe," Jocasta drew the word out. "It was just so hard! And I was so little!" They both giggled as they rounded the corner into the kitchen and Katerina got to work. Jocasta definitely knew a few good recipes, but her actual cooking skills needed some work, so Katerina usually just cooked for the both of them.

"Do you need to let your team know not to come in today?" Katerina asked as she cracked a few eggs into a pan.

"Oh no, I'm mostly supervisory at this point. An easy way to describe it is that it's like they all run data and crunch numbers and then I try to connect dots. I'll just tell Gary to make sure they don't need me for a few days." She reached into a pocket and pulled out her phone, texting Gary.

"A few days?"

"Well yeah, Marc said after the initial party thing they're throwing, if we can get more info, we'll be in the field for a few days. We have a safe apartment that we'll be in," Jocasta trailed off. "Wait, he didn't tell you that in the briefing?"

"About that," Katerina lowered her voice a little bit "I may have been distracted for a good chunk of the meeting this morning. I was kind of hoping that you would tell me what you know before the meeting with just us, Carter, and Marc this afternoon."

"Of course, but why were you distracted?" a curious and mischievous tone entered her voice "Was it about someone special?" Jocasta waggled her eyebrows.

"Yes, it was, but that conversation needs to be tabled for a little while." Katerina didn't want this to be how she asked Jocasta to take the next step with her.

"Oh, so mysterious, Katerina." And then, *Is something wrong with us?*

"Absolutely not, actually the opposite, I just want to talk to you in a more private place. You have nothing to worry about."

They ate their breakfast fairly quickly, and Katerina wondered if Jocasta was eating so fast to avoid anyone seeing them and overhearing anything or because she wanted to hurry up and get to work for the mission. As much as Jocasta said she didn't want to hide their seeing each other, she definitely seemed more comfortable doing so. Maybe if they had a more official label on the relationship, she wouldn't be so nervous for people to overhear them. Katerina didn't mind keeping things professional while they were working, but the sneaking around at night was becoming tiresome. She highly doubted anyone would even blink an eye if they saw her leaving Jocasta's room at 7am. It wasn't like there was a rule against it or anything. She did know that her work meant absolutely everything to Jocasta, so it was probably just her being extra anxious and cautious, but if it kept going on forever, Katerina was going to have a problem.

Jocasta cleaned up their dishes, taking them to the sink, so Katerina went to get a dish towel so that she could help her dry them. They cleaned the dishes in silence, but it was a comfortable silence. Katerina smiled as Jocasta wiped down the sink, always the perfectionist. "So, mission prep first, or me kicking your ass first?" She asked, grinning.

"You don't know that you'll beat me, Katerina." Jocasta crossed her arms and gave her a challenging look. "I told you, I'm going to surprise you."

"So, we're training first, then? I'll need to get my gear on."

"Me too, let's get going!" Jocasta bounded out of the kitchen and started half jogging down the hallway. "I'll race you!"

"Oh, you're on, you even have a head start!" Katerina called. As soon as she had said the first half of her sentence, Jocasta had broken into a run, so she followed. She had almost caught up to her when they got to the first landing on the staircase, but Jocasta had definitely gotten into better shape since the last time they raced. As they reached the top of the staircase though, Katerina pulled ahead and beat Jocasta to their rooms. "You put up a better fight this time, I'll give you that."

"Yeah, yeah, just be prepared to get knocked on your butt in a minute." Jocasta grinned and slipped into her room to change. When they were both changed, they headed back downstairs and to the training room. Jocasta had changed into a cropped tank top and joggers, both of which were very flattering on her, and Katerina was having trouble not staring as they made their way downstairs. They had been sleeping together a few times a week for the past few months, but she was still being distracted by how sexy Jocasta was. Maybe if they sparred now, it would be less sexy and distracting if she had to do it in the field, but Katerina was not sure, and that scared her. Jocasta bounced her way into the training room and walked over to the boxing ring in the center of the room. The training room was more like an entire gym than it was a room, but Katerina was pretty sure the team would have been just fine with the boxing ring alone. It was definitely everyone's go to. "You sure you don't need to stretch, warm up maybe?" Katerina was standing a little off to the side of the ring, stretching her arms above her head, trying not to laugh.

"Obviously, I am too good to need stretching, but I will if you really think I need to." Jocasta laughed. "I forget to stretch a lot." She bent down and touched her toes, and Jocasta sucked in a breath as more of Jocasta's already exposed stomach was revealed as her shirt slid up. She had only started training two months ago, but Jocasta had already become more taught and toned, and her muscles were becoming more and more visible. Katerina hadn't really paid attention, thinking Jocasta perfect from the moment she laid her eyes on her, but the confidence it gave Jocasta was very sexy. She was already lean, so it hadn't taken much for her to get toned and start to build some muscle, and Katerina saw how much Jocasta liked looking stronger, even if they hadn't said anything to each other. She had caught her flexing in the mirror more than once. They stretched a little more before Katerina walked over to the hanging teardrop heavy bag along the wall and started wrapping her hands to warm up a little bit. She began with a few punches, easing into the rhythm she was familiar with when warming up like this.

"That is probably the sexiest thing I have ever seen you do." Jocasta said softly from behind her, and Katerina felt her cheeks glow.

"You want a turn? With the bag I mean, not with my fists yet." She turned to see Jocasta with her hands already wrapped, bouncing up and down on the balls of her feet, punching the air. Katerina felt a flutter in her stomach. She looked just like any of the Phenoms, ready to launch into action.

"Sure!" Jocasta looked to be at ease just as much as Katerina had been, punching the bag. She *was* surprised, and they hadn't even started hand to hand. Not that she would admit it to Jocasta, yet. She would probably use the fact that she had been impressed later, to make Jocasta smile, or maybe for something a bit more explicit. The thought made her smirk as she went to a standing heavy bag to start warming up her legs a little bit. Jocasta came over to a hanging heavy bag and started kicking it, in Katerina's eye line. She felt her eyebrows raise at Jocasta's form, impressively good for such a beginner. She just kept getting more and more amazing the more they spent time together. Katerina began doing some full body warmups, punching and kicking her bag, not going too hard, but still focusing on her form, and when she felt warm, she looked up to see Jocasta doing a windmill kick and hitting her bag. Jocasta proceeded to plant her foot back down and smile at Katerina, "You ready?" Her grin was huge and mischievous. Katerina nodded and climbed into the ring, Jocasta following her.

"We can use boxing gloves if you want," she offered, but she had a feeling Jocasta didn't want to. That feeling was confirmed when Jocasta shook her head. Katerina watched her get herself into her ready position and did the same. "Okay, are you sure you're ready?"

"Yes, Katerina." Jocasta sounded a little bit impatient "Are you?" Instead of answering, Katerina swung at Jocasta, who blocked her punch. "I'll take that as a yes!" Jocasta returned a punch of her own, which Katerina blocked with ease. Jocasta's moves were fairly easy to see coming, and Katerina found that she hadn't landed a single blow on her. Jocasta on the other hand had taken quite a few hits. Almost as if Jocasta knew what she was thinking, all of a sudden, she swung her leg and took Katerina's leg out from under her, making her fall to one knee. Jocasta backed up and allowed Katerina to regain her footing, and then she was on her. Now she had more calculated moves and she was landing almost as many blows as Katerina was. It was like she had been taking it easy to get a read on Katerina's fighting style. Jocasta's hand flew past Katerina, and she grabbed her arm, spinning around and throwing her over her shoulder. Jocasta landed with a hard thud on her back, but she was smiling. "I think maybe I was a little over-confident. You win."

"You did great, Jocasta." Katerina smiled and reached down to help Jocasta to her feet, but Jocasta used her position to knock Katerina off both feet and directly onto her ass.

"I told you I'd knock you on your butt!" Jocasta laughed from deep in her belly, her shoulders shaking as she clutched her stomach and curled into herself on the mat.

"You already conceded, Jocasta, that doesn't count!" Katerina protested, but Jocasta was so cute when she really laughed like this, so she joined in. After a few minutes of them laughing on the floor of the ring, Katerina wiped a tear from her eye. "Okay, let's get up to my room so we can go over details for this evening already." She leapt to her feet but didn't offer to help Jocasta in case she got any ideas about repeating last time. Katerina climbed through the ropes and down to the floor, unwrapping her hands. She turned around to see Jocasta rolling like a log to the edge of the ring and under the bottom rope, making her think she was going to drop right to the floor. Katerina rushed over and caught her up, making Jocasta giggle.

"I wasn't going to fall, Katerina. I do that almost every day."

"Why?" Katerina let her drop to her feet.

"Because it's fun, duh." Jocasta grinned wide and started backpedaling to the door. As she was doing so, Carter walked into the training room, probably for their daily training session. "That's why I do you so much, after all." As soon as she said it, Carter dropped their water bottle, startling Jocasta, and alerting her to their presence. "Oh my god! Carter!"

"Uh, hey." They looked incredibly uncomfortable, clearly having overheard Jocasta's comment.

"*Why didn't you warn me?*" Jocasta's thoughts rang in Katerina's head.

"*Because why would I think to? And you were literally talking already when they walked in.*"

"So, um, you two?" Carter gestured between them. "That's cool, I mean, do I need to keep it to myself?"

"It's just casual. Not a big deal, so not important enough to tell anyone, really." Jocasta said it without even looking at her, and Katerina felt her heart drop. There went her hopes for their talk.

"We were just going, so." Katerina brushed past Jocasta and tried not to literally run away from her. "*I'm going to take a shower.*"

"*Should I join you?*" Katerina couldn't help but scoff to herself.

"*No.*" She was curt, and she was sure Jocasta could tell something was wrong. Then again, she was sure Jocasta thought they were more than just casual fuck buddies, too. No wonder she didn't want to tell people. No wonder she wanted to sneak around. Did she not get the hint with all of the romantic rendezvous Katerina had planned for them over the past few months?

"*Katerina, did I say something wrong?*" Jocasta's thoughts had a whimper in them that made Katerina soften just a tad. She didn't want to answer her, but Jocasta had a way of sounding so sad even in her head that made Katerina feel like she should answer her anyway.

"*Yes. Or no, I guess we just had very different ideas about what we're doing here.*" Katerina could feel the bitterness in her thoughts and wondered if that was how Jocasta heard thoughts or if it was part of her powers. They made the rest of their way to their rooms, Katerina a few yards ahead of Jocasta, completely silent. Not their usual comfortable silence anymore, but a prickly one. Katerina went to go take her shower, turning to close the door behind her, and Jocasta let her go. After a quick shower, she met Jocasta across the hall and told her that she just wanted to go over the mission. Jocasta caught her up, letting her know that the event they were attending would be a recruitment party, where the Freedom Brigade would be mingling with their followers from online and seeing if they wanted to recruit anyone into a big 'project' they had coming up. It sounded ridiculous to her, but Jocasta assured her that she had done research, and this was the second of 4 parties like this that they would be throwing. They had recruited a dozen young adults at their first party. They were to dress formally for the event, and their cover was that she and Jocasta were in town visiting Carter. Jocasta was to be Carter's sister; their names were Eleanor and Oli Smith, and to keep it simple for Jocasta's first mission, their backgrounds were pretty basic. Radicalized by the alien attacks when they were children and the way the government handled the aftermath.

The part that had Katerina's stomach in a twist was that her alias would be Jocasta's girlfriend, Wanda Karkarov. All Jocasta had said about it was that she wondered if her last name would cause suspicion, being clearly European, but Marc had mentioned to Jocasta that her accent would probably do that anyway. Their aliases had met at college. They would be meeting Marc and Carter in a few hours and then they would be heading to the apartment they would be in for a few days at the least. There, they would find clothes for the party and to 'match their aliases' as Jocasta put it. As soon as she had finished talking, Katerina had grabbed her notes and left, retreating to her room so that she could cancel the reservations she had almost forgotten about.

A few hours passed more quickly than she had thought they would, researching more about the mission and studying up on her new identity. She headed down to the meeting without running into Jocasta, and she was almost relieved to see that she wasn't at the meeting yet. *"Maybe she decided not to do it,"* she thought, sitting down next to Carter. *"Marc would have already informed you, don't get your hopes up."* And almost as if it was on cue, Jocasta walked in with Marc, laughing about something.

"Alright, Dr. Jones tells me the two of you have been discussing the details, and she feels very confident, so that's good. I had your aliases be so close to Jocasta's so that you two wouldn't look suspicious if you were close to her or checking up on her a good amount, I hope you don't mind, Katerina, playing the girlfriend."

"Of course not, Marc." she felt herself smile but inside she felt her guts wrench at the word girlfriend. They went over a few more details and Katerina found that she was getting less nervous about Jocasta as she continually asked good questions and showed that she had been well prepared for the task at hand. She felt a small swell of pride, and immediately shoved it down. Jocasta was not hers to be proud of. When the time came, the three of them headed to their safehouse. Carter let Katerina drive their car, and Jocasta hopped into the back seat, causing Carter to raise their eyebrows in surprise. As good as Carter was under cover, they were terrible at hiding their thoughts in regular everyday life. They hopped into the front seat and looked at Jocasta.

"So, little sis, you feel ready?" They grinned.

"Yea. I forgot to ask, is your alias also Nonbinary? Just making sure I use the right pronouns while we're undercover." Katerina hadn't thought about telling Jocasta, they always used the correct pronouns, no matter what, but Carter didn't look upset by the question.

"Always! Marc is good about making sure we don't use different pronouns undercover." Carter glanced back at Jocasta, who probably looked like she was thinking up another question. "Call me your big sibling if anyone asks. The big Sib to your little Sis." Carter smiled wide, and Katerina could tell they had gotten closer to Jocasta than she had realized. That would explain how baffled they had been this morning. They spent the rest of the ride talking about some show that Katerina didn't know, but she was content to just focus on the drive. When they got to the apartment building, her adrenaline was ramping up like it always did before a mission. She found their designated parking spot, a nondescript spot where they could get out easily if anything were to happen. This mission may be a low danger level intelligence gathering mission, but they could never be too careful.

Carter led the way to their door and opened the apartment with one of the three keys they had all received. It was small, but also kind of cozy. An open kitchen and living room area, one bedroom and bathroom to the left, and another set to the right. Katerina had initially volunteered to sleep on the couch, but Marc told her Jocasta would be doing that so that she would have protection from both sides. Katerina didn't think that seemed correct, but she figured Jocasta had probably told him she wanted the couch. She was never one to take the better option for herself.

Katerina headed to the bedroom on the right and found both her and Jocasta's clothes for the evening layer on the bed. They had to share the space for everything but sleeping, and Katerina didn't mind, but seeing the two suits next to each other made her muscles clench. They had a couple of hours before the party, which was a few blocks away, so Katerina just worked on making sure her gear was all ready. About an hour before they had to leave, Jocasta walked in.

"Hey, I was just gonna," she trailed off, pointing to the clothes on the bed. Katerina just nodded. Jocasta looked at the two suits to see which one was hers and retreated to the bathroom to change. Katerina was testing her communication device in her ear when Jocasta emerged. The suit was a crushed black velvet, and the lapels were a sort of silky material. Her shirt was the same silky material, but it was a red that matched the suit that Katerina would be wearing. *"How cute. Matchy couple clothes. Thanks, Marc,"* She thought with tight lips. Jocasta walked over to her and sat on the edge of the bed, looking every bit as beautiful as any magazine cover model. Katerina felt her stomach flip. "Katerina," Jocasta began, but Katerina wasn't interested in having a heart to heart right now.

"Here's your comm, it goes in your ear. I know you've probably talked to Marc or Carter about it already, so I won't bother you with the instructions." Katerina stood up and grabbed her own suit, which was also velvet, but not crushed. The red made her feel powerful as she pulled on the pants, and she looked at the hanger to see that she had two shirt options, one black and one white. She picked the white one, so they wouldn't be *too* matchy, and as she pulled the jacket off, she saw that Jocasta also had a white shirt she could have put on, and that she must have chosen to put on the matching color. The thought made Katerina feel conflicted. She pulled her hair out from between the shirt and jacket, and let it cascade down her shoulders. If the red had been any brighter, it would have looked ridiculous with her hair, but the deep tone actually looked good, she thought. The high waist on the pants was a nice touch too, it would help if they had to fight at any point. She hated fighting with a lower waistband, no need to worry about your pants falling off while you were punching an asshole.

She stepped back out of the bathroom to see that Jocasta had left the room and gathered the rest of her things for tonight. She walked out to the living room area to see Carter showing Jocasta their favorite way to hide a weapon in plain sight, not that Carter needed that, being as *they* were the weapon. They still had a few minutes before they were going to head over, but Katerina was itching to go, looking at Jocasta smiling and laughing with Carter. The sooner they were done the better. Every time Jocasta smiled, Katerina felt such a strong pang of longing that it almost made her angry.

They entered the party a few minutes later, and Katerina was genuinely impressed with the level of wealth on display here. Someone very rich was funding the Freedom Brigade. The three of them walked in together, but Carter split off almost immediately. The plan was for Jocasta to stick as close to Katerina as possible, using their 'relationship' as a reason to not stray too far. They started circling the room together, and Katerina tried to take in as much of her surroundings as she could. The room was a grand ballroom, and there was a balcony wrapping around the room where the second floor would have been. At the back of the room, a hallway led back to elevators and stairs, and she assumed there would be other rooms beyond those, and probably some on the second floor as well, though she couldn't quite see that yet. She gently touched her ear before asking Carter to check on that balcony level, and they immediately responded, 'On it!'. Next thing she knew, she could see Carter on their way up the flight of stairs in the back. The thing about this party was that they had no idea who was part of the group already or not. The website had said 'Just mingle and leave your email at the door. We will contact you.' The three of them each had a fake email attached to their alias for that purpose. Katerina felt Jocasta look her arm through her own and felt herself go a little rigid before she forced herself to relax. Tonight, she was Wanda, and Jocasta was Eleanor, and that would be fine. She would be fine. "Would you like a drink, Eleanor?" She asked, nodding to the bar.

"I think just a water is fine, Wanda." Jocasta was probably too nervous to drink right now, but Katerina was in desperate need of some liquor. Anything to steady her, really, and one drink would do just the trick. They made their way to the bar and Katerina ordered their drinks. As she handed Jocasta her water, she noticed a couple of young girls eyeing Jocasta and she slipped her arm around her waist. "Jealous of a couple of teenagers, Wanda?" Jocasta whispered softly in her ear.

"You don't have to end every sentence with 'Wanda', Casta." Carter mumbled in their comms and Katerina smirked. She had never heard anyone call Jocasta that before, and it was kind of cute the way Carter talked to her like a little sister, even outside of their roles tonight. Jocasta pulled away, apparently startled by Carter, probably forgetting that they could hear her. They spent a good amount of time mingling with the other guests, not really getting a lot of information that they didn't already know, so it seemed that the party would be a bust unless they were recruited at the end of the night. Most of the time they were just making small talk and joking with other guests, Katerina keeping a hand at the small of Jocasta's back or Jocasta linking her arm in Katerina's. Carter talked to them over the comms to let them know that they were having a similar experience, so by the time it had been a few hours, they were all feeling pretty annoyed. There was a little bit of dancing going on in the center of the ballroom, so Katerina nudged Jocasta in that direction, needing a break from the conversation they were having about the trolley problem with a couple of guys who were barely twenty-one. At least she hoped they were twenty-one, as they were both holding whiskeys. American drinking age always seemed way too high to her, but she didn't need any police showing up regardless.

"Let's dance, sweetheart. I'm feeling a bit restless." She smiled at Jocasta, but as soon as their eyes met, she felt a pang of regret at calling her sweetheart.

"Ew, boring pet name alert." Carter laughed a little in the comms.

"Okay, sure. It was nice to meet you two," Jocasta reached out and shook the hands of the guys they were talking to, and let Katerina lead her to the dance floor. As they got there, a slow song started. "*Great timing.*"

"You do know people are literally watching you, right?" Carter asked them from their bird's eye view on the landing. Katerina wrapped her arms around Jocasta's waist and pulled her close.

"Obviously." Katerina replied as Jocasta wrapped her arms around her neck and they began to dance.

"No, like a lot of people are looking at you. You're a distractingly pretty couple it looks like." Carter was watching the whole crowd from above, and as Katerina glanced around, she noticed quite a few people really were staring at them.

"Has this been going on for a while?" Jocasta asked, taking the words out of her mouth.

"Just since you got to the dance floor." Carter assured them, a smile audible in their voice. Katerina swung Jocasta around the dance floor with ease, but she almost froze when she felt Jocasta's fingers grasp the hair at the base of her neck. Jocasta held on tight as they danced, and Katerina felt like her grip was desperate, clinging to her like she wouldn't get to again. She was probably just nervous, being looked at like they were, but it made Katerina strangely angry, seeing as how Jocasta was the one that said they weren't serious.

As soon as the song was over, Katerina dropped her hands and turned to walk off of the dance floor, muttering something about needing the restroom. She heard Carter over the comms tell Jocasta they would watch out for her if she didn't want to follow Katerina, so she was surprised to feel a hand at her elbow as she made her way to the edge of the crowd. She let Jocasta hold her until they got to the restroom, where Katerina closed the door and checked for another person before locking the bathroom and turning to Jocasta. She pulled her comm from her ear and was about to say something, but instead she felt angry tears spring to her eyes, and she thought better of it. She replaced her comm and heard Carter saying that people were starting to head out, that they should probably meet up and do the same. She turned to the sink and washed her hands, steeling herself and forcing the tears back.

"Should we get going then, Wanda?" Jocasta said quietly, her hand on the door.

"Yes. Let's go find your sibling." Katerina fell into character as easily as the tears had sprung to her eyes, and they left the restroom, arms linked. They collected Carter at the bar, and the three of them made their way to the front door. Jocasta tensed up when she went to write her fake email address on the list, and Katerina put a hand on her lower back to steady her nerves before she wrote down the correct email and handed the pen to Katerina. They left the party, and all Katerina felt they had accomplished was making her feel more awkward with Jocasta. They started to walk back toward the apartment, and as soon as they were out of view, Katerina unlinked from her.

"Good party, right guys?" Carter asked, careful not to drop their ruse until they were inside their safe place.

"Very. A lot of pretty women, too." Katerina replied, making sure that she directed the comment at Carter, but also making sure that Jocasta picked up on what she was saying. "I saw you chatting up quite a few ladies, Oli."

"Not all ladies, Wanda, I had my fair share of the spectrum to flirt with, thank you very much." Carter joked. "Not that anyone cared about me when they saw my gorgeous sister dancing with you. When did you get those moves, sis?" They looked at Jocasta, who seemed a bit stiff now that Katerina had untangled herself.

"Oh, I just let Wanda lead me." The comment seemed innocent, but Katerina couldn't help thinking she was talking about what she had said that morning just as much as she was talking about the dance, as she looked into her eyes.

"You two make a good couple." Carter sounded genuine, in a way that made Katerina think that they meant the real people, not their aliases. Katerina felt her stomach tighten. As they walked into the apartment, Carter excused themself to go change, and Katerina looked at Jocasta.

"Why on earth were you holding me like that?" She asked.

"Like what, dancing with you? Acting like your girlfriend like I'm supposed to?"

"Gripping my hair like you were never going to let go. Taking every opportunity to touch me all night."

"That's what girlfriends do, Katerina. I was doing my job."

"Your job would have been accomplished with far less touching."

"Oh, I'm so sorry for committing to my role. And since when am I not allowed to touch you?"

"Since you told Carter that I don't mean anything to you!" Katerina took a breath. "We are so clearly not on the same page here." She walked to the bedroom and went to close the door behind her, but Jocasta thrust her arm out and grabbed the door, not letting her close it.

"We need to talk about this." The look in her eyes was something Katerina had never seen before. An icy determination and sincerity that was almost intimidating. *Almost.*

"I'm showering. Come back."

"No." The look intensified, and now it *was* intimidating. Katerina felt that Jocasta might actually make a scene in the living room where Carter would see, so she let her through the door.

"I'm still going to shower; I just don't want you camping out by the door." She went into her bathroom and stripped, running the shower so that Jocasta wouldn't try to talk to her for a minute. This is exactly why she should never have acted on her impulses. Now she would be compromised during the rest of their mission, and Marc would not be happy about that. Katerina wasn't happy about it either. And as much as she hated to admit it at this precise moment, it was going to put Jocasta at risk and that terrified her. She stepped into the shower and tried to let the warm water melt some of her hurt away before she talked to Jocasta, because as much as she had been hurt, it wasn't fair to attack her. As she was finishing with her conditioner, she heard the shower curtain rustle. "Jocasta, please let me have a minute." She opened her eyes to see Jocasta with tears in her eyes, poking her head into the shower. She had joined plenty of Katerina's showers before, so it wouldn't have been too out of the ordinary, but Jocasta was fully clothed, and the tears were not something she was expecting. "I'll be out in just a second, Jo." she almost whispered. She didn't want to see those tears spill out, and she felt as if speaking at full volume would have caused that for some reason. But instead of leaving, Jocasta stepped into the shower and reached for Katerina's hands.

"I panicked and so I just said the first thing that came to my mind." Jocasta began to ramble "I'm so sorry, I just I thought that maybe you didn't think we were doing anything serious and so I tried to downplay it and then I heard how upset you clearly were and I just-" She broke off, the tears spilling over her cheeks, and her breathing becoming shallow.

"Jocasta, we will talk in a minute, okay? You're going to get soaked, and you're wearing expensive velvet." Katerina hadn't remotely thought that Jocasta would panic like that, especially with just Carter. She realized that maybe Jocasta's feelings were even bigger than her own. That might explain the way she wanted to keep it quiet, if she thought it was something sacred, what they shared. Jocasta just nodded and stepped out of the shower again, and when Katerina got out, she saw that Jocasta had taken off the now wet velvet and laid it on the counter. She wrapped herself in a towel and went into the bedroom to find Jocasta sitting on the bed in her silk shirt and boxers, knees drawn up to her chest. Her eyes were focused on the window, but she wasn't really looking at anything but closed blinds.

Katerina grabbed a pair of sweatpants and a shirt and threw them on before sitting beside Jocasta.

"Jocasta, can I tell you something?"

"Please." she breathed.

"I was going to take you out tonight. Before we got the mission. I had reservations for a really nice restaurant, and a hotel room booked."

"Why?" Jocasta's eyes were growing wide as Katerina talked.

"I wanted to ask you," Katerina hesitated, trying to find the right words, "I wanted to take the next step with you and our relationship, Jo."

"You wanted to ask me to be your girlfriend?" Jocasta's eyes were saucers, her smile spreading across her whole face before dimming when she saw Katerina wasn't smiling.

"Then we got the mission, and I thought I would tell you about the date I had planned this afternoon, before we started the mission, but you said what you said to Carter, and I- I don't know how to say this."

"You don't want to see me anymore." Jocasta's eyes were still huge, but now they were full of fear.

"Not if you don't feel the way I do. And when you said that it made me realize that you might not. And then the way you were clutching me on the dance floor, and the way you were touching me I thought you were just toying with me. But just now, in the shower, I don't know what to think, Jocasta, and the mixed emotions and signals are tearing me apart because all I wanted this morning was you and I thought you felt the same."

"Katerina, I-I royally fucked up this morning, I know I did. I should have told Carter we are seeing each other and that you make me feel like the only person in any room, and I couldn't be happier with you, and they could tell anyone they want, because I want to shout it from the rooftops."

"But you didn't."

"I know. I'm sorry. I think that I had you in a little box in my heart and I was nurturing that and I wanted the box to be all pretty and figured out with a little bow on it before I shared it with anyone because my feelings for you are so messy and big, and when Carter overheard me, the box split open and all of those big feelings hadn't actually been fitting in that little box after all, but that made me panic and say something absurdly untrue for me, let alone you."

"What are you trying to say?" Katerina usually thought Jocasta's ramblings were cute, but she was becoming confused.

"As soon as someone else saw us in that frame, it made me realize my feelings for you were way more serious than I thought, and it scared me."

"So, are you breaking up with me because you have commitment issues or something?" Katerina sincerely hoped she would make an understandable point in the next few seconds.

"No! No, I'm not. I swear, I don't know how to talk. I'm trying to say that I'm in love with you, Katerina." Katerina's heart stopped, and Jocasta looked at her, her eyes shimmering with tears. There was a beat of silence, and then, "So, I don't know if you feel the same way, like you said, but I'm really hoping you'll want to keep seeing me, because I really don't want to stop seeing you." The caramel of her eyes darkened to a chocolate as her tears started to well up and spill over. Katerina still couldn't make herself respond, just stunned by the realization that she felt the exact same way, and Jocasta's declaration had only just opened her eyes to it. "Please don't say you want to stop." Jocasta choked out between breaths, as she was full blown sobbing now. Katerina's heart hadn't quite re-started yet, and she was struggling to breathe herself, but she wrapped her arms around Jocasta and pressed her lips to the crown of her head.

"Jo, I think I love you too," she whispered, threading her fingers through Jocasta's hair with one hand and holding her face with the other.

"Really?" Her eyes were full of hope and her brows stitched together.

"Yes, really. I love you, Jocasta Jones." And as she said it, she felt her heart float up out of her chest. She rested her forehead on Jocasta's and closed her eyes. "I love you."

"Then kiss me already, Katerina." And she did, but everything about this kiss was different than the countless kisses they had shared up until this point. It was sweet and tender in a whole new way, and she felt like she was sitting on a cloud. Jocasta's tears were mixing into their kiss, making her taste salt, and making her hope she never made Jocasta cry like that again. Happy tears only for her love, *her* Jocasta. The kiss probably only lasted thirty seconds, but it felt like hours, as they poured their hearts into each other. When they finally broke apart, Jocasta smiled.

"Maybe we should go strategize with Carter now," she said, standing up and going to grab some pants.

"Probably should. Are we ever going to eat dinner?" Katerina smiled at her and couldn't help but think about how absolutely incredible she was.

"I'm not sure." Jocasta sidled up to her and pressed their hips together, wrapping her arms around Katerina's waist. "So, am I your girlfriend now?" Jocasta drew out girlfriend, teasing her.

"Well, when you say it like that, it sounds like we're teenagers, so maybe not." Katerina poked Jocasta's nose, making her giggle. "Yes, I'd like that, Jo. Very much." They walked toward the door, and Katerina went out into the living room where Carter was sitting on the couch. Jocasta lingered in the door frame.

"Ooh! My girlfriend is so hot!" She announced it to the room like some sort of school age jock in an old movie.

"Jocasta, please, we are working now." Katerina nodded toward Carter, whose face had taken on quite a bright red hue.

"So, uh," they cleared their throat, "Not as casual as you said, Jocasta? Or was that just because of the mission?"

"The former, Carter." Katerina answered for her and motioned for her to sit down. "Now, what have we compiled thus far?"

"Not a lot, that's for sure. I don't think they tell anyone much at these shindigs, we'll probably just have to keep going until one of us gets in, I'd say.

"I heard one of the guys by the door mention a Jax when we were leaving, and it sounded like whoever they are is pretty important," Jocasta offered. "I don't see that on your list of info, sorry to interrupt. I just thought you guys heard too." Katerina allowed herself to feel the pride this time.

"Is that why you tensed up? I thought you had forgotten your email," Katerina smiled, and Carter added it to the list.

"Good catch, Jocasta." Carter beamed. "I'll forward the list to Marc and tell him that we will update if one of us gets contacted." They typed a little bit more on their screen and hit send with a flourish. "Now. Pizza, anyone?" Carter smiled wide.

"Absolutely!" Jocasta exclaimed, clapping her hands together and rubbing her palms.

"Good, because I ordered some while you two were making out or whatever it was you were doing." Katerina blushed at their comment, feeling strangely vulnerable.

"Thank you, Carter." They nodded and waved on their way out the door, going to pick up the pizza, as delivery could be a risk when they were undercover. She was nervous for them to go alone, as they usually wouldn't allow that for an undercover situation, but Marc had made it clear that one of them always needed to be with Jocasta. As soon as they closed the door, Jocasta came over to sit on Katerina's lap on the couch.

"Well, hello there. Who are you, miss PDA?" Katerina laughed, putting her arms around Jocasta.

"I told you I didn't wanna hide it, and if you're my girlfriend now, not only do I not want to hide, but I also want to flaunt it." Jocasta giggled. "I want everyone to know you're mine and I'm yours."

"This feels like a one-eighty of how I thought you felt this morning."

"I know. I'm sorry I let my nerves get the best of me. Plus, I never wanted to be sneaking around, I just worked so late a lot, and it seemed easier for some reason."

"Good to know. You've been apologizing a lot tonight, you know." Katerina kissed her softly. "You don't have to say sorry anymore, I know we just weren't communicating well enough. We're good." Jocasta leaned down for another kiss, and Katerina happily obliged.

"Promise?" Jocasta asked against her lips.

"Promise." Katerina pulled her down to lay on the couch and kissed her, playfully. "We don't have forever while they're getting pizza, Jo." She crushed her mouth to Jocasta's, who reciprocated the intensity. They were kissing like they never had, a sense of giddiness permeating the air. Jocasta's lips felt soft and tasted sweet, and it took a lot for Katerina not to rip her clothes off right there in the living room before Carter came back, but the promise of pizza was keeping her in check. She really needed some sustenance. Carter returned to find them on the floor, having fallen off the couch at the sound of the keys in the lock. They laughed so hard they almost dropped the pizza, but they assured Katerina it was fine, they didn't mind as long as they were happy. They ate pretty quickly, and Jocasta told Carter that she would be sleeping with Katerina rather than the couch, to which Carter replied.

"Obviously."

They all retired after they ate, throwing the leftovers in the fridge for Carter's breakfast. Katerina offered to make them all something, but they had insisted that they loved leftover pizza for breakfast, so she didn't fight them on it. Jocasta went to brush her teeth while Katerina changed into some underwear and a tank top to sleep in. When Katerina went to the bathroom to wash her face and brush her teeth, Jocasta giggled around her toothbrush.

"What?" Katerina looked down at herself to see if she had something on her shirt or something. Jocasta spit and rinsed out her mouth before answering.

"You're like, really pretty." Jocasta turned around and grabbed Katerina's hips. "I must be so lucky." She gave Katerina a peck on the lips and left the bathroom, smiling wide. Katerina washed her face and brushed her teeth as fast as she could while still assuring she felt clean, and when she left the bathroom, she found Jocasta cuddled under the blankets.

"I'm the lucky one, Jo." Katerina said softly, slipping under the covers to cuddle with Jocasta. She kissed her one more time before she succumbed to sleep, the exhaustion of the day finally weighing on her.

Jocasta

Jocasta woke up with a start, hearing shuffling in the living room of the safe house. She looked over to see Katerina had also been startled awake, she was sitting next to her on the bed with an intense look in her eyes. She glanced at Jocasta and put a finger to her lips before slipping out of bed and pulling her sweatpants back on. Jocasta pulled the blankets up to her chin and followed directions, feeling something horrible rise in her gut.

"Not her, just some dude." A masculine voice came from the living room. Jocasta felt fear and rage at the realization that the person was talking about Carter. They were not a 'dude'. But who on Earth was that? Katerina met her eyes and motioned for her to hide, making her way to the door. Jocasta slid behind the bed, glad that she had worn clothes to sleep. That was not always the case, but being away from home, she hadn't wanted to sleep naked. She heard someone turn the doorknob, and Katerina hissed "Outside, Jo. Now." Jocasta didn't hesitate to climb out the window and as she landed on the landing of the fire escape, she heard someone kick down the bedroom door. She saw the car keys float out the window, no doubt Katerina's doing, and reached out for them. She looked back into the window to see Katerina fighting the person they had heard and panicked when they used some sort of weapon to shock her, and she crumpled to the ground.

Jocasta refrained from screaming, somehow, and started sprinting down the fire escape. She heard the intruder at the top of the staircase, gaining on her, and decided to launch herself over the railing of the last flight. Her bare feet hit the concrete, and she felt a sting go up her legs. Not the best landing. She tried as hard as she could to get to the car, but the intruder was right on her heels, and before she knew it, something hard was swinging into her side, and she smacked the ground with a thud.

She scrambled to her feet and swung at the intruder, who caught her fist with one hand and almost crushed it. She felt terror rise in her as she tried to free her hand by punching the intruder's arm but was met with what felt like metal. She felt herself leave the ground as the intruder threw her over their shoulder, and she threw the car keys toward the building, so Katerina would immediately know she'd been taken when she woke up. If she woke up from whatever this person had shocked her with. Jocasta felt sick to her stomach.

It was too dark to see much of anything, but an upcoming streetlamp gave her hope that she would be able to tell the direction she was being taken in, As they approached, Jocasta felt her stomach drop. It was the building the party had been in. As the intruder pushed through the doors, she saw the ball room, just as grand as it had been earlier, but entirely empty. The lights were off, and now instead of feeling like a cool party space, it felt eerie, almost haunted. There was a light on in the upstairs hallway, so she was not at all surprised to be carried up the stairs.

Her hand was still being crushed in the intruder's, and she felt the bones start to crack. When they got upstairs, they went further into the building and stopped at a door on the right side of the hallway. Inside, there was a desk, a chair behind the desk, and a chair in front of the desk with restraints attached. The intruder threw her into the chair with restraints and she felt her back smack the chair with such force she hoped that it wasn't bruised. She tried again to free her hand by kicking the intruder's arm, but their grip just tightened, and she heard the bones in her hand snap before she felt it. Jocasta had never broken a bone in her life, and this hurt much more than she ever thought it would. She cried out before she could stop herself, and the intruder chuckled.

Once her restraints were secured, they released her hand and stood back, and Jocasta got a good look at them for the first time. They were smaller than she had initially realized, but the arm that had held her was entirely made of metal, as was part of their face, and if Jocasta was guessing right, one of their legs. Someone had experimented with making a cyborg, and it had worked. She wondered if this poor soul had volunteered or if they were a victim of something devious, then she had to check herself for pitying her kidnapper.

"What are you looking at?" They growled, and Jocasta jumped in her seat.

"I've never seen someone who was half metal before. I was looking at the skin to metal joints. I had no idea it could be so seamless." She half-lied. She definitely had noticed how seamless it was, if 'seamless' meant jagged and painful looking.

"You really are a scientist, huh?" Their voice sounded garbled, like their tongue was half metal and half flesh as well. Jocasta just nodded. "I didn't think a woman could be smart enough to be worth our time, but the boss insists that I'm an old-fashioned idiot. We'll see who's right." Jocasta's jaw dropped at the blatant sexism. She hadn't heard a comment like that in years since she had become so renowned in her field. People tended to let her reputation speak for itself at this point, and she never heard any comments like that from colleagues, at least not directly. She would always have a tech tell her that someone had said something to them questioning her methods or her results because of her sex, but these cowards never said anything to her face, because they knew she wouldn't stand for it. Here was a man, she assumed now from the comment, that thought his physical power over her was enough for him to be superior to her. It was archaic and repulsive. Before she could formulate a response, the door opened, and she heard another masculine voice.

"That will be all, Cyrus." The intruder, Cyrus apparently, left the room, and she waited for the other voice to come into her line of sight. When they did, she sucked in a breath. It was one of her students from her first semester teaching. She strained to remember his name for a moment before it came to her.

"Brian? Brian Michaelson?" He smirked at her remembering his name. He had been a senior when she had taught him, taking the introductory class as an easy credit to fill out his schedule. He was barely two years younger than her, and here he was, some evil mastermind or something.

"Brian. What a boring, bland name. No, I go by Jax here. I needed a better name if I was going to run the Freedom Brigade." He circled the desk and sat down on it rather than the chair on the other side. "Surprised, Doc?"

"What is going on here?"

"Well Doc, I'm trying to start a revolution. Enhanced folx are going to rule the world. And you're going to help me."

"Why on Earth would I do that? And isn't the Freedom Brigade an anti-government group?"

"The anti-government mantra is just a ruse to gather people who want to shake up the way of the world. We hold these parties to find people who we think would be on board with the real plan, and then we tell them what we really want."

"And if you misjudged them?"

"We kill them." He smiled. "I have a small army of Enhanced folx who need a little boost to their powers, so we can take out your little Phenoms easily when the time comes. That's what you're here for. That and to give me some enhancements for myself."

"I don't know how to do that, and if I did, what makes you think I would help you?" Jocasta felt a panic at the idea that he would just dispose of her the way he did the other people he mentioned, but she controlled her face into a mask of indifference as well as she could.

"Oh Doc, You were well on your way at that mansion up state. We've got most of your work here, you just need to continue what you've already started."

"How did you get my files?"

"I have some incredibly skilled hackers in my employ, Doctor Jones. Although none of my hackers and spies warned me that you'd be sleeping with one of the most powerful Phenoms. Good thing she tried mind control on Cyrus, or I probably wouldn't have gotten you as easily. Who knows what would have happened if she used telekinesis instead? Good on you though, she's a hot piece."

"What on Earth are you talking about?"

"Well, Cyrus is a cyborg, so mind control doesn't work on him." Jocasta gave him a glare. "Oh, you mean how do I know you were sleeping with Katerina?"

"Don't say her name."

"Oh, more than sleeping with her I see. I was watching from Cyrus's point of view. Great thing about a cyborg, they can't hide anything from you. No turning off that body cam." Jocasta felt sick to her stomach again and forced bile down her throat. This was not the lazy senior who skated through her class.

"How did you find me?"

"I was expecting to see someone from the mansion at one of my parties, but I was very surprised to see them let you into the field. I was always planning on kidnapping you at some point, but it felt like fate when I saw you walk in. I called Cyrus in and told him to follow you. Didn't want to be too obvious though, so instead, we used the city's traffic cams to track where you went. Cyrus saw your buddy, the Crusher walk inside with a pizza and figured out which apartment you were in. He also saw two people absolutely all over each other. You and Katerina, obviously."

"All of the blinds were closed; you're not telling me he has x-ray vision?"

"Infrared. Strong enough to pierce through that beat up old building, that's for sure. Definitely strong enough to look through a window and see two bodies tangled together on a couch." The bile rose in her throat again. "Honestly, Doctor, I had no idea you were into women, that was hot."

"Don't make me vomit on you, Brian."

"Oh! and surprisingly feisty. You are much cooler than I thought you were as a teacher."

"I still don't see why I would help you."

"Oh, because if you don't, I'll send my little Cyborg buddy to end your girlfriend."

"He couldn't kill her if he tried."

"Oh, did you forget what just happened?" Suddenly a screen popped to life on the wall, showing footage of Katerina slumping to the floor on repeat. "Don't worry, she's okay, just enough of a shock to put her out so she couldn't use her more effective powers on him."

"What makes you think she wouldn't be ready next time? The Phenoms are really good at their jobs, you know."

"Because if you don't help me, I'll use you as bait and then kill her. And don't tell me she wouldn't run to your arms the first chance she got." He was underestimating Katerina, she knew, but she also knew that fighting him on it would just give away more of her cards than she wanted. Then it hit her.

"If you didn't know about my relationship with Katerina, how were you planning on getting my help before?" She knew the answer before he said it, his lips curling into a cruel smile.

"I would have just tortured you until you gave in, Doc."

"You would have had to kill me."

"Then how would I get what I want?" He laughed and walked out of the room, but he stopped before closing the door behind him. "You'll start tomorrow." And then he was gone. She had no idea how long Katerina would be unconscious, but she closed her eyes and tried to project her thoughts so she would hear her. '*Katerina, love. I'm okay. Jax is really Brian Michaelson, an old student of mine. I'm in the building where the party was held. Don't use suggestion, he has someone who is immune. I love you.*' She repeated a variant of that for what felt like hours before giving her brain a rest. Her hand was throbbing, and she looked down to see that her left hand was about twice the size of her right hand, and it was bruised and purple, almost black. That was not good. Her right hand was also a little swollen, her knuckles red and raw from punching Cyrus's metal arm. She was just glad both hands weren't broken, and that she had thrown with her left fist first. At least her writing hand was okay.

After assessing the damage to her hands, she looked around the room again, noticing that there were a few screens on both sides of her. One of them big enough that she thought it might actually be a two-way mirror. She couldn't imagine that Brian would keep her in here, surely there was a cell or something where she didn't need to be actively tied down. How would she be expected to do any work like this? She felt her right foot throb, and realized that she probably bruised that up too, having kicked Cyrus with bare feet. So much for feeling confident to go in the field. Hopefully, she wouldn't find more bruises from when he knocked her to the ground, but she wasn't holding out any hope. She should have waited and trained more before telling Marc she was ready. She was supposed to be an observer more than anything, and now she had been kidnapped. She felt hot tears spring to her eyes as her shame set in. Jocasta would not let them fall. Brian did not deserve those tears, and she was sure he was watching her, or one of his cronies. Did people still say that? Cronies? She would.

After trying to sleep to no avail, Jocasta tried to get Katerina to hear her again. '*Katerina? Please, Kat, hear me. Katerina? Are you okay?*' She waited, but no response. Maybe she was too far, or maybe there was some sort of barrier. Hell, maybe Jocasta was not as good at projecting her thoughts as she thought, just like she wasn't as good at fighting as she thought. She wouldn't let herself think about the idea that maybe Katerina was not okay. Maybe she wasn't answering because she was dead. Maybe Brian had lied to her, and that shock had killed Katerina right in front of her. No. Those things were not possible.

She needed to focus on right now, on what was going on in the moment that she could see. Focus on the things she could control. Like her breathing, and her right hand opening and closing. Probably also not looking at the meat blob that was her left hand. She tried to wiggle the fingers of her left hand and had to bite her cheek to keep from screaming. One finger twitched, but that was it. Looking at it had made her want to vomit. Brian had better get her some medical attention, or she was going to have some serious problems. With the idea that he could hear and see her, she decided to demand just that. "Hey!" she shouted "I need a doctor for my fucking hand! I can't very well work without my left hand! Hello?"

"Aren't you a doctor?" she heard a voice through a screen on her left.

"Not a medical doctor, more like an anthropologist and biologist. And even if I was a medical doctor, I would need some help fixing my hand."

"Fair." This voice was not familiar. It was also more feminine, which gave her a little bit of relief for some reason. There was a twang to it that made Jocasta think whoever they were was from somewhere in the South. Georgia maybe? There was silence for a few moments before she heard "Jax is sending you a doctor soon. I just thought you would want to know."

"Thank you." Jocasta could feel herself falling asleep before the doctor finally arrived, quietly walking to her side, and checking her hand without looking at her face. He was slight and young, and had a cute little pronoun badge on his jacket. A little figure with he/him/his written across its chest. "Hey, Doctor. How bad does it look?" she smiled at him, but his face remained trained on her hand.

"I have to put some pressure on it." His expression was unreadable.

"Okay." She sucked in a breath as he put pressure on her hand. The pain exploded out from his touch, and she cursed herself as a tear snuck out of her eye.

"I can't quite tell about the distal metacarpal, but the three middle ones are definitely broken through. The swelling is pretty extensive."

"You're gonna have to open my hand up, aren't you?" she asked, and he just nodded.

"I'll have to cast it too."

"Can you even do that here?" She couldn't believe he would be able to access the medical supplies needed for that through the Freedom Brigade.

"Yes, of course, I have a fully funded emergency clinic here, just for the Brigade." He looked like he said a little too much and trained his face to look even more stoic. "Let's get you down to my operating room."

"Right now?"

"Obviously, how else do you think you'll have time to start working today?" The doctor nodded to a screen, and two guards came into the room. They unlocked the restraints holding her down and each grabbed one of her arms to take her to the operating room. Before they left the room, one of them produced a blindfold and they obscured her vision.

"Oh, so I don't need blindfolded to be brought to the secret lair, but I do need blindfolded to get surgery? You people are very inconsistent." Nobody responded. She felt like a rag doll, being toted around like this. They must have arrived though because she felt herself get lifted onto a surgical table, and then her blindfold was removed as she was strapped down yet again, but since she had to have one hand relatively free to be worked on, she had a strap around her waist now. Someone she couldn't see put a mask over her face, and the next thing she knew, she was out cold. She dreamt of Katerina, soft and warm, holding her. She tried to cling tightly to her, but was dragged away, unable to reach her or call out for her. When she woke, she had tears in her eyes, but not from the anesthesia. She screamed out to Katerina in her mind. '*Please, Katerina, be okay. I love you. I will make it back to you.*'

"Are you the one I've been hearing screams from?" A voice in the corner startled her. The same voice from behind the screens that had sent her a doctor. Jocasta tried to turn to the person talking, but she was strapped down tightly to what seemed to be a hospital bed. She was in the same room as before, but the table had been replaced by this bed.

"I beg your pardon?"

"Ah, yep, the voice matches the thoughts. Who's Katerina?"

"Who are you?" Jocasta felt violated, knowing someone was able to hear the messages she was trying to get to Katerina.

"Right. I'm Brittany. I read minds." Brittany stepped from the shadows into the light. She was probably about twenty, tall and pretty, with long platinum blonde hair. "Don't worry, I can't control them or anything. I also can't move things. Just read minds. Which I also can't help. I always hear everyone's thoughts. Thanks for thinking I'm pretty. And I'm 21."

"Oh, sorry." Jocasta felt herself blush and cursed herself for it.

"Katerina, she's your girlfriend?" Brittany tilted her head quizzically. "Yes. And you're screaming thoughts to her because she can hear them too, right?" Jocasta opened her mouth to answer but decided against it. "I see."

"Do I even need to respond?"

"No. I prefer it if you do, but if you feel like you would be compromising your morals to offer me the information that I can take freely, I understand." Jocasta felt herself wondering if Brittany could project thoughts as well, and then quickly tried to conceal that thought. Of course, Brittany heard it all anyway. "Oh wow, she can project thoughts into other people's heads? That sounds so cool. No, I can't, to answer your question. Although I've never really tried. May I?" Jocasta fixed her with an icy glare.

'Do I really have a choice?'

"No, I guess not." Brittany looked at her for a long moment. "Hear anything?"

"No." Jocasta was exhausted. How would she be able to reach Katerina now, knowing this woman was listening in?

"Oh, I wouldn't even try anymore. I can't hear anything outside the building, even standing by a window. I think there's some sort of spell on it. Open windows *might* be an option, but trust me, you will never be allowed near one of those. Jocasta tried desperately to hide her thoughts, but that led her to thinking about how much she wished she had worked on that instead of projecting them to Katerina.

"You guys talk in your heads? That would be so cute! Like having your own language." Brittany was smiling at her, not menacingly, but it still made her sick to her stomach.

"You *really* can't control it? Like, not even a little bit?" Jocasta was getting irritated.

"No. Sorry. I guess Jax was right about this being bothersome for you. He sent me in here as your guard because he thought it would be kind of like torture for you."

"Yes, well he is smarter than I gave him credit for in class, that's for sure."

"Oh yeah! You taught him in college! Bad student?"

"He didn't care about my course. Well, he acted like he didn't care, but apparently I was way off the mark."

"Suprology, huh? Yea, I didn't think anyone who wasn't Enhanced would really give a shit." Brittany's face grew sad. "But Jax says you'll come around because you're a real ally to us."

"Brittany," Jocasta began.

"Don't." Brittany held up a hand to stop her. "I can already hear your thoughts."

"Of course. Was that Jax's plan anyway? To get you to come in here and pick me apart mentally so that he really doesn't need me, and since I refuse to help him, he would rather just kill me if it'll spare him the work of torturing me?"

"Oh no, Jax doesn't want to kill you at all. In fact," Brittany lowered her voice to a whisper, leaning in toward Jocasta, "I think he has quite the crush on you." Jocasta shuddered at the thought. "But you're a lesbian, so I'll try to make sure he doesn't cross that line."

"I hope you would be opposed to him doing that to anyone he was holding captive regardless of their sexuality."

"Oh yeah of course, it's just that most straight girls would probably melt if they knew he had a crush on them. I mean, he's hot, he's wealthy, he's smart," Jocasta noted that Brittany clearly had a crush, and since she was so busy talking about him, Brittany hadn't noticed her thought, which meant she could use that knowledge, as long as she didn't think about it in front of her.

"How far is your range of thought reading? Because Katerina's is quite wide."

"Oh, usually just a room over or so. I guess like 100 feet. Why do you ask?"

"Professional curiosity." Jocasta wasn't lying, and Brittany seemed to believe the answer.

"Well, I am supposed to take you to your new lab in a minute, so get ready! Ooh! Maybe you can expand my powers to be like Katerina's! Maybe I could start controlling mine like she does." Brittany came over and started unlatching Jocasta's restraints, and Jocasta felt pity rising in her for this girl, who seemed like such a nice person, in a place like this. "Don't worry. I'm very happy here. And I'm not so innocent as you perceive me to be, Doc."

"Right. Also, do you mind not talking about her with her first name? It just." Jocasta trailed off, trying not to think about how intimate Katerina's name was to her.

"Would you feel more comfortable if we call her Crimson Mystic? That's her superhero name, right? Kind of creepy for a hero if you asked me." The name had been coined by a reporter after seeing Katerina in action publicly with the Phenoms, and Jocasta hated using it herself, but it felt less personal, so.

"Actually, yes. It isn't her name by choice, by the way."

"I heard."

"Right."

"Let's get you downstairs, then." Brittany rapped on the door and the same two guards from before entered, grabbing her by the arms again. Brittany procured a bag from somewhere and put it over her head. Great, another blindfolded jaunt through the building. She heard Brittany chuckle, probably at her thoughts, and so she focused on the emptiness behind her mask until they came to a stop. She felt her feet hit the floor again and Brittany removed the bag. The room was almost an exact replica of her lab at the mansion. A large, L shaped room, with machines buzzing in the back, and desks lined up with various lab equipment closer to her, facing an observation area and a wall of windows and one glass door. It was just like where she normally would run tests on Phenoms. Here, all she could see out the windows was a doorless hallway. She had a flash of that last day running tests with Katerina during phase one, her flirting as she moved tables and chairs, and she could feel tears starting to come to the surface.

"How?" She asked it to no one, really, but it was all that she could think, looking at this room that so resembled her own lab.

"I told you, I've got spies and hackers, Doc." Brian's voice came into the room from behind her, and she saw Brittany stiffen, whether at Jocasta's thought of Brian by his real name or at his entering the room, she wasn't sure. "Now, I know you've spent many a night in your lab at the mansion,

110

so we have a cot down here for you. You have free range of the lab, but there will be guards at the doors at all times. Don't try anything. We have loaded up your information onto these computers. Get to work." She heard him leave the room, and he must have motioned for Brittany to follow, because she walked past her toward the door as well. Her guards released her arms and went to stand by the doors. She turned around to see Brian and Brittany talking outside the door, and she found that the glass was soundproof, because she couldn't hear anything at all.

To the right of the door, in the corner, was her cot. Great. She moseyed around the lab, checking out the equipment and feeling a pit forming in her stomach. It was uncanny. Every piece of equipment was exactly where it would have been in her real lab. When she got to the desk she would have labeled as her desk, even the pens were the same brand and in the right place. Someone very intimately familiar with her lab had to be the spy. The cameras couldn't have shown them the right pen brand. The pit in her stomach grew as she sat down in the chair and went through the contents of her desk. The top of the desk was exactly how she left her real desk, and when she opened the top drawer, she froze, baffled. There was no one that worked in her lab that she could imagine knew she kept a photo of her mother in her top drawer except for one tech. Gary. Gary, who she trusted with everything in the lab, who she left in charge when she was gone. Gary, who she had laughed and joked with, and even teased about how anxious he was at times. Gary, who now she knew, must have been anxious because he had been spying on her the whole time. Looking at the picture, her stomach roiled, and she felt like she was going to vomit right there. How the fuck would she be able to tell someone to take Gary off her team from in here? She would continue to get information directly from her actual lab with him still in charge. She would literally be doing her job remotely, and for the bad guys. She felt the room start to spin and she suddenly couldn't catch her breath. She clutched at the desk and tried to steady herself, to make a plan, anything. Her vision went black, and she felt her head hit the desk, and then everything was gone.

Jocasta dreamt of Katerina again, but this time the dream was soft and warm and full of all the things she needed right now. She was in Katerina's bed back at the mansion, curled up with her as Katerina stroked her hair and sang a Borovian lullaby. She broke off the song and looked down into

Jocasta's eyes. "You'll be okay, Jo. My sweet, beautiful Jocasta." Katerina kissed her forehead, warmth flooding through her, and Jocasta closed her eyes.

"I love you, Katerina."

"I love you too." Katerina's arms wrapped around her, squeezing tight, and Jocasta felt peace. She snuggled into her and let herself rest.

When Jocasta woke up, she was laying on the cot in the corner of her fake lab. She looked around, bleary eyed and dazed, and saw Brittany in the corner opposite her, sitting in a chair. "What the fuck happened?" She asked her, sitting up on the cot.

"You had a panic attack, I think. Passed out. I was told to make sure you start working as soon as you wake up. Jax is not too happy about this."

"I've uh, never passed out from a panic attack. Ever. And I have had my fair share of them. That was wicked bad."

"Well, you'd be wise to try not to do it again."

"Right." Jocasta stood up next to her cot and walked over to the desk. Brittany stayed where she was, but her eyeline followed Jocasta. She wondered if Brittany could see her dreams when she was asleep.

"No. I can only read conscious thoughts, dreams are subconscious."

"Oh. Interesting."

"Yeah, not powerful enough to be cool, just enough to be weird and annoying." Brittany looked at her while she sat down at the desk and started going through some data that was pulled up on the computer screen. Something shifted in Brittany's demeanor as Jocasta looked over the screen. It was her data, collected from phase one with the Phenoms, she had finished that collection a few months ago now, and was at the point where she was almost done with Phase two. Who had pulled this up? "I pulled it up. While you were asleep. I wanted to see the videos of Crimson Mystic. See what the mysterious and beautiful doctor saw."

"Did you just call me mysterious and beautiful?"

"I mean, not mysterious to me, I can hear your thoughts. Mysterious to others. But beautiful to anyone with eyes."

"Are you flirting with me, Brittany?" She tried not to think about how she thought Brittany had a crush on Brian, but she couldn't help the thought half forming in her mind.

"Jax is an incredible man, and I would love to be with him, but that doesn't mean I can't find other people attractive, Doctor Jones."

"Well, I would appreciate if you didn't flirt with me, as I am very much taken."

"You're not married to her."

"Not the point." Jocasta closed out of the data set and opened up a more recent one. This was not the nice, sweet girl from yesterday.

"I told you," Brittany laughed, "I'm not the innocent girl you think I am. You don't become Jax's right hand by being sweet all the time." So yesterday had been an act, then.

"This place is a fucking madhouse." Jocasta mumbled under her breath. She started working, thinking that maybe her work could distract her, even if it was for the wrong people.

"Oh, Doctor J. You really don't know how to read people, do you?" I mean, throw on some of my southern charm, and you were pitying me and telling me things I could have just read your mind for. Jax felt the ruse was no longer necessary, and he was right since you can't hide a damn thought in your head."

"How do you know I won't learn to, now that you've shown me you aren't someone to be trusted?" Jocasta knew she had learned to do the opposite, why couldn't she learn to hide her thoughts?

"You won't. Because now you're afraid I was lying about the spell around the building. You're going to be mentally screaming for your precious Mystic til the end of time." Brittany laughed, and Jocasta knew she was right. She turned back to her work and desperately tried to forget where she was. She would not satisfy Brittany with her thoughts of Katerina, so she thought it would be good to occupy her mind with work and bore her to death.

"You know, Doc," Brittany called to her from the corner, hours later, "I bet your girlfriend wouldn't mind if you kissed me a little, just tell her you were trying to use me to escape or something." This was worse than annoying, sweet Brittany by a mile. She was fuming by the time she was done for the day; Brittany having made a dozen comments like that over the course of the afternoon, or at least what Jocasta thought was the afternoon. Before she left for the evening, Brittany walked over to Jocasta, who was closing the tab on her computer. Jocasta flinched as Brittany reached out and put a hand on her shoulder. "Don't worry, Doc, I won't do anything unless you ask me to. I just enjoy the teasing."

"Just leave, please."

"See you in the morning." Brittany winked at her and left, and Jocasta felt her insides clench. What the fuck was going on? She couldn't help but think that the entire organization was either incredibly disorganized and lacking any form of real leadership or plan, or Brian was an evil mastermind who designed it to look that way but was really calculating and plotting behind closed doors. Based on this lab, she genuinely feared it was the latter. She didn't sleep, just laid there on the cot, trying, and failing to think of a way out, while guards stood watch outside her door. Figuring Katerina would be back at the mansion by now, she tried not to call for her, but every once in a while, she felt herself projecting to her. Telling her she loved her, that she was physically okay, and that she knew Katerina would find her soon. By the time she saw Brittany coming back to the lab to babysit her, Jocasta was starting to think her calling for Katerina might actually summon her. Tonight, she would force herself to sleep.

The next few weeks went by just like that. Her trying to focus on work to distract herself from where she was and Brittany's incessant and aggressive flirting. The flirting was only made worse when Jocasta had to take her weekly shower under Brittany's supervision. The only good thing that had come from Brittany's interest in her was a small toothbrush and tube of toothpaste that was now hidden in her desk drawer. Every so often, Jax would become impatient with her progress, and would send Cyrus to "teach her to value Jax's time". With her hand in a cast, it had been a slow go, and the bruises she was gaining from those little visits were not helping either.

After a month of working with the data she had collected, and a little bit of new data sent over from the spy who was definitely Gary, Jocasta made a breakthrough. If she was right, she might be able to make a serum to give someone powers. It turned out, even those who weren't born with their powers had developed a genetic anomaly, and whatever had given them their powers had simply triggered the DNA to produce that anomaly, in one way or another. If she could make a serum to trigger the body to have the same response, it would unlock someone's powers that were already inside them. Anyone could be an Enhanced individual. She almost screamed when the realization hit her, and Brittany's head popped up from where she was resting in her corner chair. "Would your serum upgrade already Enhanced people?"

"There's no way to tell at this point. Regardless of the level of power, the anomaly looks the same, so I am inclined to say no, but I am not sure." Jocasta's blood was racing, and though she was terrified about her predicament, she was overjoyed to be having a breakthrough like this so soon. This was something big enough that she was expecting it would take years, and it had taken her months. She would need to do more research before making a serum, so that she could be sure, but it was an incredible breakthrough, nonetheless. She felt like she was flying for a moment before Brittany broke her train of thought.

"I'm going to let Jax know. How much longer until you are sure and can make a serum?"

"Oh, Um, I'm not sure, maybe a month more of research, more specific to the theory, and then the serum, I honestly have no idea yet."

"I'll tell him I've given you the rest of the night to think about what you'll need. See you bright and early." Brittany turned on her heel and speed walked out of the lab. Not that Jocasta had any sense of bright and early anymore. Being down here in the lab had given her a strange sense of passing time. She knew how many days it had been because of meals and Brittany's observing her daily, but she hadn't seen the sun in who knew how long. She was starting to think that Katerina would never find her. Not that anyone would tell her if the Phenoms were getting anywhere close to the Freedom Brigade. She still had some hope, just not very much.

Working had started to become her safe place, but now that her research was progressing, she found that she was terrified to start again tomorrow. How could she keep this up with Jax and Brittany keeping her like this? Would Katerina and the rest of the Phenoms ever forgive her? Would they understand she did it because she thought it would eventually help them, even if she was researching here? Well, that and because they had directly threatened Kat. She thought of Arthur, coming into the lab to talk to her every day, Vik, quietly teasing her about Katerina, Carter, and Austin, smiling as they discussed the latest episode of whatever show the three of them were currently obsessed with, and Marc, sweet Marc, who had been her friend and colleague for so long, she thought of him as family. She felt tears spring to her eyes as she thought of all the Phenoms, how they took her in and made her feel like family in such a short time. Even the team members who didn't live at the mansion felt like family. She hadn't done it in a while, but she felt herself projecting her thoughts. *"Katerina Gradoff, if you don't come find me soon, I don't know what will happen. I love you. fiercely. Please, hear this."*

And then it hit her. If she perfected this serum, she could take it herself before letting Jax know it was ready. She could destroy the remaining formula, and she could escape, using whatever enhancement it gave her. Maybe. There would at least be an element of surprise. It was a huge, long shot, but she felt like she could make it work. There were an incredible number of variables in that plan, but she could probably do it. Maybe. She looked at the computer in front of her, incredibly unsure, and opened the top drawer of the desk. Her mother's face looked up at her, and she felt a sense of calm as she opened a new document and started a list. She was going to do this. Jocasta Jones would be saving herself. She had never depended on someone else to save her before, and now that she had a plan, she wouldn't ever be doing so again.

KATERINA

Katerina was pacing around the meeting room. Marc told her they had some intel on Jocasta's whereabouts, but he was going to check it out himself before the whole team should make a plan. He left a few hours ago, and Katerina was on edge. She couldn't stop thinking about the night she had been taken. How she couldn't get in the assailant's head, crumpling to the ground, shocked and helpless, and then the assailant following Jocasta out onto the fire escape. Her blood curdled when she remembered the morning, when she came to, running outside to find the keys she had sent out the window to Jocasta, flung next to the building. She ran back inside to find Carter, okay, but confused about what happened. They had been drugged while they were asleep, and she had to fill them in on what happened to Jocasta. Or what she thought had happened to her. They got back to the mansion in record time and started an investigation that day. It had been well over a month now, and Katerina was still a mess. The team had put it down to her feeling like it was her fault, which she did, but her heart was being ripped in half constantly. She had talked to Vik and Carter about it a little bit at first, but now she felt like talking wouldn't help. The thought of the woman she loved being shackled and being held against her will gave her nightmares. She needed Marc to come back and tell her he found something. She needed a light in the darkness, or she was going to march into another Freedom Brigade party and fight the first person that looked at her.

They had held two more parties since the one she and Jocasta had attended with Carter, and Katerina had been banned from going to the second one, as she was 'too volatile' according to Carter. Then, the Brigade had announced another round of recruitment parties, and Carter had been going with Austin. The parties had moved location every time, and

Carter said they thought there was something special about the one they had been to, the rest felt slightly less grand, but Katerina thought they were just being dramatic, maybe trying to make her feel better for getting kicked off the mission.

She continued pacing for another hour before she finally had enough and went down to the training room. She started punching a hanging bag, and before she knew it, she was sweating. She punched until she felt like she had some semblance of control over her thoughts, and she took a minute to rest.

"You good?" Vik popped out from behind her punching bag. "You've been punching that bag like it killed your dog."

"Yes, Viktoria. I am okay." Katerina walked over to sit on the edge of the boxing ring. Vik followed her and sat next to her, clearly not buying it.

"Is it about Jocasta? Marc is on his way back."

"I'm fine. I just want her home."

"Listen, I know you blame yourself; I know you think it is taking too long to get her back, but I also know that we *will* find her." Viktoria put a hand on her back.

"What if she blames me too, and she doesn't want me anymore?" Katerina felt the words spill out without realizing she had been thinking that.

"Jocasta is a grown woman. If it is her decision to blame you for what happens, it is on her, and it is also wrong." Viktoria stood up and reached a hand to Katerina. "Do you want to go wait for Marc?"

"Yes." Katerina nodded and took Vik's outstretched hand. They walked side by side to the meeting room, and Katerina felt some of her anxiety come back the closer they got. If they didn't find Jo soon, she was going to develop a heart condition. She realized that was something Jocasta would say, and she felt her heartstrings tighten some more. She had developed such strong feelings for Jocasta so quickly it seemed, and she felt like a cliche for it. Maybe that was okay, maybe it was irrational, and she was overthinking her way into feelings that were not justified, but then, Jocasta had said it. Said it first, even. Said it before Katerina had put a name to the feelings and made her happier than she had ever been. She stopped her thoughts from scrambling too much and looked at Viktoria. She had such a surety about her that Katerina and Jocasta both found themselves looking up to, and she never seemed to question herself. Maybe that was why the moment they entered the room to see Marc, white as a sheet and sweating like he had seen a ghost, Viktoria just calmly sat down and asked him what happened. Katerina thought she was going to vomit.

"She's in a lab. Just like downstairs. It looks like she's still working, but the Freedom Brigade is a much bigger threat than we ever knew. They're not just trying to take over the government. They want to rule the world. Enhanced individuals above everyone else. I couldn't see what she was working on with my spy bot, and I didn't have audio inside the building, but it seemed like she might be continuing her work from here. She's working for them. They're going to try and create an army." Marc stopped for a moment before repeating himself, "She's working for them."

"Hold on Marc, are we sure she's doing it willingly?" Vik tried to calm him down a bit.

"She was smiling at her computer, a pretty big smile."

"That doesn't mean she is working for them willingly, Marc. Let Katerina and I see the footage."

"I don't need to see any footage. She would never willingly work for someone who was trying to instill any kind of supremacy. Enhanced or not." Katerina put her hand on the table. "Now Marc, where is she?"

"Katerina, I know you two were close, but you didn't know each other for that long, could she have been playing you?" Marc had genuine concern in his eyes, but Katerina was one straw away from telekinetically ripping his fancy little super suit in half.

"Marc, I didn't want to tell you this way, but I'm pretty sure that when she told me she loves me, she wasn't lying. Also, I've read her mind." She watched Marc's mouth drop open a little bit, and she repeated her question, each word its own sentence. "Where. Is. She?"

"The building that that first Brigade party was in. A basement level, pretty far down."

"I'm going there."

"No, Katerina, you are not." Vik grabbed her arm. "We need a plan and a whole team."

"There is something else," Marc began, and they both looked at him. "The building is really screwy. Something is off about it, I mean. My tech became more and more unreliable as it went further into the building, cutting out and things, and my infrared camera said the building was empty when I was outside, but my bot camera begged to differ."

"So, what you're saying is, we can't rely on any sort of surveillance?" Katerina looked confused.

"I wouldn't trust it." Marc started trying to come up with some sort of solution, and Katerina became overwhelmed suddenly. This was it. They had found Jocasta, and they were going to bring her the fuck home. Then, she felt something tighten around her heart.

Marc," she interrupted, "Did she look okay? Was she okay?" She felt tears spring up at the idea of Jocasta having been tortured to get her to work.

"She had a cast on her left arm, and she was in some raggedy looking clothes and no shoes, but she looked physically okay. Not starved or anything, no big bruises that I could see."

"They must be threatening her with something, though, right?" Viktoria looked at Katerina.

"You don't think-?" Katerina met Vik's eyes, and she knew Vik could see her tears.

"That they're threatening you?" she asked softly, and Katerina just nodded.

"How would they know that you are that important to her?" Marc asked, as he was trying to find some other thing Jocasta would do that for.

"Um, we were in bed together when they took her. If they had infrared cameras, they would have seen, plus, I know the intruder had some sort of camera or something on his head. I saw the red light. I'm sure he wasn't that oblivious as to why two grown women were sharing a bed." She felt the heat rush to her cheeks as she admitted to Marc that they had been sleeping together, but she forced herself to get through without full blown blushing.

"Oh. Well, she doesn't have any family, and I don't think she would be motivated by money so, honestly Katerina, I think it is you." Marc ran a hand down his face.

"Marc, I have to get her out. I have to. Please." She felt her chest constrict and then just break open when Vik put her arm around her.

"We'll get her, I promise, but I am not losing anyone else because we went in totally blind. I'll start on a plan. If you need a minute, take one, but I need the rest of the team in here, right now." Marc looked to Viktoria, who pulled out her phone and texted everyone the 911 message. Katerina felt her phone buzz and looked at Vik.

"Would you mind coming with me to get a drink?" She didn't think she should be alone right now. Vik looked to Marc, who nodded, and she ushered Katerina to the kitchen. "Vik, I-I think I might be losing it."

"Well, if you want to save her, you need to find it." Vik smirked. "I know you blame yourself even more now. I know your feelings for her are the biggest thing you've felt in a long time," Vik paused, "Maybe ever. Use that. Rally, and get in that room so you can fight for her."

"What would I do without these rousing speeches?" Katerina smiled, drank a glass of water, and steeled herself. "Let's go save Jocasta."

They had spent weeks now planning the mission, and it still wasn't remotely close to being good enough. Jocasta was being held underground, there was some sort of anomaly around the building, possibly magic, that they had yet to figure out a way around, and they had absolutely no way of surveilling anything, inside of the building or outside. They had an agent in the field, keeping an eye on the building, telling them how many people went in and out all day, but nothing could give them any insight on what they should do once inside. Katerina was getting frustrated, and she told Marc during their planning session that day that she would be doing a solo suicide mission if they didn't think of something soon. Marc then allowed her to visit their field agent and check out the building herself, to see if she could get anything he wasn't. That's how she got to be where she was now. Across the street from the massive building that she knew had a ballroom right inside, and her heart in the basement.

She couldn't sense anyone's thoughts inside and couldn't grasp onto anything past the doors. Whatever they were using to block powers and cameras was definitely working. She didn't know much about magic, but this was probably it. She watched as a group of teenagers walked into the building, laughing, and pushing each other, and felt herself disconnect from their minds as they crossed the threshold. Then she got the idea to try connecting to people's minds before they walked in, try to get deep in there, and see if she could maintain a connection that way. She did that for a few hours, using quite a few people, and it didn't work. Then, a pretty blonde girl walked by, and Katerina tried to use her suggestion, hoping if she went that far, it would work.

As soon as she entered her mind, Katerina could feel something strange. She was hearing other thoughts, anyone near her. Or anyone near the girl, rather. This was new, but she felt as if it wasn't her power, but the girl's. She took over and found that she had no idea how to turn off other thoughts the way Katerina could. She pushed the girl through the doors of the building, bracing herself to become thrown out of her mind. But this time, she wasn't. She made her way through the familiar ballroom in her mind's eye, and to the elevator where she had no idea what button to push. She dug through the girl's mind and found Jocasta, and a floor number: B 10. As soon as the elevator doors closed, Katerina felt her grip on the girl being forcefully removed. By the time the girl had gone down one floor, Katerina had lost her. But she had something. She had a floor number. And she had placed a thought in the girl's head to explain her going downstairs, in case that wasn't where she had been going of her own volition. Hopefully, that was enough for now.

She immediately called Marc and filled him in, but he was much more worried that this girl was also a telepath, and she would know that her own mind was being messed with. Katerina had to admit nobody had ever tried to use telepathy on her, so she was not positive, but she had covered her tracks the best she knew how. She returned to the mansion to find everyone hunched over blueprints and working on their plan. She knew they would be ready soon.

JOCASTA

Jocasta saw something strange in Brittany's eyes when she came downstairs, but she felt it might be better not to ask. That thought didn't matter though, because as soon as she entered the lab, she grabbed Jocasta by the elbow and whispered in her ear. "I think your little girlfriend was just in *my* fucking mind. Got anything to say about it?" and Jocasta was stunned into silence. Brittany gripped her harder.

"Uh, I-I don't know."

"I can see that's true." Brittany sighed and pushed her away.

"What did it feel like?" Jocasta was desperate for any news about Katerina, even if it meant she might get locked further away from her.

"It hurt like a motherfucker." Brittany was still whispering. "Two people are not meant to occupy one mind." She ran a hand through her hair.

"Are you gonna tell Jax?"

"Tell Jax that I was compromised? Are you a fucking idiot?" Jocasta realized she had never heard Brittany curse so many times in a row. "What's worse is that I have no idea what she got before I forced her out. I couldn't hear her thoughts back. Either she was out of my range, or her powers are way crazy."

"Why are you telling me this?"

"Because you won't fucking snitch on me, that would hurt your Crimson bitch." Jocasta flinched at the latest of twists on Katerina's name. "And I needed to tell someone, because I'm freaking the fuck out."

"You're saying fuck a lot." Jocasta felt like a young kid, commenting on Brittany's cursing, but she genuinely could not form complex thoughts at the moment. What did this mean? Were the Phenoms still looking for her, or was this a coincidence? Was Katerina looking alone? Honestly, who knew? But knowing Katerina was alive was enough to keep her happy for the time being.

"I don't know what the hell to do," Brittany sighed. "Just get back to work, doc."

"Right." Jocasta turned to her computer and tried to run a simulation with the most recent updates to her serum. It still looked like it was going to cause too many side effects. Great. At least she had gotten past the formulas that would have a high chance of death. Jax had told her she wasn't going to get a chance to do any more research, so the day after her breakthrough, she had started on the serum. It was a rough start. The first week felt like she was never going to be able to get anywhere, and after accumulating some very large bruises on her rib cage, and a deep cut on her left bicep, she had become discouraged. But whatever this program was that she was using now, it was really helpful.

Doing this alone was daunting regardless. Even now with her cast finally off, at the rate she was going, she wouldn't have a vaguely viable formula for a long time. She needed biologists and medical doctors helping her, but that would mean getting more people to work for Jax, and she didn't want to do that. Hopefully, she could do it in his time frame. Which, of course, she didn't know what that was, and she wouldn't know until he just got fed up with waiting. She ran a few more variations through the program and decided she should take a break and maybe get some sleep. As soon as Brittany left her, she let herself circle back to their earlier conversation. Katerina. For the first time in a while, she let herself think about holding her, and her dreams that night were warm. Katerina sitting by the window of her bedroom, early morning light bathing her features, and the two of them cooking breakfast together, happiness permeating every minute.

The next day, she woke up and started working, an even greater sense of urgency thrumming through her. She started running her new formula through the program, as she had created it just before turning in, before the last one's results came in. As it was going, she started on another formula. She decided to throw the model she had been working out the window, and start fresh, just to keep herself on her toes, and so she wouldn't go too far down one path.

Something about this one felt right for some reason. When the testing was complete on the first serum, her screen showing similar results from yesterday's tests, she knew she was right to change tactics. She must have gotten up extra early because Brittany was still nowhere to be seen, and the guards didn't look like the ones she normally saw in the morning. She ran this most recent serum, hoping that if her gut feeling was right, she would be able to hide it before Brittany or anyone else saw. As that serum ran through the program, Jocasta looked through her notes and some data, trying to keep herself occupied. By the time it was finished, she had re-read a month's worth of notes. She looked up and saw that this serum was almost perfect. All of the issues she had been having were gone except one. The program said there was a more than slight chance that this serum would cause loss of speech. It was a 50% probability of temporary speech loss; 30% it would be permanent. To her, that sounded like something she could fix.

Before she had a chance to go through and tweak it, she heard a big crash, gunshots, and Jax's voice from upstairs, yelling at someone to get the doctor and get the hell out of there. Jocasta knew that this was her chance to escape. Brittany came running down the hall, and before she could think about what she was doing, Jocasta swallowed the serum. As Brittany was coming in, she deleted her files on the new formula as fast as she could.

"Come on, Doc, time to go." Brittany was out of breath and when she grabbed Jocasta's shoulder, there was no room for negotiation. Brittany dragged her out of the lab, and Jocasta felt her feet touch carpet for the first time in almost 2 months. As they got to the elevator, Brittany pulled her to the side, toward a door that must have been the stairs. Before she could open the door though, an explosion shook the ground, causing Brittany to lose her grip as they both fell to the floor. Jocasta scrambled away from Brittany and tried to grab the door handle, but her hand went right through it. She turned to see Brittany, eyes wide, looking around herself.

"Doctor Jones? Where the fuck did you go? We have to get out of here! Now!" She was panicking, and as she looked at Jocasta, she continued to panic. "How did you get out of range so fast?" she said more quietly, and Jocasta looked down at herself to find that she could literally see through her own body, like an apparition. Brittany disappeared back toward the lab, and Jocasta tried the door handle again. She started to panic as her hand again went through it. She thought about the idea that she was dead, but then, Brittany would have seen a body. So, the next logical step was just to try walking through the door, and it worked! She had been right, there were stairs on the other side. She sprinted up as fast as her legs would carry her, and as she came to the third landing, she stopped dead in her tracks. Standing in front of her, sweating and with a cut bleeding on her forehead, was Katerina. The commotion was being caused by the Phenoms. She tried to call out, but she couldn't form the words. Again, a wave of panic rushed through her, this time, bringing her to her knees on the stairs as Katerina called out to someone above them. Well, she definitely had powers, but the 30% must have happened to her, and she started to spiral. Then, she desperately pleaded for Katerina to see her when suddenly, Katerina turned, and her eyes widened.

"Jo?" Katerina's eyes brimmed with tears. Jocasta looked down and saw that she was no longer a ghost, and then looked back up at Katerina, who scooped her up in her arms and started sprinting up the stairs. Jocasta tried to make a sound, to tell Katerina she could run too, that she was okay, and that she loved her, but it was like her tongue was dead in her mouth.

"*Kat, baby. I can't talk, but I'm okay, okay?*" She projected the thought, watching Katerina's tears start to spill.

"What do you mean you can't talk?" Katerina was knocking people over, still running up the stairs, and still holding Jocasta. This woman was magnificent.

"*It's a long story, but I promise, I am okay. Let me help you fight.*"

"You can run by yourself, but do not engage anyone, love. You've been in captivity for two months and you do not look as okay as you say."

"*Yes, ma'am.*" Jocasta pried herself out of Katerina's arms at the 6th landing they had come to, and got behind her, gripping Katerina's jacket and letting her protect her as they continued up two more flights of stairs. The free arms were definitely helping Katerina to use her powers to take people out. The staircase was littered with unconscious bodies at this point. They burst through another door and Jocasta recognized where they were. The ballroom where that first party had been held was still dark and creepy looking like the last time she saw it, but now there was a fight going on. She saw Marc and Carter, fighting about 10 goons together to her right, and another group of Jax's soldiers fighting someone else to the left. There were people on the second level as well, but she couldn't make anything out in the dark. She felt a rush of wind and heard Katerina say "Austin, slow down and get Jocasta out of here."

"No, I need you to stay with me, Katerina."

"I have to help the rest of the team get out, my love. I will see you at home soon."

"I love you so much." Jocasta kissed her as passionately as she could before Katerina pulled away. She had a brief moment of gratitude for the toothbrush and toothpaste that Brittany had snuck to her.

"I love you, too. Now let them get you home." Katerina looked to Jocasta's left side and smiled. "No pit stops, buddy. Get home and stay there."

"Sir, Yes, Sir!" Austin saluted to Katerina before picking up Jocasta and placing a hand behind her head. She felt like an infant. "I have to hold your head for whiplash," they explained to her. She just nodded and held tight. Austin started running, and everything became a blur.

Wind rushed in her ears, and she felt the sun almost instantly, but other than that, all she could see was color. Before she was even used to the speed, they had stopped, and there was the Mansion. Austin let her down and she immediately fell to her knees, sobbing. She was finally home, but she was definitely not safe. Not yet. Austin knelt down beside her and wrapped their arms around her. "Hey, it's okay, you'll be alright. Do you want to head inside?" She nodded and realized the team didn't know about the spy. She motioned to Austin that she needed to write something down, and their eyes widened. "What's wrong? Can't you talk?" She shook her head at them, and their eyes became filled with anger. "What did they do to you?" She waved them off and motioned toward the mansion, miming writing again. "Right." They walked inside with her and led her to the meeting room. I'll be right back! They disappeared for about 2 seconds and returned with a stack of notebooks and pens. "Tell me what you can."

Gary. He's a spy.

"Are you sure?"

He's the only one that could have known about the details that they knew. They recreated my lab almost exactly. Even my desk was exactly how I keep it, down to my mom's picture in the drawer. They had all of my notes and research. It has to be Gary.

"Shit," Austin breathed. "We'll probably have to wait for Marc before we confront him. Or at least some more people that can help to restrain him if we need to." Jocasta just nodded and wrote down that she wanted to go upstairs. Austin grabbed a couple of the notebooks and pens and they headed up. She held the notebook that she had already started writing in and braced herself to go up the stairs and enter her room again. When they got to her door, she looked at Katerina's door across the hall, and felt herself going toward it instead.

"You want to go into Katerina's room instead? I doubt she would mind, but why?"

I know you overheard us, Austin.

"I mean, I overheard Katerina, and I may have accidentally looked over while you were kissing her, but I was being polite, thank you very much." Austin followed as she pushed the door open, and they shut the door behind them. She looked around the room and tried not to let the tears stream down her face as she remembered the dreams that she had of this room over the past couple of months. The dreams of Katerina that had given her hope. She sat on the bed and crossed her legs, running her hands over the comforter. Suddenly she realized how gross she probably was. She had only gotten one uncomfortable and violating shower every week or so while at the Brigade headquarters, and being supervised by Brittany, she had kept them very short. She quickly grabbed the notebook and turned to Austin.

I need a shower. Please stay in here though.

"Absolutely, do you need anything from your room? Clothes?" Austin was eager to help her, but she shook her head and grabbed a change of clothes from Katerina's dresser. She figured the smell of her would be comforting. Austin settled into Katerina's armchair as she closed herself into the restroom and turned on the shower.

Her clothes felt like there was a full layer of dirt on top of the fabric as she took them off. Two months without a wash had her pj's grimy and threadbare. She laid them in a pile, thinking that she should throw them away, but something stopped her from putting them in the trash can. Jocasta reached her hand into the shower, testing the temperature of the water. She shivered at the warm water touching her skin and stepped into the stream. She felt the warmth of the water pierce her skin, the pressure making her feel pinpricks of heat dig into her. She maneuvered her head under the shower head, feeling the grime start to wash away. Her undercut had grown out much too long, and she made a mental note to fix that ASAP. By the time she turned off the shower, she had washed her hair 3 times and her skin was pruny. She was pretty sure she smelled like Katerina's soap had exploded on her, but she finally felt clean.

As she got dressed, she wondered how long she had been in there, and realized that Katerina and the others might be back, but when she opened the bathroom door, it was just Austin sitting there. She tried to ask if the team would be back soon, but her tongue still felt like a useless log. She needed to get with a medical doctor and see if they would be able to tell if it was temporary or if she needed to learn ASL. She could just barely swallow, but beyond that, her tongue didn't want to articulate. Austin raised an eyebrow at her, so she grabbed a pad of paper again and asked them if they had heard from the team. They nodded, and she felt a breath release that she didn't even realize she was holding.

"They are on their way. It sounded like everyone is okay. Do you wanna tell me why you can't talk?"

I'm going to tell Katerina with my thoughts so she can just tell everyone when they get here. I assume we'll do a debrief.

"That makes sense. Do you want to go to the meeting room and wait? I bet they'll be here in a few minutes." Austin ran a hand through their hair and stood up when Jocasta nodded. They walked side by side downstairs, but when they were down the hall from the room, Jocasta heard voices coming from the other end of the hall. Before she could register who the voices were, Katerina and Carter came around the corner, and she sprinted as fast as she could toward them.

Katerina turned at the sound of her hurried footsteps and her smile lit up her face just before Jocasta launched herself into her arms. Carter laughed as Jocasta pulled away just enough to kiss Katerina, who lifted Jocasta into the air before gently setting her back on her feet. Katerina pulled away first, stroking Jocasta's cheek with one hand, tears threatening to spill down her cheeks.

"Jocasta, I'm so sorry."

"No, none of what happened is your fault, Katerina. I'm just so happy to be home." Jocasta let her own tears spill and clutched onto Katerina like she was never going to see her again. *"I love you so much."*

"Oh, Jocasta, I love you too." Katerina spoke softly, rubbing her back with one hand, and stroking her hair with the other.

"As much as I love a romantic reunion," Carter spoke up, "I do think we need to get debriefing." They paused for a moment before adding, "Plus, it isn't as good when you can only hear half of it." Jocasta very reluctantly pulled away from Katerina to hug Carter before gesturing back down the hall. The four of them entered the room, which was already full of the rest of the team that had come to her rescue. Arthur, Viktoria, and Marc sat on one end of the table, hunched over in deep discussion. When she entered the room, all three of them jumped up. Marc hugged her fiercely, Arthur gave her a gentle pat when he got his turn, and Viktoria hugged her with a squeeze that surprisingly didn't break her spine. As everyone got settled in their seats, Jocasta reached for Katerina's hand.

"I need you to talk for me." Jocasta gave her hand a slight squeeze, and Katerina nodded.

"As Austin and Carter already were witness to, Jocasta can't talk." Katerina's voice broke as she said it. "She wants me to speak for her as she projects her thoughts to me. Is everyone okay with that for now?" Katerina had controlled her emotions again, and her eyes were a mask of concentration as everyone agreed. Arthur was sitting directly across from Jocasta, and he met her eyes. He glanced to her hand clasped tightly in Katerina's and back to her eyes before smiling. She returned the smile and thought to Katerina *"Who else other than Arthur was unaware of our relationship this whole time?"* Katerina blushed a little bit before thinking back.

"Everyone who knows is in this room. Even the team that worked on the plan with us didn't know. It didn't feel right to tell them without you. Marc only knew because he wanted to know why I was so sure you weren't a spy. You know when everyone else found out." Jocasta gave her a small smile before beginning.

"Okay. Well, I'm sure you all know by now how I got into their facility. What you don't know yet is that they had been plotting to kidnap me for a while. Their basement had a lab that was almost exactly the lab I have here. The details were incredibly accurate, down to the picture in my desk." She paused a moment, letting Katerina finish relaying.

"Does that mean there's a spy?" Arthur looked at her, even though the words had come from Katerina.

"*Yes. And I know who it is. Nobody knew about the picture in my desk except for one of my techs, Gary. Not even Katerina would be able to tell them what picture of my mother it was unless she read my mind. The drawer is always locked, and only myself and Gary have keys. I know it has to be him.*"

"I'll send a team down to your lab to arrest him now. You left Gary in charge, right?" Marc was typing furiously into his personal computer, but he saw her nod.

"*I don't know what all you guys know, but their leader was a student of mine. His codename is Jax, but his real name is Brian Michaelson. He wants to lead an uprising of Enhanced individuals to rule over non enhanced people. He has a telepath in his employ, Brittany, who can't control her powers, but she can only hear about a football field's distance. He also has a guy named Cyrus, codename Cyborg, who is the person responsible for kidnapping me. That's why he could get the jump on you, Kat. When they saw you with me at the party, they sent him, hoping you would go for the mind before going for telekinesis.*" Katerina relayed, leaving out her nickname, and adding that unfortunately, that had been exactly what happened. That as soon as she had realized she couldn't reach the assailant's mind, he had electrocuted her unconscious. Everyone continued to listen intently, as Jocasta explained why Jax had wanted her. When the moment came to tell them what she had done, why she couldn't get her tongue to work, she felt so ashamed that she had panicked and dosed herself that she was struggling to continue.

"Were you at all successful with the serum?" Marc asked, and when she didn't answer, he added, "Do we need to be prepared for the worst, Jocasta?"

"She is trying to put her thoughts together." Katerina held a hand to stop him from asking more questions, then thought "*Don't be ashamed, love. None of this is your fault.*"

"*I was working toward a dead end, so early this morning, I switched it up. The formula was close, the risk of death was incredibly slim, but the other complications were still too much. I was checking that out when you all came into the building. I heard the commotion and thought that maybe I could escape, so I deleted the progress I had made with the newest serum, and.*" Jocasta stopped herself again, scared of what the team would say.

"And what, Jocasta?" Viktoria looked deeply into her eyes, and the comfort in her stare told Jocasta that she didn't need to worry.

"*I swallowed the serum.*" Jocasta thought it, and Katerina looked shocked. Instead of repeating it to them, she looked at Jocasta, her brows furrowed.

"You *SWALLOWED* it?" Katerina sounded incredulous, maybe even furious, but she was no match for Marc.

"JOCASTA ALEXANDRA JONES!" He stood up, his eyes practically glowing the way Katerina's did when she used a lot of power. "YOU ARE NOT A PHENOM. YOU ARE NOT A SOLDIER, OR AN AGENT, OR WHAT HAVE YOU. WHY ON THIS GOOD, GREEN EARTH WOULD YOU, A FUCKING DOCTOR, DO SOMETHING SO STUPID?" Marc was pacing now, talking with his hands. Arthur reached up and grasped his arm gently.

"Marc, I'm sure she knows it was not the smartest thing to do but think about her situation. And sit down so she can explain herself before you start yelling like a surrogate father again." Arthur released his arm, and Marc's face flushed, but he sat back down and gestured for her to continue.

"*I don't know what came over me, I didn't even think really, I just knew they couldn't get this serum, so close to perfect. They would easily be able to finish it. Now, with the other ones, I doubt very highly that they will be able to create a working serum.*"

"What did it do to you, Casta?" Carter asked softly, reaching to grasp her hand from their seat next to Arthur.

"*Well, I know I gained some sort of Enhancement. But my research had shown that a short- term loss of speech would affect at least 50% of people who took it, and there was a 30% chance that whoever took this serum would never speak again. As I am the only person who has ever taken it, there is really no way for me to know if I will gain my speech back until it happens. Or doesn't happen.*" Jocasta waited for Katerina to catch up but held out a finger to let everyone know to wait before they asked any questions. "*A medical doctor could be able to see what the damage is, exactly, and* might *be able to predict an outcome. They could also help with physical therapy if that would be a good option, but I honestly have no idea right now.*" Katerina looked at her, the tears returning to her eyes.

"Okay, not to be that bitch, but what powers did it give you?" Austin spoke up for the first time since they started the meeting.

"I am not quite sure how to do it, and I don't know if it has to be simultaneous, but as of right now, I can turn invisible and phase through things. I passed through a door on the way out of the building. I had to focus incredibly hard to come back into view when I saw Katerina on the staircase. Also, when I was invisible, Brittany couldn't hear my thoughts."

"We will test your abilities tomorrow in the training room. For now, I think we all need some rest. Everyone, meet in the training room at 8am. And do not tell anyone about what Jocasta has just said. The people in this room are the only Phenoms or W.E.I.R.D. agents that are allowed to know anything about this." Marc ran a hand over his face. "Until I tell you otherwise, that is."

Everyone started to file out of the room, but Jocasta stayed seated, gripping Katerina's arm when she stood up. Marc noticed and hung back for a moment. *"Tell him I'm sorry. I am so grateful for him, Katerina, I don't want to lose the mutual respect and great relationship I've built with him."* Katerina complied, and Marc leaned down to hug Jocasta.

"You've lost enough, kid. You're not gonna lose me." He whispered in her ear, and she felt a tear escape her eye. Marc kissed her cheek before leaving her and Katerina alone.

"You see him as a father figure." Katerina's thought entered her mind, as soft as if she had been whispering to her.

"Marc has always been there for me. Ever since we met. He was the first person I looked up to in that way since I was 10. With my mom it was a little different, I don't think I will ever see someone else as a mother figure, but yea, I guess you're right." It was strange sometimes, talking to Katerina with thoughts. She couldn't quite measure out her words the way she did when speaking aloud, so she tended to ramble quite a lot. Sometimes, Katerina would tell her that, but sometimes she would just let her talk.

"You know, if you never talk again, my head is going to be very loud."

"We'll learn sign language, Katerina. A loss of speech is not the worst thing."

"I know, Jocasta." Katerina's expression turned unreadable. "I-" She took a breath. "I have been dreaming, for months, of hearing you say you love me again. And now, the first time I heard you say it might also be the only time." Jocasta felt her mouth drop open. How could she have been so selfish as to tell her at the same time as everyone else? Of course, Katerina would be upset.

"*Kat, I am so sorry.*" She started, but Katerina kept talking.

"I can hear anyone's thoughts, at my leisure. I have literally heard people thinking about how much they love me or hate me in crowds while I'm fighting for their safety. I stopped a falling truck, midair, from hitting a girl, and she proposed to me in her mind. Hearing you, out loud, free of me in your head, telling me how you felt? That was once in a lifetime incredible for me. And now, you come home, finally, and I've missed you *so much*, Jo. And you tell me that you swallowed your own concoction of chemicals, by *choice*, making yourself Enhanced, and taking that from me, possibly forever." She paused, and Jocasta tried to formulate a sentence in her head, but Katerina put a hand up. "I know, you had no idea. It just hurts me."

"*Katerina, I do love you. Kind of an insane amount, honestly. And I know, it's a whole other conversation, but I never thought about making myself enhanced before I was in there. And even then, it was only as a last-ditch escape plan. When I heard explosions, I didn't have time to worry about the complications of if the serum was ready or not, I just had to* do *something.*"

"*You were going to take the serum anyway? You were planning on taking it yourself the whole time you were working on it over there? Jocasta, why?*" Katerina was communicating nonverbally now, even though they were still the only people in the meeting room. "*That's kind of fucked up. It's literally doing what the Brigade wants to do.*"

"*Katerina, all I wanted was to get out of there, and not let them use the serum they were forcing me to create. The only way I thought I stood a chance of doing that was to enhance myself so I could fight against them enough to do that, and it would give me an element of surprise.*"

"*You could have trusted that we would find you! Your whole life has been about making people see that Enhanced people are just like everyone else. That thought process is exactly what makes people scared of us. Of our power. The idea that you couldn't fight back makes what Jax wants to do all the more possible, and what demonizes us to so many people.*"

"*I know, Katerina! But I couldn't really contemplate the moral conundrum that I was putting myself in when the people holding me made it abundantly clear that they would kill you, and if I had done enough work, me as well, if*

I tried to get out. At least if I did that, I would stand half a chance against trained guards and enhanced soldiers!" Jocasta knew what she had done was idiotic. She knew it was something she never would have had half of a thought to do before she was kidnapped, but she wasn't about to let Katerina shame her for it. And then a thought hit her. *"Honestly, it proves the theory that we're all the same. Anyone can be enhanced. Some people could choose it, with the serum, some people can't, but the DNA is in all of us. That's what my research says."*

"Jocasta." Katerina gave her a withering look, as if to say that she was arguing herself into a corner with this.

"I mean it. That's the revelation that made Jax order me to make the serum in the first place. Trauma can trigger the gene anomaly, some people are born with the anomaly already triggered, and the finished serum was going to be designed to trigger it, but everyone has the capability." Katerina's expression made Jocasta stop. *"I never would have taken it myself in normal circumstances, Katerina. You know that. Especially not the unfinished one."*

"We would have at least talked about it, Jo. Your whole life is dedicated to enhanced people, don't tell me you never dreamed of being one of us." Katerina stood up, and Jocasta felt herself turn pink with embarrassment and shame. Katerina wasn't wrong, but Jocasta wasn't lying to her, either. Her dreams of having powers had been as a child, before she had thought it impossible to have them herself. She took Katerina's outstretched hand, and they started walking toward their rooms. *"I believe you though. And I forgive you, even though you didn't mean to hurt me, or what was it? 'Put yourself in a moral dilemma'? I can't imagine what that was like, wearing the same dirty clothes for so long, being held in the same room, forced to do your work for bad intentions. Please tell me they let you shower, at least."*

"Supervised by Brittany, and then I put the same Pj's on so, really, not a lot of cleaning happening. I did have a secret toothbrush though."

"I'm glad to see you in my clothes anyway. Did you not go to your own room?"

"Yours feels more like home to me." Jocasta thought it without filtering, which was not uncommon, but it felt like such an intimate thing to say.

"You're welcome to stay with me if you want to, Jocasta." Katerina spoke out loud, as they got to their doors. Instead of thinking at her, Jocasta just nodded, and followed her into her bedroom. She sat on the bed as Katerina started to get undressed, throwing her suit in a corner. The whole team had stayed in their fighting garb except for Marc, who had an automated removal situation as soon as he landed anywhere. "I am going to take a quick shower. You can join me," Jocasta noticed that the blood on her forehead was dry now, the cut not very deep. Katerina leaned over to kiss the top of her head and chuckled, "If I have any soap left. Your hair smells like a whole bottle of my shampoo." She smiled and turned to go into the bathroom, pulling her bra and underwear off and throwing them in her laundry basket before walking over to the faucet. "Or, you know, you could just join me because you missed me." She called, and Jocasta felt a garbled laugh come out of her throat. Katerina bolted up and out of the bathroom. "Did you just laugh?" Jocasta nodded. "Is that like a sign of something?" Jocasta gave her a tiny smile and shrugged. She nodded toward the shower and stood up, undressing herself.

"*I have no idea, Kat. Let's just play it by ear until I get a doctor to check me out.*"

"*Okay, but I think I'm doing a good job of checking you out myself, Jocasta.*"

"*Come on, you had a long day, you need a shower. Let me clean that cut for you.*" Jocasta gently touched Katerina's forehead. "*And I want to hold you. Wet, naked, dry, in bed, fully clothed, I don't care, just let me hold you!*" Jocasta stepped into Katerina's shower, and Katerina was close behind.

KATERINA

Katerina watched as Jocasta tried to make herself invisible. They had been in the training room for at least 10 minutes, and all she had accomplished was one hand flickering out of existence for a few minutes, and now, as Marc was asking her how she had done it before, it came back. This was going to be a long morning.

I don't know, I got thrown by an explosion and it just happened. I had to fall on the ground begging to come back into view when I saw Katerina. Jocasta's thoughts came to her, and she called to Marc to tell him what she said. He nodded and turned to Jocasta, blasting her with some weapon that 'wouldn't hurt her, but would knock her off her feet' according to Marc. It looked like he was shooting her with an air cannon that was maxed out to absurd power levels. She felt herself flinch as it hit Jocasta, knowing that there were quite a few bruises underneath her clothes, hoping that they wouldn't be worse later. The rest of the team watched as Jocasta flew into the air and disappeared as she hit the ground.

"Holy shit!" Austin jumped up.

"Hey, it worked!" Carter pumped their fist.

"Jocasta, where are you?" Marc called and looked to Katerina for the answer.

"I-I can't hear her." Katerina listened as hard as she could, and after a few more seconds of silence, she tried to find her, rather than letting Jocasta project her thoughts. There was absolutely nothing. She couldn't feel her, see her, or hear her. "I can't find her, Marc, she has to come back on her own." Katerina felt her heart rate spike as she waited for Jocasta to come back into view. After a full five minutes, everyone decided to start looking for her through touch. Katerina pointed out that it might not work if Jocasta was also phasing, but they tried anyway. After another excruciatingly long minute, Jocasta's hand appeared, sticking out of the side of the boxing ring. Katerina ran over and touched her hand, hoping to hear her thoughts. Her hand went right through Jocasta's, and Katerina looked over to see Jocasta's head, also partially inside the ring.

"I'm not stuck, I am just trying to come into view while phasing." Jocasta's thoughts came to Katerina, and she breathed out a breath she hadn't realized she was holding in. The rest of the team made it over to them, and Katerina relayed the message. They cheered her on as she came fully into view, her other arm sticking out by her head, and walked out of the side of the boxing ring. It took some time, but she did it. Jocasta beamed at Katerina, and she could feel her apprehensive pride.

"Nice job, Jocasta." Marc nodded in approval and playfully smacked Jo's shoulder, but his hand went through her. "Please tell me that's on purpose."

"It is. Phasing is proving to be a lot easier than invisibility." Jocasta let out the odd little laugh that came with her 'log tongue' as she had described it to Katerina.

"She said Phasing is easier than Invisibility." Katerina couldn't help but smile.

"This might sound like a crazy idea," Viktoria said, sitting on the edge of the boxing ring. "But these powers seem an awful lot like a cartoon ghost, yes? Should we test to see if you can also fly?" Jocasta's eyes grew about four times bigger, and she nodded vigorously.

"You can catch me if I actually fall, right?"

"I can catch you as long as you don't go invisible. Work on that first, then we will test it."

"But first, Jocasta, I want you to go see Doctor Barrister, in my lab. Katerina, go with her please, to translate." Marc smiled. "I'll set up training with each of us, every day, to help Jocasta master these powers, and get her in tip top Phenom shape."

"Yes, because before the mission, I was in bottom barrel Phenom shape." Jocasta joked, and Katerina laughed before telling the others what she had said.

"I'm glad you can joke about it." Marc led everyone out of the training room and walked with Katerina and Jocasta to his lab. "I'll wait outside in case you need anything." Jocasta nodded and patted him on the shoulder before stepping into Marc's lab. It looked like a super high-tech garage, but he had a hospital bed brought up from the infirmary so that they could have a more private meeting with the doctor. It looked incredibly out of place. The doctor stood by a computer screen to the left of the hospital bed.

"Hey there, Doctor Jones." Doctor Barrister smiled and held out her hand. "What on Earth did you do to yourself?"

"I wish I fuckin knew, Barri." Katerina figured they knew each other but decided to make the response a bit more professional, since Katerina herself barely knew Doctor Barrister.

"Uh, she says she wishes she knew." Katerina smiled at her.

"Kat, I've known Barri since undergrad, you can say word for word what I say." Katerina gave her a look.

"Well, Jocasta, I have not known her for that long, so forgive me for not wanting to call her by a nickname I have literally never heard." Katerina joked aloud, earning a chuckle from the Doctor.

"You can just call me Rachel, Miss Gradoff." She held her hand out to Katerina, giving her a conspiratorial smile, "Good to see you again."

"Katerina, please." She shook her hand.

"Alright, Jonesy, have you even seen a doctor in the past 3 years?" Rachel turned to Jocasta and patted the hospital bed.

"I am a Doctor."

"She says she is a Doctor, but I presume that means nothing." Katerina pointed the last part of the sentence at Jocasta, who blushed, and Rachel laughed again.

"Okay, I'm just going to do a basic checkup to start out, then I'll run some tests. If something hurts, just tap my shoulder. Otherwise, I'll ask yes or no questions. Katerina can leave if you're more comfortable that way, Jocasta."

"Tell her you've seen it all."

"Um, she wants me to stay." Katerina croaked *"I am* not *saying that, Jo."* Jo harrumphed and nodded at Rachel.

"She wanted you to say something embarrassing, didn't she?" Rachel chuckled and shook her head at Jocasta. She started checking Jocasta's vitals and things and leaned in toward her to say quietly "I cannot believe you, Jocasta Jones. Sleeping with the most powerful human being on Earth and not even telling your oldest friend."

"How did you know?" Katerina blurted out.

"You have a very protective aura, and almost every time she talks to you, you get flustered. I may not treat you often, Katerina, but I have never seen you flustered. And I have pulled a bullet out of you."

"Well, to my credit, Jocasta has a much bolder sense of humor in her head, and even more so when talking to you. Old friends do that to people."

"Yes, well." Rachel turned back to Jocasta, "I am proud of you for not shouting to the mountains, you've grown since undergrad."

"I was very embarrassingly loud about my love life. Everyone always knew who I was sleeping with. But it was undergrad, nobody seemed to care. The frat boys used to try to see who would rack up more girls than me. I am very much not proud of it. Also, it was just the first half! Say that to her!"

"She says only the first half of undergrad. She's very embarrassed."

"See, Jonesey, how does it feel? Be nicer. Katerina is a powerful lady." Katerina laughed. She said she wanted Jocasta to at least try to keep the bruises under control while she jumped into training, but that she thought they would heal up well as long as she didn't abuse herself. She also pointed out that the cut on her arm was going to scar, a nice match with the massive scar she had gained on her left hand. By the time they had finished with Jocasta's tests, Rachel had practically told Katerina every detail of her and Jocasta's college friendship. Rachel was funny, and Katerina liked this bold, witty side of Jocasta. It was something she had only glimpsed before, but with Rachel, it was like a switch turned on, and her outgoing college days were happening right before Katerina's eyes. It was sweet.

"Kat, baby? Ask her when we'll know about my speech."

"Rachel? Jocasta wants to know when we might know anything about her speech."

"I want to do a few more tests. We need my stuff from the infirmary though. Would Marc be okay with that?"

"He's outside, I'll get him." Katerina walked over to the door and poked her head out. Marc had been leaning on the wall, and the sound made him jump. "We need you in here."

"Absolutely!" He followed her inside, and he and Rachel discussed the logistics of getting Jocasta downstairs and in the infirmary with discretion. While they were talking, Jocasta gave Katerina a look and gestured for her to sit on the hospital bed with her. She obliged, and let Jocasta snuggle into her chest.

"*Kat? You're incredible, you know that?*" Jocasta held her tightly.

"*Thank you, Jo. You're pretty great yourself.*" Katerina spoke in Jocasta's mind, not wanting to bother the others.

"*I'm going to tell you I love you. I promise. I'm going to say it out loud again.*"

"*Don't promise, Jo. You can't promise anything right now.*"

"*Katerina.*" Jocasta's thoughts came in slower this time. "*Will you still want me if I can't do it?*" Katerina could feel the fear in her thoughts, tinged with loneliness.

"*Of course I will, Jo. You can't get rid of me that easily.*" She kissed the crown of Jocasta's head and squeezed her a little tighter. "*We'll figure it out.*" She held Jocasta for a few more minutes until Marc left the room and Rachel came back over to them.

"Katerina, you wait here, I won't need you, and Marc wants as few bodies as possible. Jocasta, I am going to have to ask you yes and no questions, blink once for yes, and twice for no. You won't be able to move your head in the machines. Got it?" Jocasta blinked once. "Good. Let's get this done." Then, the two of them walked out, and Katerina was left alone. She sat on the hospital bed, trying to wrap her head around all of the events of the past few days. She and Jocasta had spent almost as much time apart as they had together, and yet she still felt as close to her as she had the day she was taken.

Even if things had changed, she still felt these enormous feelings, and she didn't know what to do with herself. This was foreign territory for her. Usually, she adapted, she was trained, great in the field, she could do anything, but this was different. She was *visibly* flustered, for fuck's sake. Jo made her feel so secure, and safe, and brave, but simultaneously, the opposite. There was so much more she was afraid of now, so much that she couldn't explain. It had been so hard to focus when Jo was gone, the one thing she could accomplish was finding her, and then, as soon as she was back, Katerina was still distracted by Jo's well-being. The whole time they had been wrapping up with the Brigade, all she could think about was getting home and making sure Jocasta was okay. It was exhausting, caring about someone's safety so much.

At the same time, it came with the feeling of butterflies when Jocasta looked at her a certain way. It came with the way Jocasta's eyes melted from caramel to chocolate when they kissed. It came with tender kisses, and fluttering eyelashes in the early morning light, with laughter, and smiles, and joy, spreading through her chest. As much as the worry and the fear gnawed at her, Jocasta was the best thing that had happened to her in a long time. She knew that, but they had only been together for such a short time, and the idea of her having to help Jocasta, and translate for her for so long was terrifying. All of her thoughts and emotions swam through her head in circles, and when the door finally opened, she felt a bit dizzy.

Rachel walked straight to her computer and Jocasta made a beeline for Katerina. As soon as her arms wrapped around Jocasta, the dizziness went away, replaced with a surety that startled her. "Jocasta, would you like me to tell you what I've found alone, or do you want Katerina here?" Rachel asked, and Jocasta just pulled Katerina closer to her in response. "Okay. Well. I think I can fix this. The thing is, there is a chance you'll get your speech back naturally, I just have no idea when. Or I can give you a shot that will either reverse the loss completely, or make it permanent. This serum was a little bit nutso, Jonesey."

"*What are the odds? The percentages?*" Jocasta asked, and Katerina relayed.

"I'd say it's roughly 50/50. If we let it go, it could be days, months, years, I have no idea, honestly. It could also be never."

"*Katerina, I'd rather do it and know for sure, one way or the other. How do you feel about it?*" Katerina felt her stomach flip at Jocasta asking her opinion. However, this was a huge deal, and regardless of what she thought, it would make an impact on Jocasta's health. If it were her, she would take her chances, but she could communicate nonverbally with anyone. Jocasta didn't have that luxury.

"*I am here for you no matter what, Jocasta. I think it might be better to know too.*" She thought, and Jocasta smiled. "She wants to try the shot."

"Okay, I am going to go get that prepared then. It can take up to 48 hours to go into effect, but after that, you'll know for sure if it worked or not."

"What is the soonest it might kick in?" Katerina asked without waiting for Jocasta.

"Any time after 24 hours and before 48 hours." Rachel told them, and then she was gone again. Katerina let out a shaky breath. Between one and two days. This would be interesting. Maybe she could distract Jocasta or something. Or maybe they would be busy with training. She was starting to get antsy when Jocasta's thoughts entered her head.

"I do not expect anything from you. If this becomes too real, you can leave, I'll understand. If you stay, I'll be overjoyed, but if you can't, it's okay." Katerina looked at her to see her eyes filled with tears, the beautiful brown pools wobbling beneath the water.

"Jo, I'll admit I'm scared, but I'm more worried about getting through the next two days than I am about the 'what if'. We're lucky. I can hear your thoughts, babe. We can communicate still, even before learning sign language. We have got this. Plus, if we need help with it Vik knows how to sign, and I think Austin does as well. I'm terrified, Jocasta, but I am not going anywhere."

"I can't get rid of you that easy, huh?"

"Exactly." And Katerina knew that what she said was true. No matter how scared she was, or how many times she doubted herself, she was in this. Jocasta was worth it to her. "I love you, Jocasta. More than I thought was possible, especially after such a short time."

"Me too, Katerina. It's kind of scary, honestly."

"Good to know we're on the same page." Katerina smiled and kissed Jocasta, just a soft kiss, but she felt her heart flutter all the same. "How do you want to approach these two days? Hardcore training? Distraction dates?" Katerina paused for effect. "Distraction sex?"

"Oh, definitely option three! But I think some training will also have to happen. Marc seemed like he was already making spreadsheets for me."

"Are you ready for that? You were still a prisoner yesterday, and you have bruises all over. Speaking of which, Marc saw a cast when we found out where you were, but it was gone when we got you out. Is that what the scar on your hand is from?"

"Cyrus broke my hand when he kidnapped me. Definitely effective. Three of my bones were snapped. But I'm all healed now! The scar is from surgery." Jocasta held out her left hand and flexed it. Katerina made a mental note to keep an eye on that. Before she could flirt with Jocasta some more, the door opened, and Dr. Barrister returned.

"Okay, Jocasta. Are you ready?" She held up a syringe, and waggled her eyebrows at Jo, who nodded. Katerina stood up, attempting to give them room, but Jocasta reached out and grabbed her hand. She held tight as Rachel counted down from three and gave her the shot. Jocasta's face scrunched up when the needle went in, but other than that, she didn't seem to be in any pain. "You feel alright? It might bruise a little bit, but you shouldn't have any pain."

"*Tell her I feel great.*" Jocasta's thoughts were impatient now. "*Can we go now? I'm hungry.*"

"She says she feels great, and wants to know if we can go eat," Katerina smiled, and Rachel gave a soft laugh.

"Get out of here you two. I'm getting hungry myself." She waved them out the door, and as they exited, Katerina saw Marc leaning against the wall in the same position he had been in before.

"Lab is all yours, Marc." Katerina told him as Jocasta pulled her down the hall and toward the kitchen. He smiled and made his way into his lab. "You really are hungry all of a sudden!"

"*The morning workout just hit me I think.*" Jocasta pulled her into the kitchen and turned to look at her. "*I have no idea what I want.*"

"I know what *I* want." Katerina grinned, and Jocasta tilted her head curiously. Before Jocasta could ask her what that was, she grabbed her face and kissed her, pressing her lips as hard as she could to Jocasta's. She broke away, smiling, and made her way to the fridge. "But I know you're hungry, so I'll just make us a couple of sandwiches. Those shouldn't take too much time." Jocasta just nodded quickly and launched herself onto the counter, swinging her legs. Katerina felt her eyes on her as she made them a couple of sandwiches, throwing some deli meat and cheese onto the bread as fast as she could without making a mess. She gestured to the condiments to ask Jocasta if she wanted anything else on hers, and she shook her head, so Katerina grabbed a couple glasses and filled them with water before presenting Jocasta's sandwich to her. She grinned as Jocasta took a bite with a smile and made a little sound of pleasure. Katerina placed herself between Jocasta's knees and took a bite of her own sandwich. She gave Jocasta's nose a little boop, which earned her a strange giggle before she stepped back and leaned against the island opposite Jocasta. They finished their sandwiches pretty quickly, and Katerina asked Jocasta if she wanted another one.

"I mean, could I eat another sandwich? Yes. Do I want to be down here eating when I could be in your room, being eaten? No." Jocasta smiled as Katerina choked on her water.

"You know, you are a LOT more forward in your head." Katerina reached around Jocasta and lifted her off the counter, letting her wrap her legs around Katerina's waist. "Let's get upstairs, you insufferable flirt." She gave Jocasta a peck on the nose and started carrying her up to her room.

"I could really get used to this. You should carry me everywhere." Jocasta nuzzled into Katerina's neck, and Katerina giggled. She sped up, and when she got to the stairs, she decided to be impressive and take them. It was only one floor, but she knew Jocasta would get a kick out of it. Almost on cue, Jocasta thought, *"Oh wow, my girlfriend is extra strong, okay! Sexy!"*

"You're cute." As they got to the top of the stairs and turned toward her bedroom, she almost ran into Jeremy, one of the kids that trained with them on the weekends. "Woah! Hey, Jer. Sorry about that." She side-stepped him as Jocasta buried a laugh in her neck.

"It's okay Ms. Gradoff. What's wrong with Dr. Jones? Is she sick?"

"Oh, no, we're just goofing off." Katerina set her down. "She did lose her voice, but she's alright."

"Goofin off, huh?" Jeremy smiled at them. "Y'all are cute together."

"Oh, get out of here, kid. You've got some training to do!" Katerina waved him off, blushing. She turned to see Jocasta grinning ear to ear. *"What are you smiling about?"*

"He thinks we're cute! Do you think everyone thinks so?"

"Of course they do, now come on." Katerina walked over and opened her door for Jocasta, who bounced in and flung herself onto the bed. The ordeal with the doctor had taken longer than she thought, and as she looked at her alarm clock, she was surprised to see it was late afternoon now. She had a sudden urge to do something. "Jocasta, what would you say to doing something a little different?"

"Depends. What would that something be?"

"Let's go swimming." Katerina smiled as Jocasta's eyes lit up. "I know you thought the tennis court pool was pretty cool, so, what do you say?"

"Absolutely. OOH! I want to try phasing in water! I bet it feels super weird."

"Does it not feel 'super weird' anyway?" Katerina smirked.

"*Well, yes, but going through an object feels different than if I'm just doing it while I'm standing or something. So, it stands to reason that allowing the water to move through me would feel different too.*" Jocasta always sounded so cute when she talked about science, or a theory she had, but just hearing it in her thoughts was not as good as when she got all animated talking about it. Katerina really hoped the shot worked.

"Okay then, just don't do anything super noticeable. We don't need anybody asking questions." Katerina walked over to get her swimsuit, and Jocasta gave her a look.

"*I know, Kat, I'll be careful. I'm going to grab a suit from my bedroom.*" Jocasta sprang off the bed and sped out the door to her room, and Katerina chuckled. She was clearly excited to go swimming. She changed quickly and grabbed a couple of towels before throwing on a sheer robe. Jocasta hadn't returned yet, so she went ahead and walked across the hall. She knocked softly and let herself in.

Jocasta's room was familiar to her, but it always felt a little strange to be in there. They tended to retreat to the safety of her soundproof wall and lack of a neighbor, so they spent much less time here. When Jocasta was gone, she had only been in a few times to clean or to sit on her bed for a moment. She hadn't wanted to intrude on her space when she wasn't there. Jocasta was in her bathroom, trying to squeeze into a bathing suit top. She had the bottoms on, but they seemed a little bit small on her, and she was genuinely struggling with the top. "You okay in here?" Katerina asked, trying not to giggle at her with the straps all wrapped around her head.

"*I haven't used a swimsuit in years, so this is kind of old, and also I think my butt is bigger. My boobs are definitely bigger than they used to be.*" Jocasta got the top around her, but she was right, her chest was spilling out of the cups. Katerina held in a giggle as she tried to shove herself in, but it was probably two cup sizes too small.

"How old is this?" Katerina had to let herself laugh a little bit.

"*Well, the bottoms are less old, but my newer top broke, so this is literally from when I was like 18.*" Jocasta grimaced when she thought it. "*Maybe I can wear like a sports bra? I have one that's almost swimwear material.*"

"Okay, well let me help you out of this, and help *it* into the garbage. This is much too old for you to be holding on to. And *much* too small. Seriously, why would you keep a swimsuit that old?"

"It's cute! I could never find one this cute again!" Jocasta was laughing now, but her laugh still sounded odd.

"Love, your chest will never fit in this again. I should know. This top is probably two cup sizes too small, and it isn't like you have excess weight in your chest. That is all breast tissue." Katerina giggled and tried to untie the straps in the back, but it was like the knot was fused together. "These straps are a monstrosity."

"Why do you think I was pulling it over my head?" Jocasta turned around and rested her head on Katerina's shoulder. *"I'm going to be stuck in this forever."*

"No, you're not." Katerina rubbed her back. "I'll cut the strings, okay? And then we'll grab you something that fits, whether it's waterproof or not, and I'm taking you swimming." Jocasta nodded on her shoulder and stood back up. She looked Katerina up and down for a moment.

"You look incredibly sexy, by the way," She thought, her eyebrows raising.

"Thank you, Jo." Katerina felt herself blush and went in search of something to cut the strings off with. She found some scissors in a drawer next to the sink and motioned for Jocasta to turn around. She paused for a moment when she looked at the bruises around her ribs, some of them still purple. Once she had cut through, the top fell to the floor, and Jocasta's shoulders rose and fell with a deep breath of relief. She turned around, and Katerina sucked in a breath herself. Seeing Jocasta shirtless was something that always gave her a thrill, no matter how many times she did. The sight had effectively distracted her from the bruises she had been looking at. She felt herself getting hot, so she bent down to grab the fallen top.

"Something making you flustered, Kat? Don't think I didn't see you turning red." Katerina could hear the flirtation in Jocasta's thoughts, so when she stood back up to see her winking at her, she wasn't surprised.

"You know how hot you are, Jo. Go get a bra on so we can swim." She tried to get back on track, because if Jocasta stood there much longer, she was going to want to skip the pool entirely.

"Yes, ma'am." Jocasta smiled and saluted at her before marching over to her dresser and digging around for a suitable bra. Katerina watched her face as she picked through her drawer, scrunching up her nose and looking for one that would work for swimming. She shook her head and pulled out a tank top instead. She pulled it on and opened another drawer, producing

an oversized t-shirt. *"Let's get going,"* she thought, throwing the t-shirt on over her clothes.

"After you, Milady." Katerina opened Jocasta's door for her and smiled. They made their way out back to the tennis court without running into anyone, and when Katerina hit the switch for the court to retract into the ground, Jocasta gasped. "Is it that impressive?" Katerina joked, and Jocasta nodded in return. It really was amazing. The court split in half and retracted into the ground, and when it was all the way in, flaps came out to cover the holes for safety. Underneath was a huge pool, and ladders extended from underwater on either end of it. She looked at Jocasta, who looked dumbfounded.

"It is never going to be unimpressive, honestly," she thought, and then *"Kind of like you, Katerina."* The compliment made Katerina blush, like so many things Jocasta did. She took her robe off and jumped into the pool, pushing her hair back as she resurfaced. *"See, you continue to prove that point."*

"Shut up and join me, Jocasta," Katerina called to her. Jocasta gave her a flabbergasted look and held her hand to her chest dramatically.

"First of all, I am literally not even speaking. Secondly, I am complimenting you! You'd think I would get a thank you!" She was joking, she had seen Katerina blush. Jocasta pulled her t-shirt off and dove into the water, surfacing inches from Katerina and kissing her. Katerina was tempted to deepen the kiss, but she refrained, instead pulling away and starting a lap around the pool. She swam on her back, lazily kicking to propel herself.

"I forgot how calming the water is. I'm glad the pool is heated though; it is starting to get chilly outside." She looked toward Jocasta, who was leaning on the edge of the pool, kicking her legs, and leaning her head out onto the concrete.

"Yea, Fall in New England tends to get that way. Do you think it would still be warm enough in the Winter?" Jocasta lowered herself into the water, standing on the floor of the pool, and turned to rest her arms on the edge, laying her head on her arms.

"Maybe not, it does tend to get pretty snowy. We might have to plow a few feet off before we even got to the pool."

"You mean Marc doesn't have a temperature controlling bubble around the compound? I am shocked." Her sarcasm was audible in her thoughts,

dripping from them, really. Katerina was on the opposite end of the pool from Jocasta now, and she dipped underwater, pushing off the wall and swimming toward her. She made it all the way to her before coming up for air, putting her hands on Jocasta's hips as she did so. *"Jesus, how did you get over here so fast?"* Jocasta jumped a little bit.

"I swam, Jo." Katerina laughed and put her forehead to Jocasta's back, between her shoulder blades, and wrapped her arms around her. "Something I think you should do more of." Katerina held her tight and lifted up, pulling Jocasta underwater with her. She let go, and when they surfaced, Jocasta splashed her in the face.

"How RUDE!" She was beaming. *"I can't believe you would enter a dunking match with me!"* She swam a little closer to Katerina.

"What is a dunking match?" Katerina asked, and instead of answering, Jocasta launched herself at Katerina, pushing her down underwater by her shoulders. Katerina spluttered as she resurfaced.

"Now you have one point and I have one point. Need further explanation?" Jocasta started swimming away from Katerina.

"Are there any rules?" Katerina laughed, chasing Jocasta.

"Your head has to be all the way under for a dunk to count, and no messing with someone's swimsuit as a distraction. That second rule comes from boys in high school pulling the string ties of a girl's bottoms. Which is gross." Jocasta pulled her foot out of Katerina's grasp and turned on her, mischief in her eyes. Jocasta looked around before she tried to grab Katerina's arm, but she wasn't quick enough, and Katerina swung her leg to knock her off balance. Just as she was about to push her under again, Jocasta phased, and Katerina's own momentum caused her to fall in.

"That has to be cheating!"

"It is not in the official rules, so unfortunately that does have to count against you." Jocasta was walking backward bouncing her shoulders.

"It better be in the rules now. Unfair advantages and all that." Katerina grinned at her and swam underwater, circling Jocasta and hooking the backs of her knees on her shoulders before coming to the surface, knocking Jocasta in on her back.

"It might be the only way I can escape you! But, fine, I won't do it again." Jocasta smiled and swam up to Katerina, playfully kissing her before trying to pick her up, and they began a tussle for control. The game went on like

that for a while, and when Katerina had 14 dunks to her 15, Jocasta was breathing hard. *"Okay, I think it is time to be done with that game."*

"You only want to be done because you're winning," Katerina smirked. They had their arms wrapped around each other now.

"Well, that, and I would much rather be doing something else right now."

"Oh?" Katerina raised her eyebrows, and Jocasta kissed her deeply. She felt Jocasta's hand move from her waist up her back and into her hair, and she shivered, pulling her closer. She bit Jocasta's bottom lip, tasting the chlorine on her skin. Jocasta wrapped her legs around her, and she started walking toward the edge of the pool. Jocasta pulled back a little bit, gasping for air before kissing her again, and she started to explore Katerina's body with her hands. Katerina pushed Jocasta against the edge of the pool, shifting so that she was holding her with one hand so she could run her fingers through Jocasta's hair. When things started to get really heated, Katerina went to ask Jocasta if she wanted to go upstairs, but as she pulled away, she heard slow clapping.

"Really not hiding anything now, are you?" She heard Vik laugh, and opened her eyes to see Vik, Arthur, Carter, and Austin watching them, holding tennis rackets.

"Good thing the kids are all off the campus on a field trip right now," Austin added. "They would have gotten quite the show." Arthur and Carter were bright red. Jocasta slid down and hid in Katerina's chest.

"Right, well, we were just about to-" Katerina started, but Vik interrupted her.

"Get it on in the pool?" She laughed again, and Arthur genuinely choked.

"We were leaving, actually. Have fun playing tennis!" Katerina felt the blood pumping in her face as she grabbed Jocasta's wrist and swam to the ladder. She climbed out and Jocasta followed, running over to her towel and T-shirt while Katerina closed up the pool.

"You know guys, it is getting pretty late, maybe we should reschedule this tennis game." Arthur was twisting his racket in his hands.

"Did you plan this?" Katerina asked Viktoria, gesturing at the group. "Since when do you all plan tennis games?"

"Well, I may have seen the two of you playing around down here, and wanted to mess with you, but little did I know that by the time I got these slowpokes out here, you'd be displaying such," Vik blushed a bit as she found the words, "intense affection."

"We were going to pelt you with tennis balls. Arthur was just gonna hit them into the water and make big splashes, cause he thought he might hurt you otherwise." Carter smiled sheepishly.

"Well, that'll teach you all." Katerina felt the heat leaving her cheeks a bit and went over to grab her own towel and cover up.

"Why is it that every time we kiss anywhere on the grounds outside of our rooms, Vik is there?" Jocasta wondered to her, and Katerina tilted her head, interested by the observation.

"Jocasta noticed that any time we have kissed outside of our rooms, you've interrupted, Vik. What a strange coincidence, I would almost say it isn't one." Katerina jabbed Vik in the side as they all started walking back inside.

"It's almost as if you've made it your mission to ruin my day with your happy relationship." Vik joked back.

"If only we could all have happy relationships with beautiful women," Austin sighed and patted Vik on the back.

"Yes, if only the women of the world wanted me for more than my body." Vik laughed and wrapped an arm around Austin's shoulder.

"They do!" Carter chimed in. "They want you because you're famous, too!" They all laughed, and Arthur shook his head.

"If only I was young enough to still care about having a relationship," he lamented, making them all laugh even harder.

"Aw, poor Art." Jocasta smiled and put her arm around Katerina's waist. *"Hey, will you carry me upstairs again? That was fun."*

"I will only carry you upstairs if you change into your own clothes when we get there. I have about two shirts that are clean at this point, Jocasta." Katerina spoke aloud, and Vik chuckled.

"I have literally been back for a day, *Kat, that is hardly my fault."* Jocasta chided, and Katerina laughed.

"What did she say?" Carter asked.

"She said 'I've only been back for a *day*, it's hardly my fault'," Katerina mocked, earning another laugh, courtesy of Jocasta. They all made their way inside, and she and Jocasta broke off from the group to head upstairs, Katerina scooping her into her arms as they went.

"Get a room, honestly!" Vik called as she followed the others toward the common area and kitchen.

"We are headed there!" Katerina yelled back and started up the stairs. Jocasta buried her face in Katerina's neck as they climbed and pouted when let her down by her bedroom door. She looked up at Katerina, with her eyes wide and her bottom lip sticking out, batting her eyelashes.

"Aw, can't you just hold me a little longer?" Jocasta wiggled her chin.

"Go change first, then I'll think about it." Katerina booped her nose and turned to enter her own room. She opened the door and heard Jocasta do the same, sighing heavily. She was so dramatic. Katerina threw her wet clothes into the basket and grabbed the softest pair of sweatpants she could find, and a t-shirt of Jocasta's she had taken and hidden in the bottom of one of her drawers. Jocasta had told her once that she bought it in high school, and there was a faded and chipped picture of a few of the Phenoms on the front. A couple of the guys on it had retired before Katerina ever joined, but Marc, Vik, and Arthur were all there, Marc front and center. It had made Katerina laugh when she had pulled it out of a box on that first day, while helping Jocasta unpack. Now, it was comforting to her as she slid it over her head. She heard soft rap on the door, and turned as Jo let herself in. Her eyes widened almost imperceptibly when they landed on the shirt. "Do you like this shirt? I stole it from someone." Katerina winked, showing off the front of the shirt to Jocasta.

"I bet that person is really missing it. It looks incredible on you." Jocasta smiled and walked over to Katerina, sliding her hands around her waist. *"Too bad I'm going to have to rip it off."* Jocasta thought, as she nuzzled into Katerina's neck.

"Oh, I'd like to see you try, Jo." Katerina laughed, placing her hands on Jocasta's hips, and pushing her away, just a little bit. Jocasta pouted and looked up at her, making Katerina smirk. "You're cute when you pout, but I'm pretty sure you already know that." Jocasta just smiled, and grabbed her hand, leading her to the bed. They both curled up under the covers, and Katerina realized that she was much more tired than she had thought she was. The stress of the past few days starting to melt away showed her just how much she had been running herself ragged. "Jocasta?"

"Yes?"

"Are you as exhausted as I am?" Katerina asked her, stroking Jocasta's hair. Jocasta nodded, placing her head on Katerina's chest. "Are you okay if we just cuddle again?" They had taken a quick shower last night, wanting to talk about everything they had missed with each other, and Katerina had just held her as tightly as possible as they talked, right up until they fell asleep. She knew Jocasta had been craving a more intimate physical affection just as much as she was, but at this point, her eyes were beginning to close.

"*Yes, Kat, this is perfect. I missed you so much.*" Jocasta tangled her legs with Katerina's and held her tightly by the waist. Katerina put her arm that wasn't already around Jocasta over her, holding her close. She kissed the top of her head.

"I missed you too, love." She threaded her fingers into Jocasta's undercut, which was much longer than she normally kept it, and Katerina felt a wave of guilt. Her hair was this long because she had been taken. "Do you want to get your hair cut tomorrow?"

"*Yes, please. It feels so weird.*" Jocasta sounded relieved. Katerina felt Jocasta's chest expand as she took a deep breath. "*I dreamt about this. You, holding me in your bed. It makes me feel so safe.*"

"I don't know why, you were taken from me when we were in bed, and I didn't quite stop it from happening." Katerina said it without thinking, and Jocasta lifted her head to look at her.

"*Kat, you can't seriously be blaming yourself. You couldn't have known the intruder was half computer, and you couldn't have done a better job of getting me out of the room. If it was anyone else, you would have saved me. And, now you know that there are people who you can't use suggestion or reading on, and you can prepare for that scenario. I cannot imagine a safer place than your arms.*" Jocasta's brows were knit together, and her expression earnest. Katerina felt tears forming in her eyes.

"Your faith in me is astounding, Jocasta."

"*You earned my faith in you, fair and square.*" Jocasta kissed her, soft and tender. "*I love you, Katerina.*"

"*I love you too.*" Katerina placed the thought in her head, squeezing her tight, and they fell asleep like that.

Katerina slept through the night without dreaming, and when she woke up, she was feeling better than ever. She looked over toward where Jocasta had been when they fell asleep, and she didn't see her. Panic started to creep in on her, but she shoved it down. She reached over and felt for Jocasta, thinking maybe she was turning invisible in her sleep, but she felt nothing. "Jocasta?" She called, and cursed herself for the tinge of fear she could hear in her own voice. Jocasta was making her a bit soft. She almost jumped out of her skin when Jocasta appeared right in front of her, Katerina's hand stuck through her chest. Jocasta's eyes were opening slowly, like she had just woken her up. She pulled her hand back, and Jocasta's eyes filled with surprise.

"*Was I just invisible?*" Jocasta thought, just as Katerina said, "Are you okay?"

"*Yes, I'm okay, I was phased until your hand was out of the area. Not on purpose, but, thankfully, I was.*"

"Were you having a bad dream or something?"

"*I don't know.*" Jocasta's mouth opened and closed as she was thinking, and Katerina wondered if she had almost forgotten that she couldn't talk. Yet. Hopefully.

"Okay, well you're okay." Katerina pulled her into her arms and kissed her cheek. Jocasta nodded against her and pulled away just as a knock came on the door.

"Hey, Katerina! I am going to assume Jocasta is also in there because she isn't in her room. Come downstairs, Marc wants to go over a new training schedule over breakfast he ordered from somewhere." Carter's voice carried through the door, and Katerina heard someone, probably Austin, giggle. Katerina felt herself getting embarrassed and placed a thought into Carter's head.

"*I'm pretty sure you shouldn't be yelling about the new training schedule when Jocasta's new powers aren't public knowledge.*" She teased, and heard Carter clear their throat and added "*We will be there momentarily.*" Carter's footsteps disappeared down the hall.

"Come on, love, we have to get up." Katerina was turning to Jocasta before she saw that she was already up and getting dressed. She had brought over an outfit last night, and Katerina hadn't even noticed.

"*Some of us are already up, thank you.*" Jocasta smiled at her and went into the bathroom. Katerina heard the water running as she got up to change, and when she joined Jocasta in the bathroom, she was finishing up brushing her teeth. She turned from the sink and kissed Katerina on the nose before slipping back into the bedroom, and as Katerina brushed her own teeth, she overheard Jocasta thinking to herself. *"God, I love this. I love her."* Katerina smiled to herself before turning the water back on and drowning out the loud thoughts. She left the bathroom to see Jocasta perched on the end of the bed, which she somehow made in that short amount of time. She was smiling wide. *"You're so beautiful."*

"Thank you, love. Ready to go down?" Katerina nodded toward the door, and they both made their way to the kitchen, where Marc had a catered buffet going. "I cannot believe that man." Katerina muttered under her breath, and Jocasta chuckled, nudging her gently. They both filled their plates and met up with everyone else in the boardroom.

"Okay, so we usually train by ourselves according to an arbitrary schedule designed to make sure that everyone is actually training, but we normally ignore that and you all train whenever you want. As the core group of Phenoms, I just assume you do your work." Marc was just diving right in. "Now that Jocasta needs someone to train her and we need to keep her powers under wraps, I have moved around the training schedules of everyone not in this room, and made your schedules more concrete, in order to safely work with her." He handed around pieces of paper, and Katerina smirked. It was a little old school for Marc to make a handout, he usually sent things to their individual tablets. "Jocasta is not on the official schedule that is on the network, so I printed these out for you all to memorize and then destroy. I want her as safe as possible, and to train without anyone finding out until she is ready." And now the handouts made sense. "As of right now, I am suspending Jocasta's study, since Gary was arrested, and I will be telling the higher ups at W.E.I.R.D. that she needs time off." Marc looked at Jocasta. "Paid, of course." Katerina watched Jocasta turn pink as she nodded to him. Marc continued, going over the sheets in their hands, and then he sat down to eat as they all studied the schedule.

"I am incredibly overwhelmed by this." Jocasta's thoughts came to her on accident again, and Katerina glanced over to see her struggling to pick up her paper, her hands phasing through it. She reached over and placed a steadying hand on her lower back and watched as Jocasta's hands grabbed the paper. This time the thoughts were directed at her. *"Thank you."* Katerina just nodded and continued her work. Jocasta had a session

with her and Marc today, and then she could take her to get her hair cut. But, if Marc was so worried about people knowing about her, maybe she should see about someone here cutting her hair. With her control being so limited, it would probably be safer. Katerina rubbed circles on Jocasta's back and continued down the schedule. She would be working with Jocasta almost daily, and there were always two of them scheduled to be there with Jocasta during a session. They were scheduled for two or three hour blocks every day, and Katerina was starting to get a bit overwhelmed herself. Going from a few sessions a week with just Vik to nothing, and then to this hard-core training regime was going to be difficult for Jocasta.

She made a mental note to schedule a chunk of time to make sure Jocasta was relaxing, because she knew she was going to channel all of the energy she usually put into her research into this with the study suspended. She couldn't help but notice that Jocasta was thinner than she had been before as well, and almost wanted to tell Marc that this was going to be too much on her, but Jocasta was her own person, and she would let her decide when it was too much.

They stayed like that for a while, everyone slowly finishing their plates, until Marc asked if they were all memorized, and they left. Marc had decided to burn the papers himself, so she and Jocasta went back upstairs so she could grab a hair tie before meeting him in the training room. They walked in to find Marc already warming up, so they both got to work. Marc called over and Jocasta entered the boxing ring with him. "Okay, so I want to work on you controlling your powers for a bit, then Katerina will fight you." He looked between them before adding, "All good?" to which they both nodded. Katerina watched as Jocasta gained a better understanding of how to make herself disappear and phase, but she noticed she was still having trouble returning to visibility. She also was struggling with isolating anything other than her hands. But for an hour and a half, she was really starting to learn. Katerina intermittently used a punching bag, keeping herself warm for her turn to train, but she was mostly watching Jocasta. By the time she was ready to move on, she was already pretty tired from those exercises, so Katerina suggested a break for a minute. Jocasta gladly sat down with a bottle of water and Marc pulled Katerina to the side. "Am I pushing her too hard?"

"She will tell you if it's too much."

"Well, she'll tell *you*." Marc agreed, and Katerina felt a pang in her stomach.

"Right."

"Hey, can we go ahead and get this over with? I'm really looking forward to that hair cut." Jocasta waved at her, standing in the middle of the ring.

"Shit. Marc, do you think it would be safe to take her out to get a hair cut?" The brigade was bound to be after her again, and Katerina didn't want to take any risks.

"I'd rather not risk someone seeing her out and about, honestly." He admitted, and her suspicions seemed to be confirmed.

"What do you have up your sleeve, Marc?"

"I can't tell you yet, but I can tell you that Austin cuts their own hair and does it pretty well, so I'm sure they would be happy to help."

"Hello? Kat, baby, come on!" Jocasta was jumping up and down on the balls of her feet.

"Okay, I think she wants to fight." Katerina gestured toward her, and Marc laughed. "I'm coming!" Katerina called, and the two of them went back to join her. *"Baby? That's new."* Jocasta shrugged, and Katerina entered the ring. As soon as she was standing, Jocatsa pounced. She had a scrappiness to her that hadn't been there a few months ago, and although she had lost some of the power behind her punches, she was still using good form. Katerina held back a little bit, trying to decipher whether Jocasta was really ready to spar with her again. Jocasta must have noticed, because she gave her a quizzical look before upping her game. Katerina started to fight her without holding back, but she quickly saw that she would overpower her too easily, and backed off again, not wanting to hurt her or make her bruises worse.

"Katerina, fight her. She needs to get used to really fighting someone who isn't holding back." Marc was standing a few yards away.

"It's her first session, Marc."

"Fight her, Katerina." She looked to Jocasta, who nodded, and she stopped holding back. It took about five seconds before she had Jocasta pinned, but Jocasta just jumped back up and readied herself to go again. They fought like that for another hour, Katerina defeating her in ten seconds or less, and Marc just watched silently. She tried to give Jocasta tips at first, but Marc had intervened, telling her to let Jocasta learn on her feet, through her mistakes. When she questioned him, he waved her off, and Jocasta had encouraged her to listen to him. She was thinking about calling it when suddenly Jocasta escaped her grasp and wrapped an arm around her, flipping her over her shoulder and knocking the wind out of her when she hit the ground.

Marc clapped as Katerina then swept Jocasta's feet out from under her and proceeded to pin her to the ground. Jocasta tapped out, and Marc jumped into the ring. "Great work, Jocasta. I think it is about time for the two of you to get out of here." He reached down and helped Jocasta to her feet. Jocasta stood up and held a finger up.

"One more time." She looked at Katerina.

"She wants to go one more time, Marc." Katerina looked to him, and he just held his hands up and left the ring, going back to his watching spot. Jocasta got into her ready position, and they started. Jocasta grabbed Katerina around the waist and pushed her toward the edge of the ring, but Katerina punched down onto her back, making her lose her grip, and got out of her reach. Jocasta tried to throw a punch, but Katerina caught her arm and pulled her toward herself, grabbing her around the torso and flipping her upside down, but before she could force her to the mat, Jocasta wrapped her legs around Katerina's neck and pulled herself upright. Katerina threw them both to the mat, and Jocasta slammed down hard.

"FUCK!" Jocasta gasped as she hit the mat, and Katerina lost her breath. She scrambled to Jocasta, reaching for her face.

"Jocasta! You- the shot-"

"It worked." Jocasta's smile was huge, and as Katerina held her face in her hands, tears sprung to both of their eyes. "Great first word, honestly." Jocasta laughed, her full, real laugh, and Katerina squeezed her face in her hands and kissed her. Her voice was a little gravelly, probably from the lack of use, but it was still her voice. Marc was climbing into the ring, and he stopped short for a moment, giving them some space. Jocasta broke away and looked at him, grinning ear to ear. "I think I'm good now."

"Obviously." He laughed as Katerina stood up, reaching down to pull Jocasta up with her. They all walked out of the training room, and Marc left them to head to his lab, to work on something that he described as 'above their paygrade'. Katerina reached over and linked her fingers with Jocasta's as they walked toward their rooms, very much ready for a shower.

Jocasta pulled her into the kitchen as they passed and bounced over to the fridge.

"Do you think those caterers left any leftovers in here?" She raised her eyebrows and opened the fridge without waiting for Katerina to respond. "Oh yes! Bacon, Pancakes, the whole shebang. Do you want a snack before we hit the showers?" Jocasta looked at her, and Katerina felt her stomach flip. Hearing her out loud was so surreal after not having heard her voice for months. "Hello? Kat? Food?" Jocasta waved a hand in front of her.

"Oh, yes, sure, just give me whatever you want." She watched Jocasta put together a couple of plates and heat them up, humming as she did so. She pulled the plates out and jumped up onto the island, handing Katerina her food. They ate fairly quickly, which Katerina noticed had become a habit of theirs. At least they made time for food, Vik would drink smoothies all day if you let her, and sometimes they had to remind her that protein shakes did not count as a meal. She just didn't want to waste any time. Katerina cleaned up their plates and laughed as Jocasta jumped down off the island, almost falling over. "Are you alright?"

"Well, I did just get my ass kicked about a hundred times." Jocasta leaned against the island and watched as Katerina washed their plates.

"And you took it well." Katerina smirked as Jocasta moved to stand next to her at the sink. She took the plates and sat them in the drying rack before turning to her. "Genuinely, you did well, Jocasta."

"Thank you, Katerina." Jocasta squeezed between Katerina and the counter, and Katerina grabbed the edges of the sink on either side of her. She inched closer to Jocasta and tilted her head to the side as Jocasta slid her arms around her waist.

"Are you sure you're okay with those bruises?"

"I feel fine, baby." Jocasta was being sincere, but Katerina was still a little worried. Jocasta looked up at her and bit her lip, making Katerina's stomach flutter.

"I think we should go upstairs now, don't you?" Katerina said softly, inches from Jocasta's lips. Jocasta nodded, looking up at her and biting her bottom lip.

"Please." Jocasta pushed her way out of Katerina's arms and led the way up the stairs. A group of trainees walked past them going downstairs, and two of them giggled to each other. Katerina heard someone saying "pool" and Jocasta sped up. Katerina followed suit and when they got into her room, Katerina gave her a look.

"What's wrong? You're stiff."

"Someone else saw us in the pool yesterday. Those trainees were laughing about it." Jocasta's face was turning pink, and Katerina laughed. "What's so funny? I'm embarrassed!"

"We're adults, Jo. The people in charge know, so who cares if some of the trainees are giggling? It's not like we are doing anything wrong."

"The W.E.I.R.D. officials don't know," Jocasta pointed out.

"It still isn't against the rules," Katerina retorted.

"Well, I'm still embarrassed that my coworkers are giggling about my sex life, Kat!"

"I'm more interested in giving them a better story than kissing in the pool." Katerina grabbed Jocasta's shirt and closed the space between them. She felt Jocasta's breath hitch as she pulled her shirt over her head and threw it on the floor. Jocasta bit her lip and looked at Katerina while grabbing her shirt as well.

"May I?" Jocasta asked, pulling her even closer.

"Of course, you may." Katerina held her arms up as Jocasta lifted her shirt off, and as soon as she was free, she bent down to lift Jocasta up and carry her toward the bed. Jocasta buried her hands into Katerina's hair and kissed her as Katerina sat her down gently. She guided Jocasta down onto the pillows without breaking the kiss, but when she did break the kiss, Jocasta grabbed her face, stopping her from moving.

"Wait, Katerina." She had a serious look in her eyes.

"What's wrong?" Katerina looked her up and down, scanning for something she might have been doing accidentally.

"Nothing," Jocasta let out a small laugh, "I just wanted you to hear something first." Katerina realized what she was doing and smiled. "I love you, Katerina. So much." Jocasta kissed her again, smiling into the kiss.

"I love you too, Jocasta." Katerina's smile turned into a grin as she pushed Jocasta back down onto the pillows. She watched the excitement enter Jocasta's eyes as she straddled her, and felt her heart rate spike. She bent over her and whispered in her ear "Now I just can't wait to hear you scream." Jocasta shivered beneath her, and she nibbled on her earlobe. She kissed the place between Jocasta's ear and her jaw, earning her a small gasp as she traced Jocasta's jawline with her tongue. She pulled back to watch her face as she traced her hands along her body, relishing in the way she shivered when her fingers grazed her hips.

Jocasta looked at her with greedy eyes and reached up to put her arms around Katerina's neck. She let her pull her into a kiss, passionate and fierce, and she crushed her body into Jocasta's, clashing their hips together. Jocasta pushed herself up into Katerina, but Katerina was stronger, pinning Jocasta down and pulling out of the kiss. She held one of Jocasta's wrists above her head and gripped her hip with the other hand while kissing her neck, then moving to her collar bone, and tracing that with her tongue as well. Jocasta hummed her approval, and Katerina moved her hand off of her hip and into her waistband. Jocasta gasped, and lifted her hips up in response, making Katerina chuckle. "Eager, aren't we?" Jocasta nodded and put her hand on Jocasta's wrist, pushing her further into her pants.

"I need you, Kat." Jocasta breathed out, and Katerina pulled her hand back out of her waistband so she could shift her body and take Jocasta's pants off. Jocasta smiled, and shimmied out of her pants while Katerina pulled. "You too, please." Jocasta gestured to Katerina's training joggers.

"Of course, love." Katerina winked and pulled her own pants off, throwing them to the side of the bed. She climbed back up and lowered herself over Jocasta, Kissing her lips softly before working down her body, cupping her breasts over her bra and kissing the swell of them that popped out of the top. Jocasta reached up and pulled the straps of her bra off her shoulders and arched her back up, giving Katerina room to slip her hand under and unclasp her bra. She took it off, and Jocasta pulled her back down into a kiss, biting Katerina's bottom lip as she broke away. Katerina threaded her hand into Jocasta's hair and pulled as she kissed her neck and gently nipped her, Jocasta's eyes widening in response.

"If you bite me, I bite back, Jo." Katerina told her, her lips grazing Jocasta's skin. Jocasta giggled and nodded, and Katerina moved back down to her breasts, kissing them, and teasing her nipples with her tongue. Jocasta moaned and bucked her hips up, and Katerina gently pushed her back down with one hand. She moved further down, kissing Jocasta's ribs and stomach, taking care to be extra gentle over the bruised skin, and eventually worked her way to the waistband of her boxers, playfully biting them and letting the elastic snap back before hooking her fingers in the sides and pulling them off. Jocasta gasped as Katerina bent down to kiss her again, teasing her clit with her tongue.

"God, I missed this." Jocasta threaded her fingers into Katerina's hair as she began licking her. She started off with her tongue wide and focused the pressure more when she got closer to her clit, watching her face as Jocasta bit her lip and closed her eyes. She sucked a little bit on her, savoring the taste of her juices, and Jocasta moaned again, making Katerina smile into her. Nothing was sexier than Jocasta moaning because of her, and Katerina could feel herself becoming increasingly wet as she teased her. She put her tongue inside Jocasta, who then pulled Katerina's hair, making her gasp. She moved back up to her clit and adjusted her position so that she could start teasing her with her fingers. She put one finger in her, only to the first knuckle, smiling as Jocasta tried to move so that Katerina went further in. She pulled back again and nipped the inside of Jocasta's thigh.

"You have got to learn to be patient, love." Katerina chided, meeting her eyes.

"I've been waiting for months!" Jocasta pouted, and Katerina felt herself giving in. She reached up and cupped Jocasta's breast, rubbing a thumb over her nipple before bringing her hand back down and sticking two fingers in her mouth. She kept eye contact with Jocasta, whose eyes were glistening with desire, the caramel swirls darkening as she watched Katerina. She slowly pulled her fingers out of her mouth and grinned at Jocasta.

"At least use your manners." Katerina loved teasing her, and Jocasta always took the opportunity to satisfy her, pouting and squirming until she got what she craved. And she always did what Katerina asked of her.

"Please, Katerina." Jocasta bit her bottom lip.

"Please what, Jo?" Katerina smirked and lifted a brow.

"Fuck me." Jocasta whined, "Please fuck me, Kat."

"Well, since you've asked so nicely." Katerina lowered herself back down and let the two fingers she had just prepared slide into Jocasta. She smiled with satisfaction when Jocasta's hands twisted into the sheets beneath her as she pressed on her g-spot, and she dipped down to give her clit some attention with her tongue. Jocasta sucked in a sharp breath and bit her lip again, bucking her hips up. Katerina started to work her up to an orgasm, and she reveled in the little whines and whimpers escaping her lips. As she felt Jocasta's muscles clenching and unclenching around her fingers, she lifted her eyes to look at her face just in time to hear her finally scream as she went over the edge. Looking at her in that moment was a high unlike any other. She lifted her head and kissed the inside of Jocasta's thighs, smiling wide. "Good girl," she whispered to her, and bit her lip as she responded with an aftershock and another whimper. She pulled her fingers out and licked them clean, grinning at her while she recovered.

"Holy shit, Kat." Jocasta was still breathing heavily. "You're incredible."

"I try." Katerina smiled and crawled up to lay on top of her. She kissed her softly, and gently nipped her bottom lip. "I always work well with a good listener." She winked and rolled off of her. "Want to take a shower now?"

"You don't want a turn?" Jocasta lifted herself up onto her elbows and tilted her head.

"Oh, I'll get my turn in the shower, love." Katerina traced her own teeth with her tongue and got up, unclasping her bra, and throwing it to the side as she walked toward the bathroom. She heard Jocasta scramble out of the bed and follow her as she turned on the faucet. She turned around just as she entered the bathroom and smiled as Jocasta placed her hands on Katerina's hips, pulling her towards her. "Do you mind taking those off for me?" Katerina asked her as Jocasta's fingers lighted on the waistband of her underwear.

"Yes, ma'am." Jocasta giggled a bit and dropped into a crouch before slowly pulling Katerina's underwear over her hips. Before she could move to touch her, Katerina grabbed Jocasta's jaw and lifted her up to stand again before kissing her, hard. She pulled away and stepped into the shower, Jocasta following right behind her.

~~~~~~

JOCASTA

Jocasta couldn't focus during her training session with Vik, her thoughts drifting to yesterday and this morning with Katerina. Yesterday, she had been impatient, missing Katerina's touch on her, but this morning was something else. They had worshiped every inch of each other. This morning had been sacred in a way that she couldn't stop thinking about, which was becoming more and more evident as she was caught off guard and slammed to the ground yet again. She pushed herself back up to her feet and steadied herself forcing her mind to focus. Before she could start to fight again, Vik held a hand up.

"Jocasta, you're clearly distracted. You didn't even fight this poorly the first time we trained together, and I know you're a better fighter now. Focus." Jocasta nodded and signaled her to start again. This time, she lasted about thirty seconds before Vik had her pinned. The only reason she could escape her for that long was because she had trained with Vik before she was kidnapped, so she was already familiar with her techniques. When she had trained yesterday with Kat it had been a travesty, and with Carter about an hour ago it was just as bad. She sighed as Vik helped her up and wondered how long it would be before she started to get better at this.

"How much longer are we supposed to be doing this for?" All she wanted was to go upstairs and repeat this morning with Katerina.

"Eager to get back to Katerina?" Vik teased her, but she was one hundred percent correct.

"Yes, actually," Jocasta admitted.

"I knew that was it. You have to be able to focus, Jocasta. I don't care what it is that distracts you, it could be that one of us is hurt or someone needs help, but you have to be able to push anything aside and focus when you're in the field. So, I don't care how good the sex is, it cannot distract you." Vik ran at her, sliding between her legs and knocking her feet out from under her. Jocasta quickly recovered, flipping onto her back, and springing up to her feet. She threw a punch at Vik, catching her in the side, and Vik smiled. "Okay, there you go!" They continued sparring, Jocasta holding her own much better until Vik knocked the wind out of her and she doubled over. Vik kicked her knees out and pinned her to the ground. "Out of curiosity though, how good is it?" Jocasta was thankful for her pre heated cheeks as she felt herself blush with embarrassment.

"Oh, um," she began, but Vik laughed.

"You don't have to tell me, Jocasta. But we do have a new recruit moving in soon who has super hearing, so based on the rumors from the trainees, you might want to learn how to be a bit quieter." Vik climbed out of the boxing ring, and Jocasta looked at her with her jaw on the floor.

"Um, what do you mean, 'rumors from the trainees'?"

"Oh, you haven't heard? One of the trainees overheard me planning the pool prank the other day and watched from the upstairs hallway, and then, a group of trainees saw you two headed for Katerina's room yesterday afternoon, so a couple of them took it upon themselves to listen in from the supply room next door. Very scandalous, apparently."

"Oh my god. Fantastic, just what I need, the whole mansion discussing my sex life." Jocasta dragged a hand down her face, trying to regain some semblance of dignity.

"Yes, well then I hate to tell you that they have a pool going for how long it takes for you to get caught full on having sex in a common area."

"You're not serious."

"I am very serious."

"That has to be some sort of harassment."

"Based on the very detailed account of your escapades yesterday that I overheard, I think a case could be made."

"Oh no, what are they saying? Maybe I don't want to know."

"I'll tell you this, I have heard at least four different people attempting to mimic a moan that I do not know who it is supposed to be but is incredibly close to a sound I have heard you make during a fight."

"Good fucking god."

"I may have also heard the phrase 'yes ma'am' being repeated at some point," Vik added before shutting herself up by taking a drink of her water.

"When are you overhearing this? I can't believe how far it's gotten; I mean it was yesterday!" Jocasta grabbed her water bottle and started walking toward the hallway.

"Some of us have to oversee the training groups, Jocasta."

"Oh, yeah. Well, I'm sure Katerina won't mind, but I am very embarrassed."

"Who could blame you? I know I'd be embarrassed to be such a submissive bottom." Viktoria raised an eyebrow and chuckled.

"Viktoria! What the fuck! I'm embarrassed that *everyone* knows what I sound like in bed, *not* about what I *do* in bed." Jocasta punched her in the shoulder. "How rude." She paused for a moment before adding, "That was some incredibly detailed eavesdropping, shit."

"I told you," Vik shrugged, "That'll be their good Phenom training." She laughed before peeling off into the kitchen while Jocasta headed upstairs. She made it to Katerina's room without encountering anyone and slipped inside without knocking. Katerina wasn't there, so she jumped into her shower for a quick rinse off. When she came out, she was still alone, so she sat in the chair by her window and looked out onto the grounds. This side of the building looked out over some trees, and she could *just* see a pond toward the edge of the property. It was a pretty big pond, so big she would almost call it a lake, but there wasn't a word for something in between so she stuck with 'pond'. She watched as a flock of birds flew from a tree and tried to fall asleep, hoping a nap would give her enough energy so that she wouldn't fall asleep before dinner. After Austin trimmed her undercut last night, she had told everyone she got her voice back, and Marc had immediately suggested the team make a special dinner to celebrate, but it wouldn't be until a bit later, and she was exhausted. She felt her eyelids drooping over her eyes and decided she should probably climb into bed. She fell asleep as soon as her head hit the pillow.

She woke up to the door opening, and Katerina walked in looking frustrated. She watched as she paced the floor for a moment before looking up and seeing Jocasta under the covers. She immediately climbed in and wrapped her arms around Jocasta, breathing out a sigh. Jocasta snuggled into Katerina's embrace, relishing in the warmth she brought her. "If I hear one more person's thoughts saying, 'Yes Ma'am' as I walk by them, I am going to lose my mind, Jo." Katerina kissed the top of her head, and Jocasta felt her tension start to melt a little bit.

"At least it wasn't one of the times I called you something else." She tried to make it a little better, and Katerina laughed.

"Yes, at least it wasn't a time when we were using toys or handcuffs or something."

"I cannot imagine what they'd be saying if that were the case."

"Did you know there's a pool-"

"Yes." Jocasta cut her off and snuggled closer to her. "Can we just cuddle for a little bit? I don't want to think about it." Katerina didn't answer, just rubbed circles on her back and leaned her head on Jocasta's. She breathed in the scent of her, a faint perfume and cleanliness mixed with the warmth of her skin. She couldn't figure out how to describe the smell of Katerina's skin other than that it was a warm smell, something that gave her comfort. She pressed her face into Katerina's chest, soaking her in and cherishing the moment.

"Jocasta?" Katerina moved her hand up to feel Jocasta's undercut, giving her a little tingle at the base of her neck.

"Yes?"

"Are you sure you're okay with this training regime Marc set up for you?" The question surprised her; she hadn't really given the new schedule any thought.

"Um, I mean, I haven't really thought about it. If Marc thinks I can handle it, I'll be fine. I trust his judgement. Why do you ask?"

"It just seems like a lot when you've just been without any training for so long, not to mention your fresh bruises and the fact that you had a broken hand. Does that hurt at all?"

"Um," Jocasta thought about this morning, having punched Carter with her left hand and feeling a sting, electing to throw punches with her right for the rest of the day. Neither Carter or Vik had noticed, but tomorrow she was with Katerina again, and she probably would. "It's fine."

"It hurts, doesn't it?"

"I'm sure it's just a little bit weak, that's all." Jocasta lifted her hand up and flexed it for Katerina. "I'll add hand strengthening exercises to my pre-training warmup."

"I'm keeping an eye on it." Jocasta could hear the look on Katerina's face, she didn't have to look at her. She knew her head was tilted, her brows furrowed, and one brow lifted up just a little bit. She nodded into Katerina and sighed. "You have to be kind to your body, love. It has to heal before you start abusing it in training. You heard Rachel." Katerina stroked her back again and kissed her head. They laid there for a while, just content being in each other's arms. Eventually, Katerina started to wiggle her arm out from underneath of her, and Jocasta lifted her head to look at her.

"Where are you going?" Jocasta pouted at her, knowing it made Katerina happy to see her with that specific look on her face. Katerina smiled at her and put a hand to her cheek.

"I'm going to get changed for this special dinner, Jocasta." Katerina looked at her lips, and Jocasta felt a small flutter in her stomach. Every time Katerina looked at her like that, she felt incredible. Being desired by someone, especially someone as astoundingly beautiful as Kat, made her feel like she was walking in the clouds. She couldn't fathom how Katerina could look at *her* the way that she was. Desire in her eyes, darkening them to a green so perfect that she was having trouble breathing as she looked at them. Jocasta leaned into her, kissing her softly, hoping Katerina could feel how much she cherished her. They broke apart, and Jocasta followed suit and walked across the hall to get ready as well. With Marc involved, this dinner would probably be much more elaborate than necessary, so she brushed on a bit of makeup just in case. She was finishing up styling her hair when Katerina knocked softly on her bathroom door. "You are beautiful, my love." She made her way behind Jocasta and slipped her arms around her.

"Oh, I'm nothing compared to you, Kat." Jocasta smiled and twisted around in her arms, hoping to steal another kiss before they headed to meet the others.

"That is an outlandish lie; you are absolutely gorgeous." Katerina kissed her first, and Jocasta felt a wave of joy flood through her. She would have been content to kiss like this for the rest of eternity, but Katerina pulled away. "Let's go, they will probably all be waiting for us at this point."

"Fine." Jocasta whined, earning her a laugh before Katerina turned and led the way down to the common area. When they entered the room, she was glad she had put on a button up shirt. This was ridiculous. Marc must have hired people for this dinner, because the whole room was elaborately set up with food on tables in the back, and the bar was fully stocked, with someone she didn't know standing behind it. Most of the people she had met while working here were milling about, everyone talking and laughing, and Katerina smiled at her as she took everything in. "This is not dinner. This is a whole party."

"That it is."

"Did you know he was doing this?"

"Of course I did."

"Why-?" Jocasta was starting to tear up. Marc didn't have to do this for her. Nobody had ever thrown a party this elaborate for her before, nor had they surprised her with a party successfully. Her mom had tried once and failed. She had always secretly hoped she would get a true surprise party one day, and she knew Katerina was well aware of those things. Marc appeared, seemingly out of thin air.

"Jocasta, you deserve it. We all wanted to celebrate you coming home, and I thought I should make an announcement." Before she could ask what he meant, Marc turned toward the room, "Hello everyone," his voice filled the room and Jocasta realized he must have been wearing a microphone of some sort. "I am so glad you could all make it and surprise our guest of honor," he gestured to Jocasta, and she felt herself blush. "We are overjoyed to have her back with us, and I am proud to announce that as of this morning, W.E.I.R.D. has given me the go ahead to make her a permanent fixture around here, both as a researcher, and as our newest Phenom!" Her jaw dropped as he turned back to her while everyone gave her a round of applause. Her head was swimming and she almost fell to her knees as Katerina stepped up and wrapped an arm around her waist, steadying her. Marc handed his little mic to her, and she looked at Katerina, steeling herself before addressing the room.

"Um, I'm as surprised as all of you are. This is the most incredible thing I could ever imagine, and I am honestly at a loss for words. I-uh," she paused, looking at Katerina and hoping she could help her figure out what she was trying to say. She nodded at her to keep going. "Working here has been a dream come true and being an official part of the team is something I could never have dreamed possible, so thank you all for making me feel like a part of your family." She felt tears spilling over her cheeks as she looked back at Marc, who hugged her as everyone started clapping again. "I love you, Marc. You know that, right?" She told him softly before he let her go.

"I love you too, kid. We all do." He swung his arm to indicate the rest of the team, standing close by. They each congratulated her, and she was thrust toward the food and bar shortly afterward.

"So are my new powers not a secret anymore?" she mumbled to Katerina as they found a spot to eat.

"They never were, Jo. The Brigade has surveillance cameras, they saw you phasing and disappearing when you escaped. Granted, they couldn't stop you, so that's good, but they knew the whole time."

"Did *you* know it wasn't really a secret this whole time?" Jocasta was floored by the elaborate ruse Marc had concocted to make this possible for her.

"No, Marc sat tight on it until last night. He told the team when you went up to bed, and that was also when he started planning this."

"When did you find out then? Because you came with me to bed."

"Same time as everyone else, Marc pulled me aside to tell me to listen in before we left."

"I am just absolutely flabbergasted." Jocasta was still struggling to put everything together. "Wait, so what is happening with the Brigade if they know I was successful?"

"Therein lies the rub. It looks like they've gone underground." Arthur joined them, "Very deeply underground. There is no trace of them anywhere since we got you out."

"That sounds very bad," Jocasta looked at him and started to feel her anxiety creeping in.

"Yes. But, that is why you'll be training extra hard, and we will be ready when we find them again." Art patted her knee and smiled.

"Right, okay." She nodded and looked over to see Carter and Austin playing pool and grinned at Katerina. "Well, do you think we could beat them?" she indicated the pool table with her head.

"Absolutely. Will you excuse us, Art?" She stood up and grabbed Jocasta's hand as Arthur nodded, and she felt the tension leaving her body again. They made their way across the room and Katerina grabbed two pool sticks, poking Austin's with one as they lined up a shot, making them scratch the ball.

"Hey! What was that for?" They laughed as Carter retrieved the ball and lined up their next shot.

"Two on two? We are fairly certain we can beat you," Jocasta directed the question to both of them, and Carter's eyes lit up at the challenge.

"Oh, you're on!" They began collecting the balls off of the table to start a new game, and Austin gasped.

"You didn't even want to finish our game first? I cannot believe this." They put their hand to their head dramatically, and Jocasta burst out laughing at the display.

"I would much rather play with you than against you, yes." Carter gave them a look, and Jocasta thought she could pick up a hint of flirtation between them. She looked at Katerina, and her face told her that she had the same thought.

The rest of the party went by in a bit of a blur, everyone laughing and happy, Marc making sure that the bar got its use as he asked people if they wanted a drink as soon as he saw an empty glass. She was beginning to feel like she needed to grab some more food before she could ingest any more alcohol when Katerina pulled her into the kitchen for a moment.

"Want to sneak away with me?" she giggled, placing her hands on Jocasta's hips.

"I'm the guest of honor, baby, I shouldn't." Jocasta put her arms around Katerina's neck anyway, knowing Kat would not be taking no for an answer.

"Nobody will notice, Marc has everyone so drunk they probably won't even remember the party is for you." Katerina was playing with Jocasta's hair now, making her insides start to flip.

"Can we at least grab some more food first so I can sober up a bit?" Jocasta never wanted to forget a single moment with Katerina.

"Okay," she gave in, her voice taking on a sing-songy quality Jocasta had not heard before. It was very cute. They joined back into the party, and they both switched to water after they ate, leaving again after they both felt much more in control of themselves. Jocasta tugged on Katerina's wrist as she led her to the stairs, climbing past their rooms and up to the roof. The air was crisp, and the fairy lights in the corner of the garden were as beautiful as ever as they made their way to the archway where they had their first date. Jocasta pulled Katerina into her arms and smiled.

"I can't believe I'm here with you," she whispered, and started to sway, dancing to a song in her head. She hummed, leaning her head on Katerina's shoulder, and they danced for a few moments before Katerina stopped her.

"Jocasta, you make me so happy. Happier than I ever thought I could be," Jocasta lifted her head and met Katerina's eyes, the twinkling lights playing off of them, making them sparkle.

"Me too, Kat," she whispered, feeling happy tears spring to her eyes.

"I have never felt this way about anyone before. I mean, I have been in love, but you, you consume me. You ground me and make me float in the clouds at the same time. I can't describe the intense beauty of the feelings that you have unlocked in me, and I just want you to know how much I love you." Katerina had tears in her eyes now too.

"I love you too." Jocasta smiled and lifted up to kiss her. They held each other close, and then Katerina lifted her up off of her feet, and Jocasta wrapped her legs around her waist. Jocasta leaned down as she put her hands on either side of Katerina's face, and kissed her again, harder. Katerina's power started to swirl around them just like the first time they had kissed, and Jocasta opened her eyes to see that they were hovering about a foot above the roof. She couldn't help but smile wide as she moved her hands to Katerina's shoulders. They lowered back down, and Katerina lifted a hand to caress her cheek, kissing her again softly on the lips. When she pulled away, her eyes locked onto Jocasta's. She rubbed her cheek with her thumb and curled her fingers around the curve of Jocasta's jaw, smiling that all-encompassing smile that Jocasta had first fallen in love with in this very spot.

"You are phenomenal."

EPILOGUE

Marc had just called a 911 emergency meeting of the core group of Phenoms, and Jocasta was becoming antsy. She was waiting in the boardroom for the rest of the team to arrive, her knee bouncing uncontrollably, and her mind starting to wander. She had flown down from the roof where she had been reading, and nobody else was here yet. When she first learned that she could fly, everyone had been incredibly excited, and since Vik had called it, they all decided that they should make her official super name Ghost.

Since she had honed her skills, she had been flying just about everywhere, but she had also been waiting for everyone else to show up to meetings a lot more. It definitely cut down her travel time, and although Katerina could use her powers to fly and Austin was as fast as they were, nobody else felt the need to use their abilities to get around the mansion the way she did. Everyone filed in, and Katerina put her hand on Jocasta's thigh as she sat down. As soon as she felt her touch, her knee bouncing stopped, and she smiled at her. She had been overseeing a training group, and her hands were a bit sweaty. "Were you teaching instead of observing again?" she whispered to her.

"Some of these trainees need better form!" Katerina mumbled to her, trying not to let Marc know what she was saying as he walked to the front of the room. When any of them oversaw a training group, they were only there for safety reasons, there were assigned agents for teaching the trainees. Marc tended to get a bit upset when Katerina overstepped that and taught the trainees. Apparently, she had broken someone's arm once. Jocasta wasn't allowed to oversee anything yet, but her training had been going so well over the past year that she was an official core Phenom now. This was going to be the first big mission she would be dealing with as a full-fledged member of the team.

"Listen up, guys." Marc looked serious, and Jocasta felt her light-heartedness from teasing Katerina bleed out of her chest. "So, as you all know, the Freedom Brigade went underground right after our successful infiltration of their facility when we got Jocasta back." The blood drained from her face as soon as he said, 'Freedom Brigade' and Katerina's hand had tightened around her leg. Marc made eye contact with her before continuing, and she sucked in a steadying breath. "Well, we found them. They came out of hiding yesterday with an attack on the pentagon, and this footage looks like they might have accomplished what we feared the most."

The screen behind Marc suddenly lit up with an image of Jax, and he pressed a button. The image quickly bled into a video of Jax infiltrating the pentagon with Cyrus and Brittany at his sides. It looked like they had had a rough year, but she didn't know what Marc meant about what they feared the most until she saw Jax's limbs extending, shape shifting into ropes as he tied up a platoon of men, choking them out, and dropping them to the ground, unconscious. She covered her mouth and tears filled her eyes as she realized what this meant. They had recreated her serum. Maybe even improved on it. Katerina moved to put her arm around Jocasta's shoulders, and Carter turned to look at her, tears in their eyes. The video ended, and Jocasta cleared her throat before looking at Marc.

"I'm going to stop them."

"We all are, Jocasta." Arthur met her gaze and although she blamed herself, she could tell he didn't.

"Exactly," Marc clicked another button, and pages of information popped up behind him. "Let's get to work, Phenoms."

AUTHOR'S NOTE

I started writing this book because I wanted to see more stories about queer women, especially superheroes who are queer. As a lover of all things nerdy, Superhero stories shaped me growing up, and when I started embracing my sexuality, I noticed a huge lack of representation not only for queer women, but just for women in general. Then, as I started the story, I thought about how I could bring a little more to the table with Austin and Carter's being nonbinary folx. As a cis, white woman, I don't ever want to overstep my boundaries, but I also wanted to write a story that allowed the reader to imagine themselves in my characters as much as possible, and while I was a little selfish with my two main ladies, keeping them in the same demographic, everyone else is meant to help represent as many groups of people as possible. If I succeed in making this book into a bit of a series, I hope to bring more <u>obvious</u> intersectional representation as the Phenom's story grows.

Now, I want to thank my love for being the absolute biggest cheerleader around, Olivia, *you* are truly Phenomenal! Another thank you is very much owed to my friends who encouraged me throughout the process of writing, and who helped me get through making this book a reality. I love you all so much. And finally, thank you to my readers. That feels so surreal to write! I hope that you will stick around to see more from this little universe I've created, and I hope you all find a safe space in my words. Thank you all from the bottom of my heart.

Stay WEIRD! Love, ~ Jezreel

About the Author

Hi! I'm Jezreel Jones. I'm a new author, and I am overjoyed to start this journey into literature. I have a BFA in Musical Theatre Performance, so telling stories is something I am used to, but this format has been an exciting new challenge. I live in Northern Kentucky with my incredible fiancée, Olivia, and our sweet puppy, Remy. I'm a bit obsessed with books, movies, and board games, and I will talk for hours about my theories on my favorite characters. I love cooking and baking, too, so the hours of conversation usually take place over some culinary concoction I've created.

As a lesbian, I want to bring some LGBTQIA representation and romance to the world of super heroes, which I am so fond of. I've grown up on superhero movies and stories, and I hope to give people some heroes that can represent them in a way that they haven't seen before. Who knows, maybe I'll only help one or two people, but even so, it'll be worth it.

Printed in the United States
by Baker & Taylor Publisher Services